I0671871

For Such A Time As This

Amber Wynn

COPYRIGHT

This book is a work of fiction. Names, characters, places, and incidents are either the product of the author's imagination or are used fictitiously, and any resemblance to actual persons, living or dead, events, or locales is entirely coincidental.

Copyright © 2015 by Amber Wynn
All rights reserved
No part of this book may be reproduced, scanned, or distributed in any printed or electronic form.

CHRISTOPHER RASHAD GLOBAL ENTERPRISES, INC.
First Edition: May 2015
Copyright © 2015 Amber Wynn
All rights reserved.
ISBN: 9780990519782

Cover photo by Amir Williams

DEDICATION

This book is dedicated to all of my beautiful Black men, young and old. Confused by the amount of hate the world has for you, angered by the injustice experienced because of the color of your skin, and immobilized by the fear that drives the morbid actions of Others.

And to the mothers of those slain. In honor of your pain,
your suffering, and un-vindicated justice.
Your cries have not gone unheard.
Your pain and anger is real, and valid, and justified.

#BlackLivesMatter

TABE OF CONTENTS

ACKNOWLEDGMENTS

I would like to thank my Front Row People. You know who you are.
My cheerleaders, my motivators, my "Girl, you better finish that
book"-ers, My *Family*. Thank you for always seeing beyond the here
and now, and showing your sistah love. You give me strength.
To Victoria Christopher Murray, my Soror, my love. Thank you for
your endless words of encouragement, guidance and insight.
To My Beautiful Black Kings, Christopher and Amir,
and my King in Training, Noah
your mom (and Nana) loves you.

PROLOGUE

August 3, 2014

"Hello?"

"Hey, mom, it's JJ."

"Hey, you close?"

"Yup. About to make a left on Grand in about three minutes—Shit!"

"What?"

"I just got tagged by Five-0."

"For what?" Adrian placed her hands on her hips, a scowl quickly replacing her smile. "Are you on your cell?"

"Are you serious? For driving black, in a 750 Li. C'mon now. And no, I'm not on my cell. The phone is connected to my blue tooth."

"Just pull over and give them your registration and insurance, JJ."

"I am, I am," JJ said. "It's just old already. And they're going to make me miss my curtain call."

"Yeah, well, unfortunately that's life as a black man in America. You can be late. Take your time. Don't give them any attitude, and get here when you get here."

"Hold on, mom. He's walking up." JJ rolled down the driver-side window.

"Good evening."

"Good evening, officer."

A second cop walked up along the passenger side and stood with his hand on his holster.

"How are you?" he said, looking inside JJ's vehicle.

"I'm fine. How are you?"

"Just fine." He looked over the roof of the car and nodded toward the other officer who moved in closer.

"May I have your registration and license, please?"

"Yes, sir." JJ flipped the visor down and removed the registration. He reached inside his coat jacket and retrieved his wallet. He handed the two items to the officer.

"I'll be right back."

After less than a minute, the officer returned.

"Sir, do you mind stepping outside the vehicle?"

Adrian listened to the conversation. Her stomach started doing flip-flops.

"I don't mind," JJ said, opening the door and stepping out the BMW. The officer's left eyebrow etched up as he eyed the white tuxedo jacket, black pants and black patent leather shoes. "May I ask why?"

"Sir. If you could just step away from the vehicle."

JJ stepped further into the street and away from the vehicle. The other cop moved toward the front of the car.

Adrian grabbed her purse and headed for the foyer, ear pressed closely to her cell.

"This is a nice vehicle you have here," the officer said with a smirk as he stuck his head into the car. "750Li —this is the big daddy. Has lots of power, ain't that right?"

JJ didn't reply. A scowl crossed his face. He looked down at his watch and shifted impatiently.

"You have somewhere to be?" The cop chuckled, winked and nodded at his partner.

"Yes sir, I do. I'm attending the Governor's Ball right around the corner at the Disney Concert Hall." JJ crossed his hands in front of his waist.

Adrian made it to the foyer, listening to the entire conversation as she took the steps two at a time. Her heart was racing and she was out of breath. Her flowing white floor-length dress trailed behind her as she moved toward the doors.

"Is that right?" The officer moved toward JJ. He looked him up and down. "You driving a 750 Li, attending a hoity-toity Governor's Ball, all decked out in your rented tuxedo—you some celebrity athlete or something?" He chuckled, looking once again at his partner.

"My name is Jared Jackson. The car is registered, no tickets, no warrants, and I have insurance. What is the purpose of you pulling me over, officer?"

The police officer smirked and got up in JJ's face. "We just got a call about a carjacking in the area." He glanced again at his partner. "Ain't that right, Gerry?" The officer looked up the street. "And you fit the description."

JJ rolled his eyes. "Yeah, okay."

The officer jumped in closer. "What, you don't believe me?"

"It doesn't matter what I believe. What you know is that I have no tickets, my registration is current, and I have car insurance," he said calmly. "I'm in a white tie tuxedo— that I *own*. So clearly, I haven't jacked anyone."

"No, it's not clear!" the officer screamed in his face. JJ stared him down. "But what *is* clear is that you got an attitude." He pulled out his handcuffs and attempted to turn JJ around. "Get on your knees!"

"What?" JJ screamed. "I will not. Get your supervisor down here. I demand to speak to your commanding officer right now."

Adrian ran outside the theater, she looked both ways searching for JJ. She remembered he said he was about to make a left on Grand, and she headed East in that direction, listening as the conversation escalated.

The officer yanked JJ's arm. JJ pulled away.

"Are you refusing arrest?" the officer asked, tackling JJ to the ground.

"Are you using excessive force?" JJ replied.
The police officer shoved JJ's face into the ground and
placed his knee into his back. The other officer rounded the vehicle and stood behind his partner, gun drawn down on JJ.

"You better be careful, boy. You don't know who you fuckin' with today."

JJ turned his face to the side. "No *you* better be careful. You don't know who you're fucking with today."

Adrian hit the corner just as the officer stood. JJ rolled over and attempted to stand. It all happened in slow motion. She watched the officer pull his gun from his holster just as JJ made it to his knees. But before he could fully stand, the officer fired his weapon.

Adrian screamed as she watched her son fall sideways to the ground. The traffic, the lights, the colors, all faded into a dull blur. She felt as if she were running in place with lead around her ankles. Everything went silent. The air in her lungs felt like hot flames. She couldn't breathe.

"Who am I fucking with, boy?" the officer screamed at the wounded man on the ground.

JJ smiled, infuriating the cop. He attempted to stand, the cop fired off another shot. JJ fell back onto the asphalt. The red spot near his chest quickly spread, turning the white jacket a deep dark red. JJ locked eyes with the cop.

"My . . . name . . . is . . . Ja-red . . . . Jack-son." The cop stood over JJ and shot him in the face.

"Shut the fuck up."

"Stop it!" Adrian screamed as she approached the scene. "That's my son!" The cop turned his gun on Adrian, but his partner quickly grabbed her.

"Let me go!" She struggled to get free. "That's my son, got dammit! If you don't fucking let me go, I swear to god!" The officer let her go. Adrian ran to JJ, and fell to her knees.

"JJ!" She gently lifted his head into her lap. Blood was everywhere. As much as she wiped, she couldn't see his face . . . *he had no face*. There was just a bloody mass. A piece of JJ's skull fell into AJ's hand. She looked at it and started to tremble. She pulled her son in close to her chest and rocked him as the last bit of life drained from his body.

PART ONE

"The last thing you ever want to do is piss off an educated Black woman.
She's like institutionalized racism: present, powerful—
and you're not quite sure how to fight it."

1 THE AUDACITY

August 22, 2014

Adrian

A week after the shooting, I was at the station asking to speak with Chief Bollinger.

"Ma'am, do you have an appointment?" the front desk officer asked.

"No," I replied

"Ma'am--"

"I'm Adrian Jackson. I've tried for the past three days to get on Chief Bollinger's calendar, but I've yet to receive a call back. So let Chief Bollinger know I'm here. And I'll be sitting right over there. Thank you," I said. The officer watched as I made my way to the waiting area.

"Mrs. Jackson?" the officer said.

I walked over to the counter. "I'm sorry, ma'am, but the Chief is not available to meet with you today. His scheduler has indicated that he will call you to set up an appointment in the next week or two--"

I looked at the officer's name badge.

"Officer McMillan."

"Yes, ma'am?"

"Tell Chief Bollinger he has exactly thirty minutes to speak with me, today, right here. Otherwise, I will be holding a press conference on his front steps in exactly an hour, where I will announce to the world that the officer who shot my son, in cold blood, is being protected by the Chief of Police.

"Tell him that I will produce a log documenting the number of times I have contacted his scheduler for an appointment and the number of times I have received a call back – which is zero. And that I was just informed today that I will receive a call to set up an appointment in the next week . . . or two," I said over my shoulder as I walked back to my seat and waited while the officer repeated my threats to the person on the other side of the phone.

Twenty minutes later, James Rasmussen entered the lobby.

"Mrs. Jackson?"

I stood and started to move in his direction. I watched as the man inspected me from head to toe.

My hair was pulled back neatly in a bun at the nape of my neck. Natural make up. My eyebrows were neatly arched stretching across my wide eyes, accentuated by long black lashes. I was dressed in a cream knit reverse-collar jacket, two-ply silk Georgette V-neck shell and knit pencil skirt. Each lobe held a simple ¼ " fresh water pearl earring. I was dressed to kill. I came prepared for battle.

I stopped until his eyes met mine. He flinched at the intensity of my stare.

"Ah. Hello, I'm James Rasmussen" He extended his hand. I shook it. "I am the department's Commanding Officer of Media Relations and Community Affairs Group."
I nodded.

James looked around the lobby. "Ah. Do you have your attorney with you?"

"I do not."

"Okay, great. I do apologize for the challenges with getting you into see Chief Bollinger. As you can imagine with running a police department, he's a very busy man." His smile was disingenuous.

"James, was it?" I said walking past him. "I could care less about his schedule. My taxes pay his salary. I expect the courtesy of a timely response." I stopped and looked him in the eyes. "Especially given that my son's murder is probably his most high profile case right now."

James's mouth tightened. I could see him struggling for a quick comeback, but could come up with nothing. He turned and led me down the hallway. He turned left and stopped at an office nestled in the middle.

"I've cleared the Chief's schedule so that he can meet with you." He opened the door.

"Thank you. I appreciate it."

Chief Bollinger stood behind his desk in a white button down shirt, a dark blue and green striped tie, and dark blue slacks. He extended his hand.

"Mrs. Jackson, my condolences on your loss. Please come in."

"Thank you." I shook his hand, and then sat in front of the large walnut desk. The wall behind him was splattered with a variety of awards and accommodations: the Police Academy, Rotary Club, Recognition of Service from the Mayor, Leadership Training, and on and on.

"How can I help you?" the Chief asked, glancing at James who sat at a conference table in the corner of the office.

"I'd like an update on the investigation of Jared's murder."

"*Alleged*," James said from across the room. "Ballistic reports have not concluded--"

My left eyebrow shot up, causing a deep crease over my right brow. I slowly and deliberately turned to face the man "spinning" my son's death.

"James." My voice slightly raised. "Were you there?"

"Of course not," he said, shifting in his chair. "But as I stated, ballistic reports have not--"

"I was." I gave him the same intense look I'd given him in the lobby. He stopped talking.

"Mrs. Jackson?" Chief Bollinger said. "I think what Mr. Rasmussen was trying to say is that this is an on-going investigation. And until we receive conclusive evidence from the crime scene and our lab, I'm sorry, but there's not much I can share with you—which is one of the primary reasons why we haven't met. I wanted to be able to provide you with something more than 'I don't have any new information right now.'"

I sat for half a second, then smiled. "Chief Bollinger, tell me, what is going to happen to Sergeant Carpenter if your ballistic report determines that he, in fact, did murder Jared?"

"A ballistic report cannot, in and of itself, determine whether or not Sergeant Carpenter murdered anyone," James interjected.
I smiled.

"Chief Bollinger, I'd like an update on the status of the investigation."

Chief Bollinger shot James a look.

"Mrs. Jackson. Unfortunately, because all of the evidence has not been thoroughly reviewed by Internal Affairs, I'm unable able to provide you with an update. I hate that you wasted your time coming down here. But I promise, as soon as I get any new information, I will call you." Chief Bollinger stood. James stood. I remained seated.

"Who is in charge of the investigation? Is it you? Internal Affairs? The police commission?"

"Ultimately I'm responsible, but Internal Affairs is handling the investigation right now. The police commission is more of an external body—if there is a determination of maleficence, then the police commission could be asked to review the findings." He stood with his arms folded across his chest.

"And Internal Affairs, it's an internal department?"

James started to speak, but Chief Bollinger raised his hand.

"It's a part of the department, however it functions as a separate and objective agency. Their role is to get to the truth. I assure you it's not like we're policing ourselves."

I nodded. I stood, shook the Chief's hand and turned to walk out the door, but paused a moment.

"Chief Bollinger, I see that you're a graduate of the Brandeis School of Management?"

Chief Bollinger turned to look at his plaque. He smiled.

"Yes, yes, I am. I participated in the program the latter part of 2007."

I smiled. "Take a look at President Abram's statement on duplicity in 1969 at Ford Hall." I turned, shot James a dismissive glare, and closed the door behind me.

James threw his hands up in the air. "Did you see how that condescending bitch looked at me?" His face was beet red.

"Don't let her get up under your skin Jim. She's just fishing for information. She's a very smart woman." I looked James up and down. "You let her unnerve you. What is your problem?"

James banged his fists on the conference table. "Oooh! She just makes my skin boil. All calm and collected, in her name brand suit and pearls. Ooooh!" he shouted.

I shook my head, then turned to my computer to look up the reference to Brandeis University.

Adrian

Outside Chief Bollinger's office, I walked up the long corridor. I made a right, and landed in the squad room with the desk sergeants.

"Ma'am, can I help you?" a black officer said.

As I turned to acknowledge him, I stopped in my tracks. Standing next to him was Officer Carpenter.

I walked up to him and stood directly in his face. The officers moved their hands to their holsters. The black officer held his hand up, stilling the room.

"Ma'am?" he repeated.

I turned my head in the direction of the officer. "Officer Johnson." I read his badge. I flashed him a quick smile, made direct eye contact, then turned to stare Officer Carpenter in the eyes. "I just left a meeting with Chief Bollinger. And, I must've gotten turned around."

"Yes, ma'am. The exit from his office would have been two lefts. You must've made two rights."

"Yes. I must've." I kept my left hand down at my side, the clutch in my right hand up to my shoulder.

A smug grin started to form across Carpenter's face.

"Carp . . . you good?" an officer across the room asked.

"Oh, yeah. I'm good. I'm alive and well . . . breathing. . ." He laughed.

I leaned in. Our noses were almost touching.

"And you sleep well at night?"

"Perfectly."

"Hmm." I paused as the officers looked on. "I need you to remember this moment, right here."

"Lady, you're not that important. Seriously? Get over yourself." He chuckled, quickly looking at his fellow officers.

I stood there, silent. I looked him up and down without moving my head. "This isn't about me. This is about my son that you murdered." I spoke so low, only Sergeant Carpenter could hear me.

"He's dead. You might as well get over that, too," he whispered back.

We locked eyes for a few seconds. I nodded and smiled, Turned, and walked away.

August 26, 2014

Adrian

"On December 29, 1992, I went into labor. For forty-eight hours, I experienced the most excruciating pain I'd ever felt in my life. Pain in my back, in my head – my body was racked with pain-- until 3:31 a.m. on December 31st, when I gave birth to a 7½ lbs, 21 inch baby boy." I smiled into the cameras.

Photographers were snapping pictures, flashes going off every second.

I paused as tears welled up in my eyes. "His name was Jared Jackson. He was valedictorian at Westlake Village Preparatory High School and captain of the debate team. He won over $20,000 in academic scholarships for which he applied to tuition at Claremont University where he was majoring in hydro physics-- specifically, Magnetohydrodynamics." I wiped a tear from the corner of my right eye and cleared my throat.

"JJ was interested in cancer research. The love of his life, Edith Green, his grandmother, died from breast cancer. Jared was actively engaged in research using magnetic drug targeting to study the interaction between the magnetic fluid particles in the bloodstream and the external magnetic field. Promising work with the nation's top researchers in oncology magnetohydrodynamics.

"On August 15, 2014, at 7:30 pm, Jared Jackson was brutally gunned down by Los Angeles police officer Peter Carpenter, three hundred feet away from his destination, The Disney Concert Hall.

"Jared was pulled over for driving a 2006 750 Li BMW. By witness accounts, he provided Sergeant Carpenter with his license, registration, and proof of insurance, as requested." My voice became shaky, but I did not waver.

Dressed in a navy blue suit, a crisp white blouse with large lapels and flared cuffs, a burnt orange pashmina tossed over my left shoulder, I recounted the incident free of notes.

"My son had just called me to inform me of his arrival. And so, I waited outside for him to walk me into theater . . . as he had done since age twelve. But, he never made it to my side. Instead, he was yanked out of a luxury car police officers decided he had no right to drive, forced down onto the ground where he was brutally murdered by racist cowards who believe they have the right to kill a man because his skin is black and the car he drives is more expensive than the one they own."

The reporters started hurling questions.

"Are you saying your son's death was racially motivated?"

I looked directly at the reporter. "I said what I meant."

"What makes you believe they killed Jared because they were jealous of the car he was driving? Reports from LAPD state he refused arrest."

"Since when did refusing arrest justify murder?" I stared at the reporter so intensely that he lowered his head and pretended to jot down notes. "Jared was a twenty-one year old African American male. He provided the officers with proof that the car was registered. He was impeccably dressed, no red rag, no blue rag, no sagging pants. Officer Carpenter drives a 1997 Durango. You do the math," I replied to the top of his head.

"Are there any witnesses to substantiate your claim that he was brutally murdered because of the color of his skin?" another reporter shouted.

I turned to face the woman, then moved from behind the podium. I pulled out a bloodstained ivory dress and held it up.

"*Me*. I witnessed him shooting my son. And when he tried to stand, the officer opened fire. I watched as he unloaded two rounds of gunfire into my son's body. I watched as his body bounced up from each shot and then go limp. I watched him shoot my son in his face."

The audience gasped.

"I ran to him. But before I could . . ." The words lodged in my throat. "Ahem . . . before I could get to my baby . . . these sick demented animals killed him. I watched the blood drain from his body."

I carried the bloody dress to the female reporter. The lady stood motionless.

"I held my son, but I couldn't look into his eyes and comfort him, because they had been shot out. He lay lifeless in my arms. The life I brought into this world was taken away from me. And now, I have to bury my only child in four days. His brilliance will never be felt by the world."

Complete silence.

I returned to the podium. "My name is Adrian Jackson. Jared Jackson was my son. He was brutally murdered by racist cowards who deserve to be put to death for their crime. Anything less would be our government saying it condones this murder by officers sworn to protect and serve its citizens. Anything less is a blatant statement by law enforcement that it believes black lives do *not* matter."

I paused as camera flashed. I waited until there was complete silence, then I turned and walked away. From the sideline I watched and listened as reporters framed their stories for their nationally syndicated audiences.

"And there you have it ladies and gentlemen, a play by play account of the events as witnessed by Jared Jackson's own mother," said one reporter.

"Adrian Jackson describing the amazing life of her would-be-scientist son. Researching a cure for cancer. But instead, today, as his mother so eloquently put it, his brilliance will never be experienced by the world," said another reporter.

"I don't know, Chris, the words are there. But she comes off a bit stoic. Maybe she's still in shock? I mean, we did see tears, but usually a mother would be sobbing. She appears very calm, and each one of her words seemed carefully chosen, almost calculated, to me," said yet a third reporter from Fox news.

In the background, protestors chanted. "Black Lives Matter! No Justice, No Peace! Black Lives Matter! No Justice, No Peace!"

Chief Bollinger

I sat glued to my TV screen watching the poised woman at the podium.

"Roger, did you fucking see that?" Jim said, clicking off the TV.

"She has to have a PR team behind her. That was some inflammatory *By Any Means Necessary* bullshit. It was polished, but she might as well have said, 'Okay black people, if this one ends in an acquittal, it means we have to get our own justice!'"

I sat, thinking more about the wording of Adrian Jackson's speech than James's sensationalized banter.

"It was brilliant, Jim. You gotta admit that," I said, swiveling around in my chair to meet his gaze. "She humanized him. Hell, she canonized him with that cancer research, grandmother shit." I picked up the phone. "Reyes. Get me background on that Jared kid's mother."

"Oh, she has a firm. Did you see that? She didn't read a speech for Christ's sake!" Jim stood, and shoved his chair to the other side of the room.

I watched him have his tantrum. It's what he did when he felt outdone by his opponent. And today, we both knew we had been outdone by this woman.

"What are the public opinion polls saying?" I asked.

"They're saying if we settled today, we'd have to pay out millions." He scratched his balding head. "This JJ kid wasn't a gang banger, no rap sheet. He was squeaky clean."

"So the mom was right? Trigger happy cops putting a middle-class nigger in his place?" I sighed. "You know Jim, I think those kind of cops are worse than the gangbangers. Assholes like Carpenter believe the gangbangers are worthless and deserve to die; but the JJs of the world really incenses them because they contradict everything that justifies the way they think." I leaned back into my chair and stared out of the window.

"Well Roger, when you're through with your psychoanalysis, we can start prepping for your press conference. You're up tomorrow. Your version of why your cops killed squeaky clean, 'would've found the cure for cancer' St. Jared has got to top today's Oscar winning performance."

" Fuck me!"

August 27, 2014

Chief Bollinger

"Ladies and gentlemen," I said to the crew of cameras. "Thank you for gathering here this morning." I adjusted the mic on the podium. "On the night of August 15, 2014, officers Peter Carpenter and Gerald Banton observed the erratic behavior of a 2006 BMW sedan driving westbound on First Street.

"The car was pulled over approximately five hundred feet from the intersections of First and Grand Ave. Sergeant Carpenter approached the driver-side of the vehicle and Officer Banton approached the passenger side.

"There was one person in the vehicle, twenty-one year old

African American male, Jared Jackson. Sergeant Carpenter requested the driver's license and proof of insurance--which the driver produced.

"Sergeant Carpenter, suspicious of the driver being intoxicated, requested the driver to step out of the vehicle and Sergeant Carpenter administered a battery of department approved sobriety-tests. At the last test, the suspect became agitated and refused to comply.

"Officer Banton, who observed the suspect's threatening demeanor first, pulled his firearm. Then Sergeant Carpenter drew his weapon. Sergeant Carpenter repeated the request for the suspect to get on the ground, but he refused. Sergeant Carpenter attempted to subdue and cuff the suspect at which point a struggle ensued.

"Fearing for his life, Officer Carpenter shot the suspect, disabling him. However, he continued to aggressively advance toward Sergeant Carpenter, at which point he discharged his fire arm until the suspect no longer posed a threat."

Finally, I looked up, with pain and regret covering my face. "Ladies and gentlemen. Our officers are human, with sons and daughters, nieces and nephews. Sergeant Carpenter will carry the weight of this for the rest of his life, certainly for the rest of his career. There are no winners here."

"Chief Bollinger," began one reporter, "what about allegations of racial profiling and excessive force by your officers?"

"The use of excessive force by police isn't unheard of, but to insinuate that racially motivated shootings by police are commonplace and that this was one of those situations undermines the commitment and dedication of the Los Angeles Police Department, and fans racial discord at a time when we least need it," I replied.

"But Chief Bollinger, Jared was in white tie," a female reporter shouted. "How much of a threat was this well-dressed young socialite?"

Her question made the crowd stir.

"Well-dressed aggression is aggression nonetheless," I quickly responded. "Our officers are trained to respond to actions, not appearances. Sergeant Carpenter feared for his life and responded accordingly."

"Chief Bollinger, according to Jared's mother, the officers are white supremacists who killed her son without provocation or cause."

"My condolences to Mrs. Jackson. She's suffering an unimaginable loss. As a father of a son, I can't imagine the pain she is experiencing right now.

"But contrary to the inflammatory rhetoric inciting the division of this city, my officers are not a renegade band of white supremacists, carelessly killing African American males," I said, staring into the camera. "What they are, are a cadre of the most brave, most committed men and women I know."

"They've pledged to protect and serve this community. And many of them have given their lives in the pursuit of this pledge. It's a dangerous thing to wash our department with a broad stroke of racism, as it undermines our effectiveness as a force to do what we are here to do, which is to uphold the law.

"No man or woman is above the law. As your chief, I take full responsibility for the actions of my officers. I am committed to ensuring all officers enforce and uphold the law. That's all I have right now. Thank you for your time today."

Adrian

I sat in my living room, in my red and blue-checkered flannel pajamas watching Chief Bollinger's press conference.

You are committed to ensuring all officers enforce and uphold the law, my ass. I opened my dossier on the chief and flipped through the pages. It read like a poster child for the Blue Blood Mafia.

Bollinger was appointed to the Los Angeles Police Department in March 1977 and rose up the ranks quickly becoming a Sergeant in June 1984, and serving in the department's controversial C.R.A.S.H. program under then-chief Daryl Gates.

He was promoted to Lieutenant in April 1993, to Captain in July 1999 and in August 2006, he achieved the rank of Deputy Chief, the same rank his father, a retired Los Angeles Police Officer, had attained. Roger Bollinger was appointed the LAPD's Chief of Police in November 2009.

His sister, Ashleigh, was a detective. His wife, Brooke, was a narcotics K9 handler. Two of his children, Brittany and Marshall, were LAPD officers, as was his son-in-law.

I ran my fingers through my hair and let out a deep sigh. *I can't trust this man to do anything but protect his own.* I stood and walked over to the mantel. Picking up Jared's high school graduation photo, I slowly traced the outline of his smile. My heart ached as warm tears fell from my eyes. I wiped my faced with the back of my hands. *It's all good.* I smiled. *I will be doing the same for mine.*

Ring. Ring. Ring.

"Hello?"

"Careful you mulatto nigger bitch! The brothers in blue stick together. If you don't want to see more niggers laying dead like little JJ, you better back off."

Click.

I threw the phone at the wall.

2 I SPEAK FOR ME

"God bless you, sister."

"Thank you, Pastor Mitchell."

We hugged.

"Have a seat." He motioned toward the red velvet chair in front of his mahogany desk. "How are you holding up? And what can Winston AME do to support you?"

"I'm just trying to get through JJ's funeral. If I can do that . . . if I can lay my son down to rest without breaking into a million pieces . . . I should be fine," I said, wiping tears from my face. Pastor Mitchell handed me a box of Kleenex.

"Thank you." I blew my stuffy nose. "What Winston can do to support me is allow me to have the funeral here."

"Of course!" Pastor Mitchell said. "Now, do you have a church home, or . . ."

"No, sir. I'm not a practicing Christian in that vain." I eyed the Pastor. "Yes. I believe in God and all that—but right now, I'm really not concerned about my salvation. And Bishop Brown was telling me I needed to join the church and take some classes."

Reverend Mitchell shook his head. "If you want your son to have a church burial, then your son will have a church burial. No conditions."

The tears poured from my eyes. "Thank you." I managed to force a smile. "But I do have one condition."

Reverend Mitchell paused. "What's that?"

"I'm having an open casket."

"An open casket?" he stated slowly. "Sister. Are you sure that's the way you want to have your son memorialized?"

"I am sure that I don't want this to be swept under the carpet. And the way that doesn't happen is by letting the world see the bullet holes in my son's face."

"Look, I know that you're angry--"

"No, Pastor. I'm beyond angry."

"Yes. And vengeance is mine sayeth the Lord. You have to trust that God will punish the evil. Your focus needs to be on laying your child to rest in a nice, respectable manner. This . . . this isn't the way." He shook his head.

"So are you saying that you won't allow me to have the service in your church if it's open casket?"

"I think it would do more harm than good." He looked me in the eyes. "I think it would incite a riot and we need to be about peace--"

I stood up. Pastor Mitchell stood as well.

"Thank you for your time." I turned to leave the office.

"Sister Jackson. Please. I know you're in pain, but we don't want more lives taken. You know they just need a reason. Please, just pray on it. The doors of Winston AME are always open to you."

I paused. "Thank you. Reverend. For your *unconditional* support." We locked eyes for two seconds and then I turned and walked out the door.

I met with all six of the mega churches in L.A. And they all said the same thing: We'd be happy to host brother Jared's home going, but the casket has got to be closed.

The youngest pastor, Jordan Parker, Jr. finally told me the bottom line. "Look, these politicians look to us to bring calm to the neighborhoods, not incite riots."

"Meaning, they lace the offering trays with donations to keep the house niggas in check," I said.

"No, we pick our battles. This is about winning the war."

"Well, have you been watching the news, Pastor? We're losing the war—the war on crime, drugs, health--all the wars black folks are fighting, we're losing."

"If God is for us, then who can be against us? No weapon formed against us shall prosper, sister."

I paused a moment and looked at the pastor. "So, I'm not sure where that God of yours is, but He ain't showing me He's for us right now. Because every weapon formed against us: guns, crack, AIDS, gangs, cops who are killers -- they all are prospering. But you go ahead and do you, brother."

I grabbed my jacket and walked out the sanctuary.

"Sell outs!" I screamed at the top of my lungs.

"Hello, Ms. Jackson. I am so sorry about JJ," the older woman said sitting behind her espresso brown colored desk. The office was decorated with a hodgepodge of African art and collectibles. Nothing matched; there was no rhyme or reason. It looked as if The Motherland had opened her mouth and vomited the contents of her stomach across the room.

"Thank you, Mrs. Wilson. It's been a struggle."

"Of course it has," she said in a whisper. "Is there anything I can do for you? Anything at all?" The woman was tall, thick, very light complexioned with long blonde dreadlocks past her shoulders. She smelled of musk and oil.

"Yes, I would like to rent out the Vision Center for JJ's funeral."

Mrs. Wilson paused for a moment. She turned to grab a binder off a shelf behind her. Her shelled earrings swung across her cheek as she moved. She plopped a huge book down and started flipping through the clear plastic pages. She smiled when she found the page.

"Yes! Here it is." She turned the binder toward me.

"It's Harold Hambrick's funeral." She sighed with satisfaction. "Harold was the founder of the Black Family Expo at Exposition Park. The place was packed." She flipped the pages. "I'm sure we'll be able to accommodate the crowd."

"Capacity is not my concern."

"What's your concern?"

I braced myself for the response by shifting in my seat.

"I want to have an open casket."

"Like Emmit Till?" Ms. Wilson said slowly. I nodded. She stared at me for a while. "The preachers said no?"

"They did."

"You know they get money from elected officials?"

"I figured as much."

"Yeah," she said returning the binder to its place on the shelf and pulling out another binder. "That's how they keep them on a tight leash. It's why we don't have black leaders in our community anymore. They're all on the white man's payroll."

"I believe it." I held my breath waiting for Ms. Wilson to reject me.

"How many speakers will you have?"

I gasped. "I, um . . . three. Me, his professor, and his best friend, Reggie." Tears spilled from my eyes. Ms. Wilson reached across the table and I grabbed her hands.

"Thank you," I sobbed. "Thank you so much."

Ms. Wilson flashed a warm smile. "Let's plan the most amazing home going for your son."

"My son." I started to shake. "My son!" I screamed at the top of my lungs. "Oh God! My son! My baby!"

Ms. Wilson dashed around the desk. She sat on the arm of my chair, held me close, and rocked me as I wept for my son.

Outside the Vision Center, reporters interviewed people as they exited the building with tear-stained faces.

Inside the massive auditorium, I stood stoically as the people filled the rows. I looked out from behind the heavy curtains as mothers wept as if it was their son laying lifeless in the steel grey casket. Men wept openly, knowing, but for the grace of God, it could be them laying in that box. And there were the lookie-loos who could have cared less about the life and legacy of my beloved Jared. They came so that they could say they saw that African American man who'd been shot in the face by the LAPD

They gawked, gasping and covering their mouths with their hands as they approached the casket. But I didn't care about them. They had their role. They'd tweet, pin, post about how horrific he looked. And that's exactly what I wanted them to do.

I didn't want JJ to die and have his memory fade, like a story on the evening news. So many had told me I wasn't honoring my son's memory by having him viewed this way. But I knew what I was doing. It was what I did every day on my job: saturating the market with a memorable image. Good or bad, they would remember.

JJ was impeccably dressed in white tie. His face was grossly disfigured from the gunshot wounds, but the mortician had done a fabulous job, considering. I didn't regret my decision. But I was in knots over my eulogy.

In the middle of Dr. Bryant's heart-warming speech espousing Jared's passion, intelligence, and love for science, he broke down. He couldn't compose himself enough to continue, so I stepped in and read the rest of his speech as if I had written it myself.

Then, I stepped to the side and the lights went down and the curtains slowly opened to a huge white screen. The theater filled with a hyped beat . . . followed by "O-lah, O-lah Aay!" and the voice of Jared's best friend Reggie McAllister.

JJ and I were instant best friends. He transferred to Harvard-Westlake in Spring 2007. Most new kids walk into class, shy, nervous. Not Jared Jackson. He walked in confident, assured—like he belonged. He sat next to me and flashed this big grin. 'Hi, I'm Jared Jackson!' He extended his hand like a grown man. "My friends call me JJ." I gave him dap "Then JJ it is— cuz you and me, son, we're going to be boys." And that's where it all began.

The screen showed Jared and Reggie in a homemade video.

We were the modern-day Kid 'n Play. JJ was Kid, light-skinned, freckles, with a not so high, high top fade (Mrs.   Jackson wasn't having the 'buffoonery'), and I was Play, the smoove chocolate brotha with all the moves.

Jared and Reggie were re-enacting the '80's Rollin' with Kid 'n Play video: dressed in identical black and grey shirts, baggy black pants, and high top boots, the two were lip syncing and dancing to the song. The clip showed a younger version of me in the background, laughing, and waving my hands in the air as I sang along with the boys.

Every July we'd load up Mrs. Jackson's Navigator and pile in, eight-deep, for our annual 4th of July trip out to the cabin in Running Springs.

The screen showed a collage of photos of me, Jared, Reggie, and friends: in the lake, kayaking, water skiing, lounging on a boat, on the patio, in front of a big screen playing videos, me in front of the barbecue grill, and Reggie & JJ in the middle of the room dancing together.

Most people saw JJ as this brilliant nerd—with him doing cancer research and what not--and he was. But he was also fun and funny. He loved to laugh. And he had this way about him . . . I don't know, he made everybody in his space feel special. He was authentically caring.

The last segment of the video was pictures of Jared: from baby pictures with his dad (first hair cut, first step, first day of school), to birthday parties and pictures of him with his grandparents.

I loved that dude. He was my brother. I still pick up the phone to call him 5-6 times a day like we used to do, to tell him something random . . . or get his advice . . . or hear that laugh--what I'd do to hear that laugh.

The video froze on a beautiful picture of Jared, head tossed back, laughing, looking happy and carefree.

This is how I choose to remember JJ. Happy. Full of life. Because my life would have been empty without my best friend by my side through all my tragedies and triumphs; my heartbreaks and eternal loves—and the mundane every day life occurrences that most people could care less about.
I love you JJ. Your boy, Reggie Mack.

Adrian

I took two deep breaths and approached the podium in a white knit two-piece suit with a mock turtleneck collar; square mother of pearl beads on the sleeves, pockets, and collar. I looked out into the crowd. The corners of my mouth slowly inched up.

"Thank each of you for being here today to celebrate the life and legacy of Jared Jackson." I gasped and placed my right hand over my stomach, shaken by my own words.

"He was my life." I stared out for a moment, at nothing. "After his father was killed in the Afghanistan war, JJ was my only reason for living. I threw myself into being the best mom. I felt like I had to make up for Brandon's absence. So, he had the best of everything: schools, extra-curricular activities, chemistry sets."

The audience laughed.

"But you know, despite all of my spoiling, he remained unaffected." I cleared my throat. "He wasn't a spoiled brat, or a stuck up snob—he appreciated nice things, but that's all they were to him . . . things. His joy, as Reggie said, came from his relationships.

"He loved people. He genuinely cared, about people. That's why he loved research and the hope of helping people." I removed the microphone from its stand and moved down to the now-closed casket.

On each side of the casket were life-size pictures of Jared. To the right, was a headshot resembling one a model might have in his portfolio. Jared was dressed in a white V-neck sweater. His eyes were sparkling. I stared at the photo.

It was so clear I could see the light brown that encircled the pupils of his hazel eyes. I searched for the reason he was gone, why he had been taken from me, how I would go on . . . I searched, but the sparkling eyes never answered my questions.

I moved in front of the casket and looked at the picture to the left. JJ was in a black suit, shirt, and tie--looking handsome and serious. I had the pictures so the world could see how beautiful JJ was, and the open casket to show how he looked after the police murdered him.

"There's this hole in my heart. A missing. I can't really explain. And it's deeper than the pain of death." I scanned the audience. "I've experienced death before: my husband, my dad, my mom. Brandon's was probably the closest experience that I've felt to this pain because he was also killed. But his death was *a choice* he made because he believed in this country." I chuckled "He believed in this country.

"But I tell you today, as I bury my child, that I do not. There is something fundamentally wrong with a country that turns its head to this." I turned and slowly ran my hand over JJ's casket. "I can't believe in a country that tells black mothers that the children they gave birth to, put their heart and soul into raising to be great men— that their lives simply don't matter."

The people gathered clapped.

"I cannot believe in a country that says a man whose civil rights are being violated by the very institution that his taxes support, does not have the right to get angry, speak out against, or even become aggressive and fight that injustice -- I cannot believe in that type of country."

"Alright!" an older lady said.

"And you can spin it however you want: '*Black men are threatening, they are violent, they are aggressive.*' But what is fundamentally true in relation to that statement is because of the way things are set up in this country, a black man has the right to be any one of those things. Obviously, being the opposite doesn't get you any better results."

There was more applause.

"I know that's right!" a man in the middle of the auditorium stood and clapped.

I turned to look at JJ's casket again. "This is supposed to be a home going celebration, the public honoring of an amazing human being. But my soul is not at peace, my brothers and sisters."

"Amen!" shouted a woman.

"Take your time!" said a man.

"Countless people have told me JJ is in a better place, that he's in heaven with his father. They've told me that it's not for me to understand, that God had other plans for him . . . and that I have to be strong and give my son the proper going home celebration.

"Well, this is all I got, people." I waved my hand around the room. "And I hope it's enough. Because my heart has been shattered into a million pieces. And nothing in me is celebrating. Nothing in me feels peace, or joy. I only feel anger, frustration, pain and despair." Tears welled up my eyes.

I turned back to the podium and placed the mic in its stand. "So many of you have asked how you can help me. It's simple: don't pray for me, or repeat any of those pat lines, that quite frankly sting every time I hear them. I know you mean well, but please . . . don't.

"My son is not in a better place because his place is with me. And I don't have any more strength to give. I could give a damn about having him for twenty-one years, or all the memories I have . . . none of that comforts me. None of that brings me joy. Maybe it will ten years from now when the pain isn't so raw, but right now—I can't bear to hear it.

"If you want to help me, then help me right this wrong. When it's time to vote, please go to the polls. When there is an injustice, please raise your voices. I know that I am vocal. But there are mothers out there who just can't stand. And I get it. Most days it's hard for me to get out my bed.

"So I, you, we—have to speak for them. We have to fight for them." I pointed down at JJ's casket. "We have to fight for *them*. If you want to do something for me, then be in action.

"I won't rest until I get justice for Jared. And that's not everyone's cross to bear. It's mine. But I'm asking you, I'm pleading with you, don't turn your head to the way they are killing our sons, brothers, and fathers. *Black Lives Matter.* Thank you."

Ring. Ring. Ring.
"Hello?"
"Black lives are worthless, you stupid bitch! The police need to rid the world of all
you monkeys." Click.
I slammed the phone down on the base.

"How do you feel about the open casket? What are your opinions about what Ms. Jackson said at JJ's funeral about the police and our government? Do you believe the police have waged a war on African American men in America?" a reporter asked people as they left the funeral.

Adrian

I stood to the left of JJ's open casket and greeted every person in attendance. The Vision Center reported over 1500 people. Fox News reported 500.

Finally, I left the building.

"Ms. Jackson, we spoke to several of the prominent preachers around the city and they indicated that they advised you against an open casket funeral. One said he felt it didn't honor your son's life. Another said he believed it would incite a riot. And another felt that it hindered the path to healing. What do you have to say to those remarks?"

I closed my eyes and slowly rubbed my right temple.

The reporter held up his hand for the cameraman to stop shooting.

"Adrian, I'm sorry. Go bury your son."

"That's okay, Tony." I smiled, tugging at my suit jacket. "I'm fine."

He touched my shoulder and looked into my tired eyes. "Are you sure?"

"Yes. Start the camera." The cameraman tossed the camera back up on his shoulder.

"Hello, we're live on the corner of 43rd and Degnan, at the famed Vision Center, talking to Adrian Jackson, mother of brutally murdered Jared Jackson. Ms. Jackson, our condolences on your loss."

"Thank you."

"There's been much controversy about your decision to have an open casket funeral for your son. Would you like to comment on that?

"My comment is that it's *my* son, I paid for the funeral—I could care less what anybody else thinks."

"Right, but the leaders of this community seemed to think that this act was done to incite people to riot."

"And so what if it was?" I looked around. "No one is rioting."

"No. It seems as if people are sad, hurting."

"They should be sad, angry. And the pastors should be up in arms about these senseless killings. Instead, they're vocal about how I chose to bury *my* child? This was *my* child."

"Yes, of course. No one is questioning your right to bury your child as you see fit. It's just, the pastors in the community feel like you could be more instrumental in helping the community heal. But instead, you keep promoting violence and hatred."

"*Heal?*" The camera zoomed in on my face. My eyebrows came together to form a deep crease in the center of my forehead. "This community can never heal. Not as long as our government continues to condone the brutal murder of innocent African American males. Because the minute we start to heal, another one of our children will be killed, and another, and another. It is time for this madness to stop. But it's only going to stop if we stand up and fight the corruption." The veins on my neck were bulging.

"Non-violently?"

"It seems to me the nonviolent approach is not working too well."

"So you're advocating violence?"

"I'm advocating justice. I've never known any true justice to come about by passive aggressive action. Change comes when pain comes."

"What about Dr. King's non-violent approach to civil rights?"

I looked around. "And yet, we're still addressing the same issues we were addressing back then, aren't we, Tony? I'm ready to see real change, deep systemic change. Not surface niceties."

"Your leaders have put out an open letter to the community indicating that they only support non-violent efforts for resolving these issues.

"Tony," I said. "I am a grown woman, fully capable of making my own decisions – as are the one million African Americans living in this city."

"Right, but they said..."

"I don't care what *they* said. These people don't speak for me. These are not leaders. Leaders can't be bought, or sold, or paid to sell out their community for their own personal gain."

"So--"

"Listen to me. And listen very carefully. Today, I laid my son's body to rest. But I am not done. I won't be done until I get justice. So these people can sell out if they want to, but I won't sit idly by while another child is killed and another mother feels this pain. I won't do it." I took a deep breath.

"I speak for me. And I'm only going to say this once." I spoke directly into the camera. "You racist cop killing cowards, I'm putting you on notice. One way or another, you will be stopped. Black lives *do* matter. And you're about to find out just how much."

I walked past the reporter and cameraman and slid into the waiting limousine.

3 NO JUSTICE, NO PEACE

Chief Bollinger

"What the grand jury had, that the rest of us did not have, was a set of physical facts that told a story that led them to this decision," I said. "Moreover, those facts were consistent with what the officers said under oath. Contrary to what those who want to divide our city is saying, my officers are not coldblooded killers. They were doing their job and following the law."

"And so you just heard Chief Bollinger give his explanation as to why officers Carpenter and Banton were not indicted on murder charges for the August 2014 fatal shooting of Jared Jackson," said a reporter, standing in front of the criminal court house. "As we speak, it looks as if thousands of people have converged on City Hall to protest the non-indictment of the officers."

The news anchor in the studio cut in. "Jim? We're going to cut in to the live feed to an interview with individuals from the protest."

"Hello Jason, we understand that you're there with three individuals from the protest?"

"That's right, Bob. Three local residents who say that there was enough concrete evidence to indict the officers in the fatal shooting of Jared Jackson who was unarmed at the time," Jason said. "They went on to say that while they were not surprised at the verdict, they are very angry that once again, an innocent life has been taken by local law enforcement, and once again the justice system has failed."

"Jason, I'm getting that we have footage from your interview for our listeners to view for themselves. Let's take a look."

The screen faded from the reporters to the earlier interview. "And people wonder why we're so angry? It's because things like this continue," a lady in her late fifties explained. "Our kids, gunned down for no reason at all, and these officers just get off scott free. It's a tragedy and a crying shame!"

"But the jury failed to indict because there wasn't enough evidence to prove that the officers did anything wrong," Jason said.

The woman looked at Jason indignantly.

"I'm trying to understand how one young man without a gun could have done anything so terrible that it caused another man to shoot off his face?"

Then, the screen cut to another interview.

"I expected this. I'm not surprised. White jurors, supporting white cops." This time, it was a twenty-something year old male who spoke. "A black man will never get justice in a city where the jurors don't look like him, or understand his life."

"Okay, but how does that negate evidence? If the evidence points to a fact, then the race of the jury is irrelevant, right?" Jason said.

"No, it's about the spin the prosecution puts on the story. When it's all said and done, that jury decides based on what they believe. And if they believe his life wasn't worth the cement he died on, they won't find the evidence to indict. And that's what happened today. Those white jurors didn't believe that black life had any value."

A Latina woman standing next to him, spoke up. "No, when it came down to it, it was about who they believed because it was Adrian's word against that cop's. His and his partner's And they took their word over the truth. His mother was there, she saw it with her own two eyes."

"What did their verdict say to you?" Jason prodded.

"That those people on that jury could give a damn about the truth." The woman folded her arms across her chest, turned her head and looked away from the camera.

"Jason, we're switching back to the live feed. We just got reports of rioters, overturning cars and setting them on fire. Can you confirm?" Bob asked.

"Yes, Bob, it's true. If you look . . . the camera is going to zoom in . . . the police have created a barrier between us and the growing mob . . . but if you look in middle of the street, angry protestors have toppled what looks to be a Toyota Corolla.

"Apparently the driver was screaming, 'He got what he deserved. Go back to Africa where you belong!' when someone in the crowd yanked him out of his car.

"They pulled the driver out of his car?" Bob repeated. "Did I hear you correctly?"

The crowd in the background was chanting *No Justice, No Peace! No Justice, No Peace!*

"That's right, Bob, this driver was literally yanked out of his car and pummeled by the angry protestors, after which they flipped his car over and set it on fire." Jason had to scream over the shouts of the crowd.

"Why on earth would he drive into this crowd and say that?" Bob asked his co-anchor. "Not that it justifies the attack, but clearly, he didn't think that all the way through."

"Clearly," Jason said. "A police unit was able to safely extract him, but I'd have to agree, Bob, he didn't think that all the way through. I had an opportunity to speak with Adrian Jackson before the police made us move behind this barricade, Bob, and when I asked her about the mob gathering outside, here's what she had to say."

Again, the screen cut to the previous interview.

"I don't know what you're talking about. Where is the *mob*? Where is the *riot*? Anytime there are more than three black people on one corner, we're labeled as an angry mob or rioters. This community is tired of the police using young black men for target practice. And they're vocalizing their frustration--exercising their constitutional rights."

The camera returned to the reporter. "And there you have it. This is Jason Eason reporting live from downtown Los Angeles. Bob, Ann, back to you." Jason faced the crowd marching past him.

"No justice!" a tall chocolate brother with a megaphone screamed.

"No peace!" the crowd replied.

"No justice!"

"No peace!"

Ring. Ring. Ring.

"Hello?"

"Justice was served. Killing all the black criminals who are bringing this country down selling drugs. And all the niggers on welfare draining our system. Killing niggers is the best thing we can do to keep this country pure."

"You are an ignorant ass," I said, and hung up.

Adrian

"JR, do you have the information?" I said into my cell.

"Darlin', why don't you take it easy for a while and grieve, rest, take care of you--"

"Look, Joshua Richards, I don't have time for this, okay?" I paced my office. "Either you're going to help me, or you're not. Just tell me now so I know one way or the other."

JR paused. "Of course I am going to help you. I have put my job on the line getting you this confidential information, are you seriously questioning me right now?" JR asked.

I paused and took a deep breath before I sat on the edge of my desk and stared out at the cityscape. JR was right. He was taking a huge risk sneaking me information about the cops and the case.

"I couldn't even publicly mourn Jared or hold my best friend's hand because of the shit I'm doing. So, back that shit up right now, mister sister."

"Yes, of course—you're right. I'm being foul. I am so sorry," I said, rubbing my temples. I rounded my desk and fell back into my chair. Tears formed in my eyes.

"I'm just so angry and frustrated. I need to see some movement."

"I know, baby girl. I know. As do I. But don't take that shit out on me. I'm way too fragile and don't do verbal abuse—not from my men, and I definitely ain't gone take it from no breeder!"

I laughed out loud. "You fool."

"I'm just sayin'."

Joshua and I had been friends for over four years. He worked in the mailroom of Dietrich Advertising Agency as a part of the D-Prep summer residency program in Los Angeles. It was also the same year Dietrich had its first female at the helm, Linda Lewis, who took over the role as Chairman in January 2013.

Joshua stuck his head into my office one day and said, "Excuse me, Mrs. Jackson, do you have two minutes?"

I looked up from an ad campaign I was due to pitch the next morning.

"I do. Come in."

"I am so sorry to bother you." Joshua sat in the red chair in front of my pewter metal and glass desk.

My office was very modern. Minimalist, straight lines, bright, and bold—greys, blacks, whites and reds.

"So, I was wondering. How can a brother get up out of the mailroom and into an office--heck, a cubicle would even be okay?"

I smiled. I had seen Joshua around the office. You couldn't help but notice, there weren't too many Black people at Dietrich. He was always professional, impeccably dressed. So for him to come at me with straight Ebonics tickled me.

"Would it now?" I placed the ad down, giving Joshua my full attention.

"Yes, ma'am," he said in earnest. "It's been six months. And I get it. A brotha's got to pay his dues. But, seriously? I'm wearing Hugo Boss suits. Not at all mailroom material, right?" He threw his hand up in the air in disgust.

"No, not at all." I replied.

"So, I thought I'd ask you, seein' you *boss* in your designer suits and corner office." He sat patiently as if I could honestly 'tell him' in two minutes.

"What's your major?"

"Business, with an emphasis in Economics and Forecasting from Morehouse University."

"I attended Spelman!" I screamed. I jumped up and ran around the desk.

"Hey!" I hugged him hard. He returned the hug in true Morehouse/Spelman fashion.

"You a cougar?" He laughed. "I should have known."

We laughed together as I returned to my side of the desk, a new vibe in the air.

I got right to work on it, asking him a few more questions, then giving him an assignment to prepare an analytical report on the marketing trends for the Taco Bell account that I was going to have him work. After I explained it all to him, he sat back in his chair and smiled.

"What?" I returned the smile.

"I am so grateful for a college education. Bless our HBCU founders."

I chuckled.

The following week JR presented me with the most thorough analytical report I'd seen in my entire advertising career. I was so proud.

Four years after that, JR left the ad agency and went to work for the City Attorney's Office as an Actuary. In his role, JR assessed financial security systems, focusing on their complexity, mathematics, and their mechanisms. He also had access to confidential information on police and court data.

JR was the one who told me that Officer Carpenter lied about there being a carjacking reported—the supposed reason for pulling JJ over, which I heard the officer say to Jared. And, he'd gotten me the official dossier on Chief Bollinger.

"The problem is, you can't use any of this information in court," JR commented.

"That's not the problem, son. This report is my secret weapon." I smiled broadly at my dear friend. "Knowing the truth helps me shape my strategy. Even if I can't use it in court, it keeps me ten steps ahead of those corrupt bastards."

"You got me doing some Bourne Identity shit over here."

" Just do your damn job," I replied. "Did you get a copy of the discovery and transcripts from the officer's debriefing after the shooting?"

"Of course I did. Who you think you're messing with, some amateur?" he snorted.

"No need to get your panties in a bunch. I know I can count on you," I said.

"I'll drop it off at the same location as always."

The same location was a laundromat on Vermont and Jefferson. Just across from USC. I'd go in and hand Marisol five dollars, and she'd hand me a bundle of fluff n fold laundry. Except, in between the bundle of towels was a manila folder.

I scanned through the documents until I came across what I was looking for: depositions for Sergeant Carpenter and Officer Banton. I sat in the parking lot for over an hour reading the transcription. They lied through the entire deposition. I wasn't surprised.

I highlighted the discrepancies. I had made up mind that it was time to do things differently. Waiting for justice from our criminal law enforcement agency was not going to give me the results I needed.

4 GAME ON!

"Good morning, on the *Today Show*, we have an exclusive interview with mother of brutally slain LA youth Jared Jackson. If you recall, a grand jury failed to indict twenty-year LAPD Sergeant, Peter Carpenter on felony homicide charges. Stating lack of sufficient evidence, despite first account testimony by the victim's mother."

Matt Lauer turned to Adrian and said, "Thank you Ms. Jackson for joining us this morning."

"Thank you for having me, Matt."

"Allow me to start by expressing my sincere condolences for your loss."

"Thank you."

"As I mentioned, a grand jury failed to indict Sergeant Peter Carpenter on any charges relating to the death of your twenty-one year old son…"

"Murder."

"Pardon me?"

"Murder. Death is what happens when your organs shut down; murder is what happens when another person willfully and intentionally takes another person's life." The camera zoomed in on my poker face. Not quite emotionless, but definitely no discernible emotion.

"Sergeant Carpenter was never tried in a court of law, therefore--"

"Neither was Jared. But hey . . . he's dead, so to hell with him?"

"Ms. Jackson--"

"Mr. Lauer, I came on your show today because your producers said I'd have a forum to state my case--*And* my case is this . . . my son is dead. Killed by a police officer for no reason other than he was black. And then, he was not prosecuted. Do you know what that says about our judicial system, Matt?" I answered before he could say a word. "The system failed. That failure is tantamount to a public decree that says black lives don't matter."

"Who is saying that?"

"The police department is saying it, the superior court is saying it. Cops have permission to kill at will."

"What would you like to happen, Ms. Jackson?"

"I would like for Congress to enact a law that makes it illegal for police officers to racially profile. And if convicted of racially profiling, have them charged with a felony crime."

"Yeah, I'm not so sure about that one. While it's true that not all black men are criminals, some are. If this law is enacted, it's basically saying a police officer can't question a black man--" Matt said.

"When did I say that? What *I* said was, the law would abolish racial profiling."

"Right but, every African American pulled over would cry racial profiling."

"Then the police better have a bona fide reason for pulling over African Americans." I stared at Matt for a moment. "Seems . . . reasonable to me . . . What do you think, Matt?"

"I think we'll pause for a break. But when we return, more on this heated issue about race in America. Thank you, Ms. Jackson for spending time with us this morning."

Ring. Ring. Ring.

"Hello?"

"I will shoot you between the eyes like your good for nothing son if you don't stop your whining on public television about how corrupt the police are."

"Listen, you coward. I am not scared of you! Come do it now. I'm outside waiting for you." I hung up, grabbed my .38 and walked outside.

One hour later, I walked back in the house and placed the gun back in my safe.

Chief Bollinger

I watched the *Today Show* interview with Adrian Jackson. She was becoming a major pain in my ass. This case would be the death of my career as Chief of Police if I didn't get ahead of it.

I opened up the file on Adrian Jackson. Even though I'd been given this information a few days ago, I didn't think I'd need it. But after watching her interview this morning, maybe there were a few things about Ms. Jackson that I needed to know.

I read through the pages:

Born Adrianna Isabelle Green, June 24, 1968, two minutes before her twin brother Andre Isadore at Centinela Hospital in Inglewood, CA. Andre died at age 3. The babysitter found him floating face down in his parents' swimming pool.

Adrian attended Catholic school and was an outstanding student. She was at the top of her class, the captain of her basketball, swim, and track teams.

I turned the page and took in the information about Adrian's college years:

The report said that even though she was an excellent student, Adrian was also very social. She was president of the Associated Student Body for two years at Spelman University, as well as an active member of a black sorority.

She transferred to Northwestern her junior year where she met Brandon Jackson, a pre-law student, majoring in Criminal Justice. He was also in Army ROTC. They graduated in May 1990 and were married September of that same year.

Adrian started as an intern at Cramer-Krasselt, and advanced to a mid-level management position. Brandon was commissioned as an officer in the Army. In 1995, Adrian gave birth to Jared.

In 2001, Brandon was deployed to Afghanistan. He did two tours and in 2007, was killed in combat by an Improvised Explosive

Device—a homemade bomb. Afghan insurgents claimed the bombing attack that killed six US troops.

Adrian received Dependency and Indemnity Compensation of $1,233.23 a month: full death benefits paid to spouses and children of those who died while on active duty, on top of a separate 1.5 million dollar life insurance policy.

Adrian moved back home to California with her parents for three years at which time she attended grad school and obtained her MBA in Marketing from Stanford University. She secured a lead role as Strategy Team Leader for Liquid Agency where she oversaw development of brand strategy, creative and editorial direction, and program execution for Southern California.

In the Spring of 2010 her father, Dimitri Green suffered a massive heart attack and died. In January 2012, Edith Green was diagnosed with Stage IV triple negative breast cancer. Ms. Green succumbed to cancer at age 77 in May 2012.

I closed the folder and sat staring into space for several minutes. Nothing in that report gave me insight into Adrian Jackson's thoughts, although I understood her motivation. She wanted justice. I rubbed my temples.

Getting justice for her son could result in the complete dismantling of the department. There was so much at stake. So much more than what appeared on the surface. Despite the loose cannons in the department, this police force kept the city safe. The good far outweighed the bad.

I stood and grabbed the 8 x 11 photo of Adrian Jackson. As I stared into her green eyes, I thought about my own sons and tried to imagine the pain she had to be going through.

But I had a job to do. And I would do it.

"Game on, Adrian Jackson."

"Courtney, it's been three weeks since the California grand jury decided not to indict the officers for the brutal murder of the promising young scientist, Jared Jackson, and the community is refusing to let up," said late night BET personality host, Marcus Brennan.

"That's right, Marcus. It seems as if every night the numbers are multiplying. So far, eighty die-ins have been reported across the county. The majority of them have taken place in front of the Parker police station in downtown Los Angeles.

"The protests have been vocal, but no major incidents have been reported. In larger metropolitan areas like Florida and Missouri, protestors have been met with militarized police wearing riot gear—some locations, like Cleveland, Ohio have gone so far as to deploy army tanks.

"When asked to respond to the police's reaction, Adrian Jackson replied, 'Everything they do is excessive. Pull over a young black man, kill him. Have a peaceful protest, deploy army tanks. It's overkill. If they're that trigger happy, and that damned scared, then maybe they shouldn't be on the streets. Maybe they should apply for a better suited job where they can feel secure about who is in their space, and not feel compelled to shoot everything that moves.'"

Chief Bollinger

"What the fuck, Roger?" the Mayor of LA screamed in my ear. "Shut that Adrian Jackson woman up already!"

"Yes sir, I'm trying. She does have the Freedom of Speech Act on her side," I said.

"If you keep on talking like that you will be out of a job soon! You need to stand up for and protect us!" the Mayor said. "You're the freakin' Chief of Police for heaven's sake!"

"Well of course I'm going to protect us. That's what I'm doing every day." I paced back and forth behind my desk.

"This woman is inciting a riot in our city. I'm up for re-election next year, I don't need this, and if you want to keep your job, you'd better fix it." The Mayor hung up the phone in my face. I slammed the phone on the base.

"Gonzalez!" I screamed through the door.

"Yes, Chief?" The female officer stuck her head through the door.

"Get the black church coalition in here, now!"

"Yes, Chief."

Chief Bollinger

"She doesn't listen to us," Pastor Mitchell said.

"Well who does she listen to? You're the leaders of the black community, aren't you?" I ran my fingers through my hair.

"As far as I can see she doesn't listen to anyone," Pastor Parker said. He sat in his chair with his legs crossed. "She doesn't have a spiritual counselor that she turns to during crises, at least not openly."

"Because she's cold as ice inside. She doesn't have a spirit." I said.

"She's very strong willed. Not cold," Bishop Brown corrected. The other pastors nodded. "But you are going to have a problem with her."

I slammed my hand on the table. "Going to? I am having major problems now and I need you to shut her down; that's what you're paid to do."

"We can only influence the members of our congregations, Roger. We don't have control over *all* black people, especially non-practicing ones," Bishop Jennings said.

"Then you're no good to me." I stood. "I need to be able to neutralize people whether or not they're Christian." I walked to my window and stared out. "You are supposed to be the leaders of your community, not just the leaders of your churches—that's what you told me when you were negotiating your rates, right?"

The pastors squirmed in their chairs.

"And we have been just that," Jordan Parker, Jr. replied. "Every time you've asked us to handle a situation, we have. Don't stand there and question our ability to influence the African American community because one person is giving you a run for your money. We never said we could control every black person in LA County. We're doing exactly what your donations pay us to do. Don't minimize our contributions."

I turned to look at the table of men. What I didn't need right now was for my only inside source into the black community to turn against me. "No, Pastor Parker. You're absolutely right. You help keep things calm in your communities. I do not question or minimize your influence," I said. "I am just afraid this woman is going to incite a riot."

"Has it ever occurred to you to give her what she wants?" Pastor Mitchell replied. "That's one sure way of avoiding a riot."

I shook my head. "The grand jury decided not to indict those officers. I can't undo that," I barked.

"Yes, but you know what she wants. She wants policies that protect African Americans from your trigger happy racist ass cops," Jordan Parker, Jr. retorted.

I stared at Pastor Parker, who in turn sat up straight in his chair and returned the stare. Thinking long term, I turned away first. Pastor Parker glanced at the rest of the pastors around the table who nodded.

"I don't have control over policies."

"Of course you do," Bishop Brown said. "You're the highest ranking officer in the city. If you don't, then who does?"

"She wants vindication," I said. "I can't give her that."

"She's been very clear that she wants systemic change in the violent and discriminatory policing culture of the Los Angeles Police Department. That, you have control over as Chief of Police, right?" Pastor Parker asked.

I started to respond, but thought better of it. Instead I stared out the window for a moment longer.

"Gentlemen, thank you very much for making it here under such short notice. As always, I appreciate your wise counsel. Sergeant Gonzalez will have your checks ready for you on your way out."

5 THE BAIT AND SWITCH

Chief Bollinger

"Got dammit! This bitch is out of control!" Jim screamed, storming into my office.

I looked up into a beet red face, spewing spit everywhere. I leaned back in my black leather chair and waited for Jim to give me the news.

"She's called a press conference!" Jim plopped down, exasperated, in the chair in front of my desk. I knew better than to try and get in a word until Jim had exhausted himself with at least a few tirades first.

"A press conference, like she's a politician. Like she's the Chief of Police. The nerve of this woman." He ran his fingers through his wispy, red comb over. "You know this is just to keep the rioters riled up?" He stood up and paced the area in front of the desk.

"She is a cunning and conniving bitch, but I gotta tell you--" He stopped in front of me and placed his hands on his hips.

"She's not a dumb bitch."

I laughed out loud, knowing that was high praise coming from James Rasmussen.

"When is the press conference?"

"This Wednesday at 10:00 am in front of City Hall."

"Then, get her in here at 9:00 am and let's get control of this situation once and for all. Get the comptroller in here so I can figure out the Mayor's price point."

I turned my attention back to my report and Jim left my office.

✊ ✊ ✊

Adrian

"Thank you for meeting with us, Mrs. Jackson," the mayor said. "Please have a seat."

I walked across the room to the chair Mayor Villanueva pointed to. Every eye was on me as I sauntered across the floor in a black V-neck, three quarter sleeves shift dress, with contrasting cream trim in a wide cream band.

The tiny room held about twenty-five people. From what I could see it was the mayor, the Council members, the black church leaders, and a few other people I did not recognize.

"Thank you, Mayor Villanueva." I took my seat.

"My pleasure. So, let's cut to the chase, shall we?"

"By all means, let's do," I replied.

"You're scheduled for a press conference in less than an hour, where half the city will be watching." The mayor sat on the edge of the table in front of me. "And the other half will be viewers in cities from across the country."

I didn't respond.

"You have experienced an immeasurable loss. As such, our community has experienced a major loss."

Members of the council nodded in agreement.

"Now it's time for us to rebuild our city and heal--"

"I'm not interested in healing," I said.

"Excuse me?"

"I *said*, I'm not interested in healing."

The mayor's eyebrows nearly touched his hairline. "What do you mean you're not interested in healing?" He dramatically searched the faces in the room. "You mean, you want to keep the hatred and discord going on in our great city?"

There were grunts and gasps.

"I think your officers do an adequate job of doing that, Mr. Mayor." I looked him in the eyes.

He smiled warmly, then reached over and touched my shoulder. "Adrian, I'm no stranger to racial profiling." He nodded. "I'm from East L.A. I've been pulled over for driving brown more times than I can count on both hands and feet."

The men in the room said, 'That's right' 'Me too' or 'Amen,' some form of agreement.

"I do understand the problems we face in eradicating racial profiling, excessive force, and police brutality in this city."

"I'm glad to hear that."

"But! Flaming the fire is not the way to do it," he said. "First of all, it's just going to get more people hurt unnecessarily."

The men in the room nodded.

"Secondly, it only creates divisiveness. In a major metropolitan city, you need for everyone to be on the same page. Practically speaking, you need everyone's consensus in order to bring about change. If you pit black against white, then they will take a stand along color lines—doesn't matter if they're right or wrong. What matters is which side they belong to."

I looked bored.

"Adrian. You say you don't want more black men killed. But what you're doing is a sure fire way of doing just that."

I looked at the mayor like he was crazy." Armando," I said, calling the mayor by his first name." Are you kidding me right now?"

The mayor looked confused.

"I say I don't want more black me killed *by your racist police*." I turned to face the other men in the room. "I'm not speaking Mandarin here. It's not okay that police officers have a license to kill black boys and men at will. It's not oaky that the judicial system is rigged to protect them after they commit murder. And it's not okay that you feel you can talk to me like I'm some uneducated hood rat."

The mayor stepped back as if he had just been slapped. He started to speak, but I held my hand up to his face.

"Save the theatrics for someone who gives a damn about the politics of this city. That would not be me. What I care about Mayor Villanueva, members of the Council, men of the clergy, and whoever the rest of you are, is justice." I stood up to leave.

The mayor motioned to the young white guy at the corner of the table. Two councilmen blocked the door so I could not exit.

"I know you better move," I said to the white guy. "I am not afraid of you," I said to the Latino guy.

"They aren't going to harm you, Mrs. Jackson."

I turned to face the mayor. "Oh, I know. I was warning *them*." I stood with my hands folded across my chest. "Tell your goons to move before I have to make good on my threat."

The mayor laughed. "You are a feisty one," he said. "Just give me five more minutes, and then you can be on your way to your press conference."

I looked down at my watch. They'd had me locked up in this room for nearly a half hour.

"Fine." I returned to my chair. "What?"

The mayor smiled. The young white guy, who was the assistant to the comptroller, slid a 9 x 12 manila envelope across the table in front of me.

"Open it," the Mayor said.

I opened the envelope. Inside were two stacks of bills. I was confused. I looked up at the Mayor.

"It's $50,000.00"

"For what?" I said.

"For you." The mayor walked around the table and sat next to me. "Take a trip, pay off some debt, buy a new car, start a foundation – whatever you want. The money is yours. Tax free, to do with whatever you want."

"I just have to . . ."

"You don't have to do anything." The mayor was very skillful with his language. "What we'd hope you'd consider saying at your press conference, is that you want peace. You want the city to heal. Tell them you want the rioting to stop."

I watched as the mayor practically wrote my speech. "As a matter of fact, you might want to tell them that JJ wouldn't want all of this damage and destruction to the city. Ask them for peaceful demonstrations."

"So this is how you got Rodney King and Michael Brandon's mother to give those pleas for peace?" I shook my head. It made sense now. Rodney King was still swollen from the beat down the cops had given him and he was talking about "Can't we all just get along?" That never set right with me. But now I got it. A backroom deal bought the mayor a quick and easy way to diffuse the crowd.

I shoved the money back in the envelope. I stood, placing it neatly under my arm.

A huge grin crossed the mayor's face. "If you do accept the money, the only thing we do insist on," the white guy slid a piece of paper in front of me, "is that you sign this confidentiality agreement indicating that you are not to reveal the source of that income as the City of Los Angeles, or mention that this conversation ever took place." I paused for a moment, thinking. "Can you agree to that?"

"Yes," I said. I signed the document, stood and walked toward the door.

The room broke out into chatter. The mayor raised his hands for silence.

"Very good. And thank you, Mrs. Jackson," the Mayor said.

"We're going to make changes in the police department, I assure you."

I grunted as I the left room.

✊ ✊ ✊

Adrian

"Good morning, ladies and gentlemen. Thank you so much for being here today. It's been over a month since my son JJ was brutally murdered and there has been no justice in this case." I motioned to the side of the stage. "And since his murder, three more African American men have been shot and killed.

"Joining me on stage are their mothers, Darlene, Kim and Julissa."

The women stood on both sides of me.

"Today we stand in solidarity, putting police departments across the county on high alert that we will not tolerate this blatant disregard for human life."

The crowd erupted in cheers.

Joleen looked frail, as if she were going to drop dead right there on the stage. She was dabbing the corners of her eyes with a handkerchief to catch the constant stream of tears. I hugged her.

"Mrs. Patterson. I know, honey."

She cried on my shoulder. I rubbed her back, and cried with her. The other mothers on stage embraced us. We stood for three minutes holding each other and crying tears of knowing. It was the only time during the press conference that the crowd was silent.

I pulled away from the huddle, wiped tears from my face, then returned to the microphone.

"On behalf of all the black mothers who give birth to black sons with the expectation that they are going to live happy productive and long lives, we demand legislation be passed that protects their freedoms, their rights, and their lives as American citizens."

The crowd went wild, chanting Black Lives Matter! Black Lives Matter! Black Lives Matter!

"Just Friday, the judge gave strong indications he might toss the lawsuit the four of us are seeking requesting an independent investigation of this prosecutor's handling of grand jury proceedings in our sons' shooting cases.

"California County Circuit Judge Jacob Antos told our attorneys that an outside investigation may be unnecessary since the U.S. Justice Department reached the same conclusion as the county grand jury that declined to prosecute Peter Carpenter, who shot and killed my son Jared. We requested that Judge Antos appoint a special prosecutor to investigate misconduct on county prosecutor, Mark Fontaine's part.

"We believe county prosecutor Fontaine acted in bad faith and intended to prevent all of the evidence from being presented to the grand jury to ensure Sergeant Carpenter was not charged with a crime.

"This is a perfect example as to why these prosecutors can't be partial. The police are the prosecutors' primary witnesses. These departments work closely building cases against criminals – these prosecutors cannot aggressively prosecute police, they can't be objective—they are too intricately intertwined."

The crowd clapped. "That's right!" one supporter yelled.

"That's like having the fox watch the hen house!" another screamed.

"That's why today, I am giving Mrs. Joleen Patterson, Mrs. Mable Powell, and Mrs. Belinda Carter each $15,000 to cover legal retainers for attorneys in their sons' court cases."

The crowd cheered.

"Today, Mrs. Patterson, marks the first step for seeking justice for the brutal and senseless murder of DeShaun Patterson," I said to Mrs. Patterson.

She sat speechless, then she cried and rocked in her chair.

I turned to the two hundred plus individuals holding signs and chanting.

"Fellow Americans, let's be clear about what today is. Today is a day of reckoning. We won't stop until every marginalized American, black, brown—it doesn't matter the color of skin—is given the same protections and privileges as white America. We did not give birth to our children for law enforcement to kill them. It stops today! No justice!" I shouted, fist held high in the air.

"No peace!"

"No justice!" I screamed.

"No peace!"

"Black lives matter!' I yelled.

"Black lives matter!"

"Damn straight." I left the stage holding hands with the other mothers.

✊ ✊ ✊

"That bitch, that fucking, black bitch!" Jim screamed at the TV. "Look at that shit, Chief! I knew she couldn't be trusted."

I sat silently. "You mean you knew she couldn't be bought."

"Fucking right." He paced back and forth. "She's not the type. She's not poor. She's educated. She has her own money. Fifty-thousand dollars didn't mean shit to her," Jim said.

"Because it's not about money, Jim," I replied. "This is about a grieving mother getting justice for her son's murder. It's pure and simple. And she won't be bought, or bribed, or scared into anything else. I don't know when you idiots are going to get that."

Mayor Villanueva

I watched Adrian get on stage and make a complete fool of me. First, she came off looking like St. AJ, protector of all black mothers, by giving those mothers my bribe money.

Secondly, she did the complete opposite of what I asked her to do. Instead of encouraging the rioters to have peaceful protests, she incited them and got them even more riled up.

The kicker of course, was that there was nothing I could do about it. It was bribe money, completely off the record. She could use that money any way she wanted and she used it to build her stake in the game.

It was a brilliant move. I was pissed. But I tipped my hat off to Adrian. She turned *the bait and switch* on me.

"I wonder what she was originally planning to do at the press conference before she got the money?" Councilman Warkowsky said to me. "Just stand in solidarity with the mothers?"

"Probably so," I replied. "Her goal is to not let the momentum die.

"That picture of the mothers huddled is going to be on the front page of every newspaper tomorrow. You watch and see."

"We just gave her more fuel to fan the flames. And there ain't shit we can do about it."

I threw my pen on the desk, leaned back in my chair, and rubbed my forehead.

6 MY PARTNER IN CRIME

Adrian

"Adrian Jackson is not patriotic. She's not an American and she should be ashamed of herself for inciting riots, dividing our country, and smearing the good name of our boys in blue!" Senator Walsh screamed.

I sat on my couch, reviewing an ad by one of my junior marketing specialists. I looked up into the eyes of Senator Walsh as he spoke about me as if he knew me personally.

"She is basically asking for law enforcement to give hardened criminals a pass just because they are African American," he continued.

"Senator Walsh, I'm going to ask you to stop the fear-mongering and stick to the facts, sir," correspondent Tina McFarland said. "Adrian Jackson has only asked that those representing the electorate do their jobs and protect innocent Americans."

"They police are sworn to protect and serve decent Americans, not criminals. And what Adrian Jackson is basically asking us to do is to put the lives of our police officers in jeopardy--"

"No sir. What she's demanding of you, and all those elected into office to represent *all* Americans--not just the white and privileged--is to respect black lives."

"Police officers are law abiding officers of the law."

"Until they shoot innocent victims. Then they become cold blooded murderers, Tina interjected.

"Those cases are few and far between. On the whole, the number of legally and justifiable deaths far outweigh those few, and unfortunate, might I add, unlawful ones."

"Well how unfortunate for Adrian Jackson that her only child happened to be one of those few and far between."

"Yes, it is unfortunate, and I am deeply sorry for her loss."

"And Mrs. Brown's, Senator?"

"Pardon me?"

"Are you deeply sorry for Michael Brown's mother's loss, or Eric Gardner's mother, or Trayvon Martin's mother, or Eric Grey's--"

"Of course I am deeply sorry for all of these mothers' losses," the Senator shouted. "But again, they are not the norm--"

"They *are* the norm," Tina interjected. "The malicious actions and cover ups are the culture of local police departments across the country. And Adrian Jackson, along with thousands of other Americans demand that you do your job and pass legislation that protects innocent Americans from these entitled, privileged and protected murderers."

"Ms. McFarland!" Senator Walsh said. "You paint a broad stroke of criminalized stereotypes of our officers. We have very decent, law abiding officers on the force, who work hard and respect human life.

"To lump them together with the small percent who have gone rogue is deftly unfair. It puts their character in question, and quite frankly, puts their lives at risk. But more importantly it does an injustice to the amazing Americans that they are."

"Senator Walsh, welcome to the world of a black man in America."

I laughed out loud. "You go Tina!" The telephone rang. "Hello?"

"Hey AJ, it's Linda. What's up woman? How are you doing?"

"I'm good. Redlining Channing's GroupOn revamp."

"What? Are you serious?" Linda said. "Bitch, you're supposed to be resting and recuperating."

"I am resting and recuperating, *and* redlining Channing's GroupOn presentation. What?"

"*What?* Have you taken any time for you?"

I sighed. "Time for what?" I tossed the folder on the couch next to my feet. "All I am inside is sad and angry Lindy Lu," I whispered. "Who needs to spend countless hours swimming in either of those?"

"I hear you, honey bunches. But, if you keep going a hundred miles a minute then you're going to crash and burn."

"I hope so, then maybe I'll be able to sleep." I rubbed my temples before I grabbed my purse and pulled out a pocket mirror. "I gotta do something. I'm a light-skinned sistah, you can really see the black circles under my eyes."

We laughed.

"Yeah well, I told you what to do."

"I don't want any pills." I rolled my eyes. "That's the white woman's way of handling life. I'm not a white woman."

"No shit," Linda replied. "A white woman would not be prancing around town publicly threatening the police, calling out the president, and checking prime time news anchors." I chuckled.

"Is that what I'm doing? I thought I was seeking justice."

"You know what I mean."

"I do. As a white woman, you wouldn't be doing what I'm doing." I glanced over at the TV and saw B-roll of rioters holding signs that read: *Freedom and Justice for All Torture Victims*. I turned up the volume.

"Victims of police torture under former Chicago Police Commander Jon Burge would receive an apology and access to a $5.5 million fund under a reparations package that Mayor Rahm Emanuel and a number of Chicago aldermen proposed Tuesday," the female reporter said.

"More than one hundred people have accused Burge and officers under his command of shocking, suffocating, and beating them into giving false confessions in the 1970s and 1980s. The city has so far paid about $100 million in lawsuit settlements to Burge victims."

"You'd be locked up in a room somewhere high as a kite off of vicodin or oxycontin—numb to life and pain, oblivious to anything going on in the world . . ." I said, turning my attention back to my friend.

"Yep. I'd be none the wiser, until my frail sensibilities could handle the harsh realities of this life racked with so much pain," she said dramatically.

We chuckled together.

"You pill head."

"I got it honest. My mom rolled with the best of them. She'll tell you in a minute, it's what saved her forty year marriage; that, and the fact that she was screwing her pharmacist. But she always manages to forget that second part."

"Lindy Lu, girl you are a hot mess."

"At least you laughed a little bit."

I smiled. It amazed me how many people were trying to make me smile and laugh. I wanted to scream, *laugh for what? My son was shot in the face, and his killer got off scott-free. What the hell is there to laugh about?* But I never did.

My eyes turned back to the television as the mayor of Chicago spoke into the camera.

"Today, we stand together as a city to try and right those wrongs, and to bring this dark chapter of Chicago's history to a close."

His words made me think of L.A.'s mayor. I would have been happy with a statement like that from Villanueva 'Let's right the wrongs,' that's what I wanted, some accountability.

But instead what I got was some backroom deal to try and buy off my silence. Pretend as if things were changing, but all along maintaining the status quo.

"Listen, black woman. I need you take care of yourself. I get that it's hard. I get that you're hurting. I even get that I don't really get all that you're going through and don't have the right to say anything to you. But you *have* to sleep, and eat--and guess what? You *have* to grieve."

"Listen, white woman," I said. "I know." And I did know. I'd done nothing but cry since JJ had been killed. I gasped. *JJ was dead.* Every time I said it—it just felt so unreal. I knew a part of the reason why I kept on the move was so that I wouldn't have to deal with my reality.

"So, are you still going to the cabin for a few days?" she asked me.

"Yep. I'm going to send Channing these edits and be out the door by ten-thirty. You got the landline number in case anything comes up?"

"In case there's anything I, as the CEO, can't handle, you mean?" Linda said.

"Yes. That's exactly what I mean."

7 RUNNING SPRINGS

Adrian

I packed my car with two bags of groceries and a case of water. I packed light because I had everything I needed at the cabin. The two and a half hour drive was easy in terms of traffic, but difficult emotionally as the memories of all the trips with JJ and Reggie flooded my brain.

As I rounded the winding curves up the mountain, my shoulders started to loosen. I loved Running Springs. Everything about the place was calming and relaxing. Running Springs was a mountain community in the San Bernardino Mountains, and a major gateway to Lake Arrowhead, Arrowbear, Green Valley Lake, and Big Bear.

I remembered the first time I visited the place. It was with Linda. Her parents owned a cabin there because they had season passes to Snow Valley. I fell in love with the place. With my first bonus check from Dietrich, I purchased a four-bedroom three-bath cabin off of Knoll View for a little under $280,000. It was built in 1998, and besides the cedar siding lining the three-story 2,500 sq. ft. building, nothing about it resembled a cabin. I loved the way it sat back off the street, high up on a hill.

From the street, you could see the three-car garage on the bottom level, the hundred foot deck, on the second level, and the red brick drive way that aligned the landscaped hill that led to the huge cabin.

The drive way went up an incline and then flattened out to lead to the garage and makeshift basketball court for the boys. I smiled remembering all the games JJ and Reggie played in that driveway.

The boys always complained about carrying their bags and groceries up the two flights of stairs. And I would always say the same thing, "Shut up, man up, and deal with it." After a while, I knew they complained just to hear me say that.

Inside the cabin, I put the groceries away and moved into the living room. I stretched out on the couch, grabbing a blanket that was draped along the back. I tried to close my eyes and sleep; my body was so heavy, so tired, but my brain was busy at work, churn, churn, churning thoughts and memories, thoughts and memories. I tossed and turned and eventually threw the blanket off and got up.

It was in this living room where the boys made that Kid n Play video Reggie played at the funeral. It was in this living room where they celebrated the 4th of July every year. I'd be on the deck drinking my homemade pink panties, and the boys would either be playing video games, basketball, or down on the lake.

I smiled but then a second later, I fell to the floor. It was like I was handicapped, and someone had snatched my cane from me. My legs completely gave out from under me.

I lay there for hours, sobbing, deep, dark, hollow sobs that came from my gut. I looked up and what was once bright beaming rays, had now turned to royal blue skies; a few clouds slowly made their way past my window. I just lay there. It was the first time in months that my mind was quiet, and I enjoyed the peace inside my head.

The next time I looked up, the room was dark, the blue sky was pitch black and covered with a blanket of twinkling white lights. Disoriented, I sat up and focused on my surroundings.

"Jared!" I shouted. And then it hit me, like a hard sock in the stomach.

"Got dammit!" I screamed at the top of my lungs. I peeled myself off the cold hardwood. "Ouch." My right shoulder was sore.

I walked over to the entryway, flipped on the light, picked up my bag, and walked upstairs to the master bedroom. The sensor triggered the light in the massive bedroom. I stood in the doorway for a few minutes, then walked across the room and slowly sprawled across the bed.

What am I doing here? I rolled over on my back and stared up at the cedar panels of my vaulted ceiling. I remembered purchasing this place, thinking it would be our home away from home. And it had become that.

For sure, the usual suspects would meet every Fourth of July: Jared, Reggie, JR, Linda—and if any of them had significant others at the time, then their *plus ones*. I never had a plus one. After Brandon, my heart was too fragile to try again. I filled my days with advertising, and my evenings and weekends with Jared's activities.

My mind started to drift. Finally I would find that elusive thing called sleep.

✊ ✊ ✊

I put on a fresh pot of coffee.

The sun's rays permeated the huge kitchen window, almost blinding me. I placed my hand over my eyes to block the light so I could see down the road.

It was a quiet neighborhood. Most of the neighbors on the street had lived there for over thirty years. When I bought the place, one by one, they made their way over. And one by one, told me their stories.

I ate a fried egg and avocado with sour dough toast for

breakfast, just to put something in my stomach. I hadn't had an appetite since this all began. Like my inability to sleep, I was unable to eat regularly. I ate because I had to, not because I wanted to.

I walked outside to the deck and stood in the sun. The warmth felt good. I sat on the chair and closed my eyes, not believing that this was my life. Everything in me said it wasn't real, that somehow I'd wake up and my real life would miraculously appear.

When I thought about Jared, tears started to roll down my face. I tried to stifle the scream building up in my throat, but it was erupting at warped speed.

Just as it hit the top of my throat, a wave of heat shot through my body. I jumped up and ran for the door, but before I made it two feet, I vomited all over my redwood deck. A couple of heaves had me on my knees. When I was empty, I sat for a while gathering energy.

What am I doing here? I got up and walked down the two flights of stairs. At the bottom, I unraveled the water hose, drug it up the stairs, and washed all traces of my bile from my cedar wood deck.

"Hey, kiddo!" I turned to see Bob waving.

"Bob!" I said to my next door neighbor. "Hey!" I threw the water hose over the balcony, then went downstairs and down the long driveway to meet Bob in the front of my house.

We hugged. "I wasn't expecting you guys so soon. What's the occasion?" Bob smiled.

I froze. Pain registered across my face.

"What's wrong?" Bob watched me look down at my shoes, then back up at his face.

"It's Jared," I said. "Bob, Jared was killed back in August."

Bob looked confused. He turned his back to me, then next thing I knew he was sliding down the side of the fence. I tried to grab him, but he was a solid 280 lbs. He hit the concrete with a thud.

"Bob!" I screamed. "Somebody help me!" Bob grabbed the fence and tried to pull himself up. But it was as if someone had knocked the wind out of him and he couldn't pull himself back together.

"No! No!" Bob wailed. "Not the kid. Not JJ. He was such a good boy. Such a smart and brilliant kid."

I kneeled down at his side.

"I know. He truly was."

Bob grabbed my arm. "No! This can't be true." Bob's face turned crimson red, his eyes filled with tears that instantly spilled over and down his face. He held on to my arm and pulled me down to his face.

"He's dead? JJ is really dead?" he said.

I cried. I couldn't speak the words although I knew they were true. I just nodded.

"Oh God. Oh God, no!" he sobbed. "Oh God, no."

"Bob, we have to get you to the hospital. Can you help me? Can you try and stand up?"

"I don't need a doctor," Bob said, still sobbing.

"Yes, I think . . ." I tried to place his arm around my neck, "I can help you up." I tried, but he didn't budge.

"Jared is dead?" He looked at me as if I would give him a different answer.

"Yes," I said. "He was killed by the LAPD on his way to a concert. He was to meet me . . ." The words caught in my throat. Bob watched my agony. He grabbed my arm and pulled me down to the ground with him. He held me tight and rubbed my back.

"My God," was all he could say.

We sat there for about ten minutes crying together, then Bob decided he needed to get up off the ground. "I'm going to get up and go, kiddo. Before this Arthur kicks in and I really need a doctor." Bob struggled a little, but he made it. I stood with him.

"What do you want to do?" I knew he wouldn't make it up my two flights of stairs. But there was no one around to help.

"Take me back to the Ponderosa."

"Why don't you just, stay here and I can run and call the ambulance . . . you know, just to check you out?"

"Why don't you just do what I asked and take me home. I'm an old man, I don't ask for too much. Can you just do what I asked?" Bob pleaded. He started his walk home and I moved slowly with him, but we finally made it to his cabin.

I looked around quickly for a phone.

He plopped down on an old green couch.

"There. Much better." He looked over at me. "Isn't it?"

"Yes, much better." I said.

Bob smiled. He took a deep breath.

"Now tell me what happened to my Einstein?" Tears welled up in Bob's eyes. He turned pink again.

"Okay, and then we can call the ambulance?"

"Yes, now tell me what happened?

I shared with Bob all the details about JJ's death, all I was doing, and the fund that I was supporting.

Bob sat, listened and shook his head. He couldn't believe it. "These ass holes," he said. "They need to spend one day at war. Then they'd understand that race is a man-made evil." He looked at me.

"In 'Nam, you put your life in the hands of your brother. On the field, in the rice patties, in those jungles, your brother was American. He didn't have a race, he just bled American blood." Bob sat for a moment. "They need to spend one day at war, then they'd treasure human life."

Like me, Bob was all alone. No wife or kids. Now, I had no husband, no son.

The room began to feel hot, muggy—I couldn't breathe. I looked at Bob in his grief and felt like I was suffocating.

"Bob, are you okay?" I said, moving toward the door. "I completely forgot I had something in the oven. I need to go check on it before I start a fire." But I was out the door before he could reply.

I had a quick stride that turned into a light jog, and before I knew it I was running up the street. I hadn't ran in weeks, but the thud underneath my feet and the swishing of my arms fell into place as if I had been running every day. *Because I have been.* I thought. Not just on a track either, but, I'd been running every day in my life— always in motion, always going, going, going. *I'm tired.*

I took the incline with ease, turned left and made my way down Live Oak Drive. I ran for miles on the two-lane road not made for pedestrians. But it was late afternoon and not much traffic.

As I ran, I paced myself like I used to do back in college when I ran track.

"Pace yourself, set your stride, save your energy," Coach Williams would say. "The race goes to the one who can pace herself. It's not a sprint, this is a long carefully run race."

I settled in to my stride. It felt good. Comfortable. I hadn't felt comfortable with anything in my life since . . . *Breath in through your nose, out through your mouth, in through your nose, out through your mouth.*

Track had been my life for years. It was where I met Brandon. He was a handsome man, 6' 2", all muscle. He was two shades darker than I was, but he tanned easily so he always looked much darker; smooth and creamy, like the color of a Sugar Daddy. His hair was sandy brown, thick and curly when he didn't cut it low—which he rarely ever did. It was always cut low in a fade, with waves.

Brandon had the most amazing light brown eyes. They looked like the sun was shining behind them. He had a very pronounced nose, unlike mine, his was full and distinctly African. His lips were thin, but full. All of his features seemed to fit perfectly on his long face.

On that day, I had seen him stretching on the far west side of the field by himself, but I was focused on my coach and my turn to sprint.

I was trying to beat my last time by .3 seconds. If I could do that, I would qualify for the Illinois Twilight at the University of Illinois that weekend.

"Green, you're up," the coach yelled to me, then blew his whistle.

I jogged over, stretched, then pushed my heel back into the metal plate. I bent down, placed my fingertips on the red hot earth and waited calmly for the "Beeep!" of Coach Williams' whistle.

He blew, I flew.

Something about the rhythm of running soothed my soul. The timing of my feet, hitting the ground, my arms moving; it was all like the parts of an engine. Every time my feet hit the ground it felt like I was being super charged, like spark plugs, reigniting me more and more.

I rounded the second corner, this is where I needed to push.

"Push!" I heard someone screaming. "You got this. Push. Give it all you got!"

And I did.

I dug deep and pushed, all the way to the finish line.

"Yes!" Coach Williams screamed. "You did it! You knocked off .34 seconds! You're going to the meet this weekend."

I fell to the ground, and that's when I saw his track shoes first. Then his long muscular legs. I looked up into his silhouette as the sun was shining brightly behind him. I placed my hands up over my eyes, but still ended up squinting.

"Great job." He extended his hand out to me. I grabbed it and pulled myself up.

"Thanks. Was that you cheering me on at the turn?"

"Yep." He smiled. "Brandon Jackson."

"Adrian Green." We shook hands. I felt a little spark and smiled. When his smile got wider, I couldn't help but wonder if he'd felt it, too.

We started working out together, and pretty soon hanging out after practice. Brandon was in Army ROTC, so I'd watch him on Thursdays doing his drills.

He shared his goals with me. "I want to join the US Army JAG Corps."

"What's that stand for?" I said.

"The United States Army Judge Advocate General's Corp. You're an officer and a lawyer."

So that's what he did. He graduated, and applied for JAG. He had just been accepted when he proposed.

We were walking along Lakefront Trail and he stopped and kissed me. "Adrian, I love you so much."

"I love you, too."

"Then marry me."

"What? Marry--?"

"Yes. I know there's not anyone else for me in this world but you. I'm happy when I'm with you, I'm miserable when you're not around. Please, say you'll marry me."

I hugged him tight.

"I can take care of you now," he said into the top of my hair.

"Please, Brandon. I work for one of the top advertising agencies in Chicago. I can take care of myself." I shoved him, playfully.

"I know. But as your husband, I need to be able to take care of my wife – even if she doesn't need me to do it. How about that?" He pulled me back into him and kissed me long.

We had a beautiful wedding: small and intimate. Fifty people, just close friends and family at a beautiful church in Los Angeles. The church had always been one of my favorite places with its hand carved wooden pews, and statues that looked like they were staring into your soul.

"They look creepy to me," Brandon said when I first showed him the church.

I socked him in the shoulder. "They do not!"

"They do, but hey, if this is where you want your wedding, then the creepy statues are more than happy to look over us while we make it official." He kissed me. "I just want to marry you and love you forever."

Brandon did his first tour in Afghanistan after only one year of marriage. He was an officer and didn't have to go; he volunteered. When he came home, we made Jared.

He loved his son. He would sit with him for hours playing Thomas the Train and Legos. He'd read to him every night.

I remembered saying to myself *I can't believe how happy we are* watching Brandon tickle Jared and roll on the ground rough housing with him.

When he signed up for his second tour, I was not happy. "You have a son, Brandon. It's not just about you anymore. I get it. You love your country, but you can get killed. If that happens, then what?"

"Seriously, Adrian. I'm a black man in America. I can get killed walking to the store."

I cried all that night as he held me.

For the next two months before his deployment, we spent as many moments together as we could. Brandon would take Jared to school, cook his dinner, and read him to sleep. Then, we'd spend the rest of the night, talking about our hopes, our dreams…our future.

The day he left, he kissed me and Jared and said, "I'll be back. You're my family. I'm not going to leave you alone in this world."

While he was away, I kept busy by raising Jared and juggling my career. By the time Brandon returned from the war, Jared was five and running everywhere.

"Oh my God, he's big!" Brandon said, swinging him around. Jared screamed with delight.

"Again! Again!" he squealed.

We were happy for two years. And then Brandon announced that he was going back to Afghanistan for another tour.

"Why Brandon? You've done two."

"They need soldiers to volunteer. So many have been killed, and the others have done so many tours, our numbers are low."

"Which is why you need to stay home with your son and wife," I said. "Why do you have to be the one to go?"

"I have to." Brandon looked into my eyes. "You knew this was who I was when you married me."

"I thought when you married me, you would put me and your son first. Not this war that doesn't even make sense."

Brandon held me as he said, "Babe, I love you and my son more than my life. That's why I'm going. I believe in what we're fighting for. I believe I'm fighting to keep my son safe."

Five months after being deployed on his third tour in Afghanistan, I got the visit from two officers in dress blues. Before they even spoke, I slammed the door in their faces. "No! No!" I screamed. " Get away from my door."

Jared ran into the room. "Mommie! Mommie! Why are you crying?" I pulled him as close to me as I could and cried in his chest. He stroked my hair. "It's okay, Mommie, don't cry."

The officers stood outside my door for two hours until I finally had the courage to let them in. I read the official letter. Brandon had been killed by an IED. He would be awarded a purple heart posthumously. I would receive combat battle pay . . . the rest was a blur. All I knew was that my husband was dead.

Those were my thoughts as I ran past homes that had been nestled in these mountains for decades. I loved the feel of the gravel underneath my feet.

Finally, I returned to my cabin and ran up the two-flights of stairs.

Inside, I peeled off the sweaty clothes and stood underneath the ten-inch chrome shower head.

I closed my eyes as the hot water pulsated over my head and shoulders through 120 jets.

I enjoyed the quiet and the steam for a few minutes before washing my hair. I'd kept it pulled back in a bun the last few months and when I saw my tattered ends, I made a mental note to get to the beauty shop.

I threw on a grey cotton dress, slid into flip-flops, and made my way to my bed.

Once inside my down comforter, I slept. And slept. And slept.

Bang, Bang, Bang!
Bang, Bang, Bang!

I pulled the comforter down from over my head and squinted, trying to figure out what was going on..

Bang, Bang, Bang!

The door. I threw the covers back and slid out of bed. I paused for a moment, feeling groggy. What day was this?

I walked down stairs, trying to orient myself to the bright sunlight that blanketed the open room.

Bang, Bang, Bang!

"Shut up! I'm coming," I said.

The banging stopped.

I swung open my door, scowl on my face. "What is it?" I screamed before I saw who was on the other side.

"Well, bitch, you're alive," Linda said, hands on her hip. "Your neighbors thought your ass was rotting away in there. So they called Auntie Lindy Lu." Linda pushed past me, carrying a shopping bag.

"Why did you tell these hicks my name was Lindy Lu: you know they actually believe that shit, right?" Linda dumped the contents of the bag on the coffee table.

"What is all that?" I said, plopping down on the couch.

"I don't know. The lady two cabins down from you – I can never remember her name – gave it to me. She's the one who called me. Said none of them had seen you, but your car was out front.

They were worried; so I stopped there to let her know I was here and checking on you. She gave me this bag." Linda leaned over and studied the contents. "It looks like shit from the Country store." Linda grabbed a container and opened it. "Oh shit, these look like homemade oatmeal raisin cookies!" She ate one. "These are delicious!"

"Those are from Julie." I smiled. "She bakes the best oatmeal raisin cookies ever."

"We should market these, AJ! We could make a fortune." Linda pulled cellophane from another item. "What is this?" She stared at the carved boat made out of wood.

My eyes filled with tears. "It's JJ's."

I grabbed the blanket off the back of the couch and wrapped it around my shoulders. "He and, um, Briana made them the first summer we moved here. Bear showed them how to make them from real wood."

"Holy Jellystone Park. You've got a real live Yogi Bear twiddling and carving boats out of trees?" Linda asked, shoving another cookie into her mouth.

I threw a pillow at her head, but then looked at the contents on the table. "I guess Bob told everyone about JJ." I pulled my knees to my chest and wrapped my arms around my legs. "What day is it?" I looked around the room.

"It's Wednesday, you matted hair ball of stink," Linda said, "When was the last time you bathed?"

I tried to pull my hair back, but Linda was right, it was a matted mess. "I showered . . . Sunday, I think. Yes. Sunday after my run."

"And then what?"

"And then I did what you told me to do. I've been resting."

"You've slept for three days straight?" Linda walked over and sat next to me. Her tone was softer now. "Have you eaten anything?"

I closed my eyes. "I haven't been hungry. Just tired. I got up and used the bathroom a couple of times, drank some water. But I really haven't been hungry, Lindy Lu."

Linda stood, tossed the cover off of me and grabbed my arm.

"Ouch! That arm is attached to a body."

"A stinky body." Linda led me toward the stairs, and shoved me up. "Go shower while I fix you something to eat. I told you to get some rest. I didn't tell you to go swim in a bed of stinky depression and wither away to nothingness. Jesus!"

I went upstairs and showered while Linda prepared breakfast.

"There," Linda said, grabbing my plate and scraping the crust and eggs into the garbage disposal. "Don't you feel better?"

I shrugged. "I feel better if you feel better. You feel better?"

"Yes, got dammit."

"Well then, all is well with the world, now isn't it?"

"It is according to Linda Lewis. What about Adrian Jackson?"

Linda sat at the table and stared into my hollowed eyes. It was the look I had after Brandon died. I knew I had it, because I knew how Linda looked at me back then. It was the same way she looked at me now.

I started to cry. Linda got up and got me napkins. I wiped my face.

"I'm just lost, Lin." I blew my nose. "I don't want to wake up because I'm angry every time I do." Linda nodded. "I felt this same way when daddy died. And when mommy died." I shook my head and wiped tears from my face. "And . . ." I sobbed. "When Brandon died."

"I know, baby." Linda grabbed my hand. "This is some bullshit. No doubt. This is the most fucked up shit that could ever happen to you."

"Yeah, right?" I said.

Linda said. "I was talking to the man upstairs"

My eyebrows shot up.

"Exactly!" Linda said. "But what the fuck else are you going to do driving up that scary ass windy road?" she said dramatically. I laughed. "So yeah, I was saying to the old guy, 'Seriously? What a piece of shit you must be to do this to my girl.'"

I shook my head. "This is what you said to the Creator after all these years of silence? Do you really think that was wise?"

"Well, I figure, he kind of knows me . . . what the fuck am I supposed to say? 'Dear Lord. If thine will be done--' Fuck AJ, I don't even know how to talk Bible!" We both laughed. "No seriously. I just can't begin to . . . I was relieved your ass was still alive this morning. But I had prepared myself to find you dead. That's why I stopped by your neighbor's place first. I was trying to delay what I thought was the inevitable."

"Linda!" I screamed.

"Well, bitch. This shit is enough to take any normal man down. I'm just saying." I laughed. But I couldn't argue with her. It wasn't like I hadn't thought about it. I thought about dying every day.

What *did* I have to live for? My entire family was dead. Yeah, I had friends, but there was really nothing here to keep me alive.

"No, I feel you. It's true."

"So what are you going to do with the rest of your life, Adrian Jackson?"

"What life?" I got up and moved to the family room. Linda followed.

"Your life: that living, breathing thing right there. I know you defined yourself by your roles: daughter, wife, mother, but there is more to you than those titles."

I rolled my eyes. "Like what?"

"Well, as of late, you're the new Mrs. Dr. Martin Luther King. Every time there's any story about a black man getting killed, your picture pops up. You're the new civil rights guru."

I waved my hand, brushing Linda off.

She continued, "They've been blowing up your phone at work trying to get you on this show and that show. You really have a platform if you want one."

I didn't reply. I wasn't thinking about a platform. I didn't have the energy to think about anything, or anyone. I just wanted to go back to bed and sleep, and I told Linda that.

"You want that asshole to get away with killing your son?"

I closed my eyes. Linda knew how to push my buttons. I massaged my temples. "Of course not."

"Then you need to have a platform." Linda sat back in her chair and crossed her legs.

"I don't have the energy for this, Lindy Lu. Please, let it go."

"Okay. But you know how this works. In less than thirty days your window of opportunity goes away. You won't have momentum, you won't have your community behind you – who, by the way, adores you.

"You have your foundation, all you need is your platform, and you can do this, AJ." Linda sat on the edge of her chair. "This is what you do every day. You started with the press conferences, you just need to finish working your plan."

I became agitated. "I don't have a plan."

"Then make one."

"My plan is to rest up here 'til the end of the week, then bring my black butt back to work. That is, if I still have a job?"

Linda waved the statement off. "Bitch I'm the CEO. But you need to finish this for Jared. You need to *plan your work and work your plan..*"

I sat , processing her words.

"Lindy Lu, I know you mean well. But you're going to have to put your internet psychology back in its little hole. I just don't have it in me."

Linda looked me up and down, but she didn't falter. She stood up and walked outside. A few minutes later she came back with a *Post It* flip chart. She threw markers onto the table and set the tabletop easel pad on the dining room table.

"What is this?" I said.

"It's me, helping you develop your platform." Linda grabbed a black marker. On the top of the page she wrote: *The Big Pay Back.*

I watched Linda make a chart, just like we did at work:

Goal. Audience. Markets. Data. Analysis. Outcome.

Linda turned to look at me. "You ready to do this?" I nodded.

✊ ✊ ✊

Three hours later, Linda was on the road back to Los Angeles. The plan had been made, and all that was left was for me to fill in the blanks. The blanks were the most important part. I had decided that the goal was to ink Federal legislation that criminalized racial profiling.

We both had our marching orders. Linda would return to L.A. and start booking me on talk and radio shows, and I would spend the rest of the week fine-tuning the language for the plan.

Day one: I combed through pages and pages of websites trying to understand what my best line of offense might be: An engrossed bill, an enrolled bill, a general bill, a resolution? There were over twenty types of bills. Then, I had to decide which way I should go House or Senate?

Day two: I read through several hundred bills, made lists of the elected officials, the bills they proposed, supported, and voted against.

By day three, I had whittled my legislative demands down from seventeen to three and decided on the executive order by the president because while they are subject to judicial review, and may be struck down if deemed by the courts to be unsupported by statute or the Constitution, they did not require Congressional approval.

By Friday, I had crafted my whole plan:

To be black in America means every day is a risk. In a country overcome with racism, police violence, and elected officials blocking reform, even the most simple activities — a walk down the street or the drive to work — could mean an unlawful arrest or deadly attack at the hands of law enforcement.

That is why Americans are demanding legislation designed to:

1. **Strengthen law enforcement accountability.**

2. **Request that President Obama sign an executive order enforcing and expanding Federal bans on discriminatory policing** and strengthening police accountability mechanisms nationwide. The solution to America's policing crisis is not martial law or more militarized policing, it's holding those sworn to protect and serve accountable for their criminal actions.

3. **Make sure our criminal justice system serves all and not just some.** Require a special prosecutor to conduct a public probable cause hearing when reasonable grounds exist to believe that criminal charges should be considered in a police-involved killing.

4. **Combat toxic media representations of black citizens.** Local news stations play a harmful role in shaping the narratives that exacerbate a dangerous and hostile climate for black communities.

The result is that our communities are being put in double jeopardy, first by over zealous police and then by news stations serving as PR firms by proxy.

"Linda, it's AJ," I said into my cell as I locked up the cabin. "Do you have everything lined up? I'm ready."

Adrian

I had my strategy. I knew what I had to do. For the next three months I was on a world wind tour. Linda had booked me on every radio station, news channel, talk show, and community event that would have me. I spoke at block clubs, on college campuses, you name it; I was there.

My first radio show was Killradio.com, a popular, albeit most inappropriately titled, streaming talk radio station, where I was interviewed by a 22-year old DJ who said, "*That's what's up,*" at the end every sentence.

"So, tell our listeners, what politics are you advocating?"

"I'm not advocating politics, Eric, I'm advocating social justice."

"Yeah, that's what's up."

I laid the foundation by going straight to the top of the food chain.

"Until President Obama issues an executive order we will continue to experience a nationwide culture of policing that allows corruption and racial terror to flourish unabated."

Linda scored big; she got me on with Meet The Press, with Chuck Todd. His other guests included Kansas' Secretary of State Kristoff Kolbane, and former Chief of Police, Quentin Baxter. We went toe to toe on the presidential executive order.

On the Wendy Williams show, we both let our hair down. She got on her soapbox about white people asking her why do black folks resist arrest?

"Uh, hello! Because their rights are being violated," Wendy said, staring into the camera. "I had to tell them, you wouldn't know anything about that because as a white person, you don't experience it."

"Exactly!" I said. "But let someone assault *them* for absolutely no reason— I doubt very seriously that they'd just stand there quietly and be embarrassed or harassed."

"But that's what they expect black folks to do—girl, as my grandmother used to say. 'They done lost they fool ass minds.'"

On KJLH, I was up at an abhorrently ridiculous hour on Dominique DiPrima's Front Page, expanding the conversation to include the President blocking local states from issuing equipment and riot gear to officers at rallies and protests.

Queen Latifah, who was also a guest on the six a.m. show, did an awesome job of crafting the message about the need to appoint special prosecutors.

"Government prosecutors and local law enforcement agencies usually work together in criminal cases. That obviously creates a conflict of interest for government prosecutors if they are then called in to prosecute a police officer," she said. "Seems to me like they'd *want* have a special prosecutor appointed. That way, they can still go throw back a cold one after court like they always do."

"Oh my God, AJ—you have these elected officials running scared!" Linda said into the phone.

"Doubtful. They're too arrogant to be scared."

"Meh, they may be arrogant, but they are not stupid. You're playing hard ball, and they don't know what to do with you."

"They could start by telling the truth."

"Elected officials. Telling the truth? Yeah those term don't really go together."

We laughed.

"What's my line up for the next couple of weeks?"

She told me that she had already scheduled Ellen and Steve Harvey and was working on Jimmy Kimmel and Tom Joyner. Just as she began talking about The View, her assistant buzzed in and she clicked over.

It was just seconds when she came back to me, breathless and excited.

"That was the White House calling. We just scheduled you to fly in to meet with the president and then speak in front of a Congressional hearing."

"Are you kidding me?"

"I wouldn't do that. I just spoke with his assistant; she's working on your clearances. But she's thinking mid next week."

"This is amazing!"

"This is it! This is what we've been waiting for."

"Yes," I agreed. "Yes!"

"The President has scheduled a meeting with Adrian Jackson," the White House aide announced to Senator Walsh. The Senator looked up from his stack of papers.

"When?" He looked at him over his black horn rimmed glasses.

"Thursday."

The Senator dismissed him with a wave of his hand, then picked up the phone and dialed.

"Armando, I see you can't keep your trash in your own back yard?"

"What are you talking about, Senator?" Mayor Villanueva replied.

"Adrian Jackson has a meeting with the president. I thought I told you to handle this."

"Uh. I have it under control--"

"Apparently you do not; but you damn well better get it." He hung up the phone.

.

✊ ✊ ✊

"Got damn you, Adrian fucking Jackson." Mayor Villanueva murmured under his breath as he texted. "Just couldn't leave well enough alone, could you? Well, I tried to reason with you. Now, you just have to learn the hard way."

< Armando: I have some trash I need you to clean up.

< Trash man: Send me the details.

< Armando: I need this done ASAP!

< Trash man: It's extra for a rush job. You know the drill.

< Armando: Just handle it.

< Trash man: Consider it done. Like the last clean up?

< Armando: Yes. Like the last time.

✊ ✊ ✊

Adrian

"Mrs. Jackson." President Obama stood as I entered the Oval Office. He unbuttoned his single breasted taupe jacket. He had on a light blue shirt with a multicolored gold, blue, and white tie. He extended his hand.

I wore slimming copper colored ombre eyelash knit long-sleeved jewel neckline topper jacket and sleeveless sheath dress. *Can't meet the President and First Lady looking raggedy.*

I stopped a few feet before reaching President Obama. Mrs. Obama stood next to him in a blue and white striped jacket and sheath dress.

I became choked up.

"Oh my. I'm so sorry . . . Mr. President." I turned away.

Michelle walked over and embraced me. She whispered words into my ear. I nodded as tears flowed down my cheeks. We hugged for a few minutes. When we pulled apart, the two of us, both 5'11" stood eye-to-eye, strong, tall . . . soft and vulnerable. It was an amazing moment between black women. *Mothers.*

I wiped my tears and an aide handed me Kleenex.

"Thank you." I dabbed my face. I smiled and approached the President of the United States.

He too embraced me and whispered words in my ear. And then together, the three of us sat and talked. For one of the few times since Jared had been murdered, I felt like I was heard.

"This is Janet Coley, AT&T Customer Service Number 2615, how may I provide you with excellent service today?"

"I need to change my unlisted number."

"Ma'am, I see here you've changed your number five times in the last month."

"Yes, I realize that. . However every time I pay for my number to be unlisted, it's somehow always leaked to the public. And I'm still receiving threatening calls"

"Ma'am, by law I am required to report any threatening or malicious calls to proper authorities--"

"The FBI already knows about the issue. They claim they're tracking them. Can you please just change the number again, please? Thank you."

Adrian

It had been a long grueling month, and a sistah was tired. I looked into my rearview mirror and didn't recognize the woman staring back. Her features looked familiar, but she was flat, lifeless. The makeup hid the dark circles from the constant movement and sleepless nights, but nothing could hide the emptiness that filled eyes that used to sparkle—

"Oh shoot!" I screamed, as my car swerved to the left. I was driving Northbound on the 134 freeway. I yanked the wheel back to the right, which caused me to spin out. As the car came to a sliding stop, I heard a thump, thump, then my car dropped down in the rear left corner. I looked out of my side mirror and saw my back tire rolling across the freeway!

"Oh my God!" I scanned the freeway to see if there was oncoming traffic, although I had no idea how I would warn anyone facing sideways in the middle of the slow lane.

A red SUV swerved around me, followed by a grey Honda leaning on her horn. I grabbed my head, anticipating the blow. But they just missed my rear.

The other cars were far back enough to merge into the next lane. I turned on my hazards, grabbed my purse and jumped out my vehicle.

On the side of the road, I prayed silently, thanking God for covering me. So much could have gone wrong, especially if I had been going the speed of traffic.

"Hello ma'am, you need some help?" I jumped.

It was a tow truck driver.

"Wow. Where did you come from?" I said, looking around. It was like he popped up from nowhere.

"I just got on the freeway and saw a tire in the far lane over there, and then noticed you just ahead. Let's get your vehicle out of the line of traffic. That's just an accident waiting to happen."

✊ ✊ ✊

Forty minutes later, he'd retrieved the tire, put on my spare, and was handing me a receipt. I still had time to make it to the show.

"Thank you so much. You really were a God send," I said, handing him my credit card.

"No problem. I'll be right back. The card reader is in the truck."

✊ ✊ ✊

The tow truck driver pulled out his cell and dialed a number. "Yeah, it's Antoine." He opened his door and leaned inside. "Is it taken care of?"

"No. I loosened the lug nuts on the tire and it came off, but she wasn't going fast enough. Yeah. Yes, I understand." He looked up and saw the woman waiting patiently on the side of the freeway. "You want me to cut the line? I have access to the vehicle now."

"No, that's too risky. Besides, if there are too many issues with her car, she'll take it in and might be able to tell it was tampered with."

"Well, I can just follow her home. And make it look like a robbery or--"

"No. Let her go. I have another idea."

Adrian

"Thank you for having me on your show, Ellen. I'm a big fan."

"No, thank you, Adrian. Portia and I are big fans. Your crusade to right the wrongs of injustice across the country is, is amazing."

The audience clapped.

"I understand you met with President Obama, and he's reviewing recommendations from the Task Force on 21st century policing?"

The audience clapped.

"Thank you. I'm so grateful that the President took time from his busy schedule to meet with me. And I believe he's going to do all he can to help."

"Awe. Busy schmusy. What was he doing? Just running the country?" Ellen stared into the camera.

The audience laughed.

"No seriously. He's a great man." She laughed. "So he's going to do his part, what can we do to make a difference, Adrian?"

"Yes, I'm glad you asked." The camera panned behind us to a

big screen. "Everyone can support local bills sponsored by community based organizations and elected officials that call for LAPD reform and accountability. These bills on the screen are the ones we need to pressure our elected officials to support."

- AB 953 (Weber) Law enforcement: racial profiling - Increases law enforcement transparency and accountability to communities by training police on racial/identity profiling and implicit bias.
- AB 619 (Weber) Death in law enforcement custody - Requires law enforcement to provide a comprehensive report to the Attorney General when a person dies while in custody.
- AB 1118 (Bonta) Police officer standards and training: procedural justice - Increases law enforcement transparency and accountability to communities by training police on procedural justice.
- AB 256 (Jones-Sawyer) Electronic evidence - Ensures that tampering of digital evidence by police officers qualifies as a felony.
- SB 411 (Lara) Right to film police - Protects Californians' right to film police officers.

"You can also visit EllenTV, we have the links that will take you directly to each bill, and give you step-by-step instruction on how to support this movement." Ellen reached over and shook my hand.

"Thank you, Adrian for joining me today on the show. I really appreciate it. And because of your humanitarian work, I would like to contribute $50,000 to your *#BlackLivesMatter* campaign. Because truly all lives matter and, it's a tragedy what happened to you and your amazingly brilliant son—Jared--and, other potentially brilliant young lives cut short because of hatred and bigotry. So, thank you for all you do and keep up the good work. You make me proud."

8 INTRIGUE

Francisco

"Que como o café, Senhor?" the waitress said. She was round, short and tan with waist-length blonde hair.

"Sim, preto por favor." I said

I sat at one of my favorite restaurants in my hometown of San Paolo, Brazil -- *Figueira Rubayat*. A beautiful tall, lush Figueira tree claimed its place of honor in the center of the patio, where diners could admire its huge thick branches outstretched from one end of the patio to the other, eating underneath half a century of old spirits as my mother described the souls of old trees.

I dined at many places. All of them densely populated so that I could blend into the crowd. But each one was uniquely different, and had specific sentimental value – unless I happened to be working a job.

It had been years since I had an assignment in my hometown, which gave me comfort. *Home, is where there is peace, not where blood is shed.*

I took special care to keep San Paolo off my register. Though, I was never *really* ever at peace.

"O jornal da manhã, por favor?" I said to the waitress when she placed my coffee in front of me.

She nodded, moved from the table and returned shortly with the LA Times. I took a slow slip of the steaming hot coffee and paused. I was captured by a pair of sad green eyes on the front page of the newspaper. I studied the picture, admiring the woman's style.

I sat staring at her plump nude lips, the shape, and the natural fullness. She stood holding a blood-drenched evening gown.

Intrigued by the contrast, I read the headline: *Black Mother Outraged at Alleged Cop Killing.* After reading the article, I returned to the photo. The caption read: *Adrian Jackson holds up evening gown soaked in dead son's blood.*

I sat, continuing to stare into the saddest eyes I'd ever seen.

Francisco

"*Sr. Monteserrate. You have been summoned by Ambassador Alberto Cavalcanti,*" the voice on the recording said, "*for a matter of grave importance. The honor of your presence is urgently requested.*"

I deleted the message and quickly dialed Thiago's number.

"You make your messages seem as if I have choices in these matters, my old friend," I said.

Thiago sucked his teeth.

"These things are of international importance, Sr. Monteserrate! Completely above my pay grade. However, I am a gentleman and not a rogue. I will always conduct myself as such. Despite the expectations of others for me to do otherwise."

I chuckled. "Then, my good gentleman. Where am I off to this go 'round?" I handed the waitress ten reals.

She glanced down at the money. "Obrigado, Senhor!" She nodded with a wide smile.

"O prazer foi meu, senhorita!" I said, then turned my attention back to my call.

"In ten business days, the consulate will meet you in nos Estados Unidos da America, at this location called Capitol Hill, Sr. Montesserate," Thiago said. "Why you must continue to visit such barbaric countries at this time in your career is beyond me. Surely, Comandante knows--"

"Thiago! Thiago!" I laughed into the phone. "Eu te amo irmao! But surely if o Comandante has summoned me to *America do Norte*, then it must be of major importance. Therefore, who are we to question?" Though I talked into the phone, my eyes remained fixed on the photo of Adrian Jackson.

"You sir, are Francisco Monteserrate! And I, sir, am Thiago Alexsandro Davi Pedro – of the Great Dom Pedro! Fourth child of King Dom Joao VI of Portugal and Queen Carlota Joaquina, and thus a member of the House of Braganza!" Thiago exclaimed theatrically.

I smiled broadly as I listened, for the hundredth time, as my friend detailed his ancestral legacy, "Ah yes. And yet, here you are, descendant to one of the greatest men in all of Brazil, coordinating my flight for a meeting in the barbaric Americas."

Thiago was silent.

"Thiago. My brother. Some things happen for reasons far beyond our understanding." Francisco picked up his paper and headed toward the exit. "Please can you be sure to ship me plenty of agua de cocoa and a Cajuina? The American coconut water is bestial, and I can't find Cajuina anywhere."

"Sim, claro! And at least five liters of Catuaba. The Americas would not carry our country's bebida. No alcohol, no carbonation, and blended cashew apples, I dare say are probably too bland for their taste." Thiago sighed with exasperated disgust.

"Thank you, my friend," I said. "I have a feeling that this will be a very interesting trip."

I hung up and quickly dialed another number.

"Ola! Victor. Please, I have a task for you. I need a dossier on an Adrian Jackson."

"Absolutely. What level?"

"Top level, please. I need to know everything there is to know about her."

9 ON ASSIGNMENT

"Comandante?"

The man behind the cherry wood desk looked over his progressive glasses at the woman standing in the doorway. She was stunning: 5'8", dark olive complexion. He loved the way her hair cascaded down her elongated torso, but he was especially fond of its shine.

She had beautiful trees for legs, long, lean, sturdy. They were perfectly bronzed, and looked magnificent in the pencil skirt and three inch pumps. He followed the curves up her calves to the hips underneath the black skirt, to the fullness spilling out the sheer plum-colored blouse. She was young, twenty-seven or twenty-eight, he believed. The youth showed in her pale green eyes, and the eager way she tried to please him when they made love.

"Sim, Vitoria? O `e isso?"

"Sr. Monserrate esta aqui para ve-lo."

He was a distinguished looking man. Lean, like a distance runner, dark-complexioned, with a rugged-shaped face. Despite his age, he had a full head of hair that was all white. Not the dull, dirty white, like most aging seniors. The Comandante's hair was bright white, silky soft and shiny. Against the dark blue suit, it looked even whiter--like the white of the French cuff shirt he was wearing.

The Comandante always wore a suit, except Monday, Wednesday and Friday mornings at 7:00 a.m. when he played racquetball, or Tuesdays and Thursdays at 6:00 am when he swam laps in the heated pool.

The Comandante was in his 60's, but sharp as a whistle and clean as tack. He didn't speak much, but commanded the room when he did.

She gestured for Sr. Monserrate to approach.

She watched as he strolled easily across the room. He was regal looking, tall, dark olive skin with a thick wavy head of shiny black hair. Thick eyebrows sat on a cliff-like shelf, atop small, deep-set eyes. Piercing black eyes, framed by super long perfectly curved lashes.

His five o'clock shadow fully covered his jowls—-the mustache and hair that lined his cheeks was jet black, but the chin revealed a heavy blend of grey.

He wore a black mock turtle neck sweater with black jeans and black suede loafers. His jewelry consisted of one silver bracelet on his left wrist. He was too young for her taste, but she could definitely imagine him in another ten years. She licked her lips.

"Por aqui, senhor" *Right this way sir.*

"Obrigado." *Thank you,* Sr. Monserrate said, entering the room.

The Comandante placed the book he was reading down on the desk, stood, and beamed.

Francisco

The Comandante walked around the desk and extended his hand to me.

"Ah, finalmente! O filho prodigo retorna." I paused, hurt by his statement. I hadn't been away that long, and I certainly didn't see myself as a prodigal son.

I ignored his outreached hand and walked up and embraced him.

The Comandante returned the hug with a hearty pat on my back.

He pulled back and looked me in the eyes. A slow warm smile stretched across his face.

"Filho prodigo?" I said, repeated his words that had hurt me. "Voce me estripar com seu pai palavras." We locked eyes for a moment.

"You decided to leave the business, Chico," the Comandante said sitting on the edge of his desk. He extended his right hand toward the chair in front of him. I obediently sat.

"I left the business, I did not leave you."

"My son, they are one in the same." He stood and returned to the other side of the desk. Sitting, he folded his hands in his lap and leaned back in his chair. He stared at me for a while.

"Comandante. You summoned me" I bowed. "And I am here. At your service."

"Oh Francisco Monserrate, if your loyalty was that easy."

"Comandante, I have never been disloyal"

"Calm down." The Comandante waved his hand. "You are loyal to no one but your spoiled selfish self."

"How can you say that when--"

"When you gave your entire life to serving me? Yes, yes, I've heard this bullshit line too many times to count." He looked at me over his glasses. "You're still alive. There are many more years for you to serve."

"Comandante!" I said in feigned protest. "You promised."

"Promised Schmomished!" he snorted. "You were my best General. Generals of your caliber don't just . . . just, what is the word you used?"

"Retire."

"Ah fuck that word, Retire. I hate that word, Retire! Who in the world, becomes the best, the very best, and then retires? What the fuck is this?"

I chuckled. The Comandante looked up, and I quickly turned serious.

"A man who knows too much, has done too much, and wants more of his life," I said in earnest.

The Comandante dismissed my reply with a wave. "You're fifty-two for heaven's sake! You're still young." He grabbed pieces of paper from his desk and moved them around.

"Comandante, I am here. How may I serve you?" I leaned back into the quilted chair.

"Ah yes, your service. I do need your help." He linedup the stacks of paper neatly on his desk. "I need your help."

"Of course, what must I do?"

The Comandante paused. "Only you can help me, my son," he said as if he felt I really needed to hear that again before he told me what he needed. "And, given the way you abandoned me, I feel it's the least you can do to make up for your duplicity."

I raised my left brow. "Senior Cavalcanti, high treason is a dishonorable offense. I do hope you don't seriously consider my departure from the trade as such?"

"I do indeed, Francisco Monserrate." I shook my head in disbelief. "You broke my heart with this decision." He sighed and looked off into the distance. "But I survived." He turned back to me. "And now I have an opportunity—*we* have an opportunity to make this situation right."

"Yes, Comandante. How? It burdens my heart that you consider me a traitor--"

"A traitor to your country! Not just to me, your father!"

"—because of my decision," I said. "What must I do to right this wrong, besides going back to work. Father, I love you deeply, but you do know my mind is made up. I will not rejoin the rank and file.."

"Yes, yes of course. You are *retired!* Not coming back, no longer living that type of life . . . weee weee weee. *Pansey, shit.* I got it!" he shouted. "I wouldn't dare ask you back, just so you know."

"Good."

"Ya!"

"Ya!"

The Comandante grunted. "Don't come back then. But I need you to complete this one task. And then I will never bring up anything related to *A Família* again."

I sat up, intrigued. Alberto Cavalcanti may be able to do many things, but letting go of a fight he believed he was right about was not one of them. AND, a fight about his beloved *família* – impossible.

"Do tell." I crossed my legs and listened intently.

"Do you remember the day I found you, Francisco? The Comandante asked rhetorically. "You were just a boy. Your spirit crushed at such a young age. But your eyes, your eyes were thirsty for life." He paused as he reflected.

I listened, remembering my childhood before Alberto Cavalcanti. I turned my head and squinted, looking into the bright rays of the sun beaming through the window.

"But I knew you would be a great General. Even then. In those tattered clothes, face streaked with dirt . . . I saw it in your eyes meau filho forte bonita. Such strength in a young boy. I am an expert at these things, you know? Picking good soldiers."

I nodded.

I had been with A Família all of my life. I saw what the Comandante had done. The lixo do reboque, o indesejavel, all the undesirables that he had turned into trained professionals--including myself. Though I hated to admit it, I was a most talented killer.

"Your task, my son, is to train someone to take your place," the Comandante said.

"Train someone? You and Attila do the training."

"We train on fundamentals—crafting the initiate into a powerful, dark side–fueled weapon by teaching them to draw upon their rage to use as a weapon and tool." The Comandante stared at me. "Then dominance—I focus on intellectual and psychological while Attila focuses on the physical."

"Yes, each of us underwent that training. You pushed us to almost unbearable feats. Broke us down to nothing, then built us up . . . to . . into soldiers," I replied. "Why do you need me to train anyone beyond the training The Academy provides?"

The Comandante paused for a moment. "The type of training this person requires, is not text book. It isn't taught in a simulated training room or in a staged conflict . . . What this person requires is your eye, your intuition, your sensibility. You are a natural. You know and do and say things that I would have never thought to teach you . . . you, my son, are a natural born killer."

I contemplated the Comandante's observations. I knew they were true. And it was because of those precise reasons that I had to get out of the game. I loved it too much.

Every assignment was disappointing if it wasn't more challenging than the last. I found ways to be more creative, more than the assignment called for me to be—just because. And I loved it. I loved killing.

And it *was* more than I had been taught, trained to do . . . it was as if, like walking, or talking or breathing, I killed naturally—without thinking or putting in much effort. I couldn't remember anymore when killing moved from something I did, to someone I was.

"I need a new General, filho. Someone who will step up and lead A Familia when I am dead and gone."

"Please father, you will never die," I teased.

"Everyone dies, Francisco. It is inevitable. And I need someone to take over and run the business. The business I thought for sure you would inherit," the Comandante said wistfully.

Long ago, the Comandante had selected me to replace him when the time came. At first, I was thrilled by the notion of stepping into the Comandante's shoes. But after my burn out, I decided that the business was not for me.

The Comandante had hoped time away would change my mind. But it had been two years, and I had given him no signs of me coming back to the fold.

"And so, who is this person? Is it Rafael? Antoinette? Brunaldo?" I sat, combing through the prospective successors.

The Comandante reached into his drawer and handed me a red folder. "Take a look at the next General."

I combed through the pages of the dossier for a Geovanne Affonso Azevedo.

On paper, he was quite impressive. Top among his cohorts. He mastered the art and decimated the craft. He was ruthless and a perfectionist. Meticulous and fearless.

I shifted the folder to conceal the rise in my pants. I struggled hard not show facial reaction to what I was reading. It had been a long time since something—anything—had excited me. Reading this dossier got me going.

I felt the Comandante watching me. "Geovanne needs to be your apprentice. He needs to learn to think, feel, respond, and process the way you do." He paused. " This is what I need, Francisquito. Do this, for me, and I'll never bring up The Family again."

I took a deep breath. "Eu sou pai terrivelmente triste, eu nao posso fazer isso," I apologized to my father, hoping that he would understand that I just couldn't do this. I handed Sr. Cavalcanti back the folder, stood, and walked out of the office.

✊ ✊ ✊

Atilla walked into the Comandante's office.

He was a short man, not more than five feet. He had a broad chest and large head, tanned with leather-looking skin, like he spent all his waking days baking in the sun.

He was a rather unattractive looking man, primarily because his big wide nose dominated his face, making his already small eyes seem smaller .

Bao Tingh was affectionately named Attila, after Attila the Hun. He had murdered so many during the Roman Empire, that the dead could not be numbered.

Likewise Bao had killed so many in his career that his dead could not be numbered, either and so begot the name.

Sr. Cavalcanti referred to him as The Beast. But the rest of The Family called him Atilla.

"Is he going to do it?" The Comandante swirled around in his chair.

"Oh, yes. He's definitely going to do it. Get Geovanne to the States immediately."

Francisco

I left the embassy with my brain in a whirl. I hailed a cab. "The Capitol Building, please."

On the drive over, I couldn't stop thinking about Geovanne. *He needs to learn to think, feel, respond and process the way you do.*

I thought about the training regimes under the Comandante and Atilla. They were based around a classroom mentality to keep students competitive rather than cooperative, with Academy instructors teaching several students at a time.

Under the Comandante, the standard class size was three to four individuals. Under Atilla, the number was increased to well over twenty. Under this system, the training was even more competitive with all the students vying for recognition.

The most talented students were often glorified, while the weak ones were pushed out of training. In addition to the classroom instruction, students were expected to study and practice on their own.

Also, it was not unheard of for the Captains to take an apprentice under their wing and tutor them individually. During Atilla's reign, such activities were against the rules and had to be kept secret from the Academy headmaster.

I thought about Geovanne, and what I would teach him and how. How to observe and respond to human queues without perception.

"That will be $16.47," the cab driver announced. I snapped back to reality.

"Thank you." I handed the driver a fifty-dollar bill.

I arrived at the State Capitol Building and headed toward the visitor center to identify the location of the room for the hearing in the Senate Office Building.

I turned heads as I filed through the halls. The women looked on as I moved purposefully toward my destination.

I wore a beautifully tailored smoke-grey suit, with a cream-colored silk shirt. When in the States and not on assignment, I could be visible and look like any other visiting tourist. I knew very well how to blend in and not be seen.

But today, my purpose was to be seen.

✊ ✊ ✊

Adrian

I stood before the Senate committee after speaking to the proposed legislation. I answered the Senators' questions and awaited their final decision on the matter.

Tap, Tap! Senator Franks banged his gavel. He shuffled his papers and read through them one more time. He placed his hand over the microphone and spoke to his colleague, nodded his head, and then cleared his throat.

"On the matter of Senate Bill S.178 – Justice for Victims of Discriminatory Policing, the following is the Statement of the Committee's Conclusion for floor consideration by the Senate.

"The Committee on Civil Rights Policy appreciates the problems in policing, administration, and in public policy that impel the statement of the goals specified above. We believe that as regards to 'breadth requirements' some constructive movement toward 'mutual accountability' is desirable and feasible, and we offer some concrete recommendations at the end of this report.

"However, as the committee, we believe to appoint special district attorneys for every arbitrary claim would weaken the strength of an otherwise reputable judicial system which has successfully prosecuted much more difficult problems--so difficult that the Committee on Civil Rights Policy believes it would be legally undesirable to attempt to implement these objectives." Senator Franks flipped to the next page.

"Therefore, the official findings of this committee of the 114th Congress, on the Amendment of Senate Bill 178 - Justice for Victims of Discriminatory Policing, is as follows:

"The primary obligation to protecting the populous is not to assure them that policing can be accomplished without impunity loss of life or mistakes.

"Rather, it is to be sure that legal, professional and respectful procedures, practices and are adhered to by sworn law enforcement agents" The Senator looked up at me.

"Under the order of 4/21/2015, not having achieved 60 votes in the affirmative, was not agreed to in the Senate by Yeah-Nay Vote 43-55. Record Vote Number: 156. The bill does not pass."

Tap, Tap!

I stood before the panel, making deliberate and intentional eye contact with each Senator. I gathered my things and turned around and left the building.

Francisco

I sat in the galley and watched the beautiful woman, physically dejected, exit the room. I made note of the Senators and their position on the legislation they just voted down. I moved through the aisle and followed Adrian out the Capitol.

PART TWO

10 A INTRODUÇÃO (THE INTRODUCTION)

Adrian

Two hours after the hearing, I sat in the bar at the Hotel George, drowning my rage and disgust in the bottom of four martini glasses: an apple, a cosmo, a lemon drop, and a dirty martini. I was well on my way to martini number five when a tall, lanky white guy approached my table.

"Do you mind if I take a seat?" He slid in the chair across from me.

"As a matter of fact, I do," I replied. "I would like to be alone." I waited for the man to leave, but he wasn't easily dismissed. He was a rather peculiar looking man. The first two things I noticed were his protruding ears and equally pronounced nose. I couldn't help but think, if he could somehow push those two things in, he'd be handsome, for a white guy anyways.

He had very nice hair, full-bodied, dark black. It was curly on the top and cut close on the sides. His eyes were intense, but he had a warm smile. He definitely did not fit the Hotel George look. Everyone there was in a suit and tie. This guy was in a blue button down shirt and beige Dockers, much too casual for a government suit.

"Now why would you be alone when you could have the company of a witty, funny guy like myself?" He smiled.

I looked him up and down and chuckled. "Because I could care less about wit and humor. And because I'm not interested in being entertained." I ran my fingers around the rim of my glass.

"Well, what do you care about then?" He leaned back in his chair. "And what are you interested in? I'm all ears – literally."

I laughed out loud. The guy blushed.

Across the room, a waiter presented a customer with a bill and an argument erupted. The customer insisted that he didn't order the drink, and that he thought his buddy had sent it. The waiter stated that she was about to end her shift and needed to close out her tabs.

I leaned against a pillar that was behind my table. My eyelids were heavy and I heard myself slurring. The white guy was comfortable, leaning in toward me when a beautiful bronzed complexion man tapped him on his shoulder. As the white guy turned to his left, the bronze guy grabbed something off the table and slid it into his jacket pocket. When the guy turned to his right, he met eyes with a visibly angry man.

"It's time for you to go."

"Says who? I'm having drinks with the lady here."

Before I could reply, the beautiful man had the white guy by the thumb; he was on his feet, but leaning back in excruciating pain.

"Says me. Drinks are over." The bronze guy turned to me. "He's a reporter. He's been taping your conversation the entire time." The reporter frantically searched the table.

"Where's my recorder? That's personal property, you can't just take it!"

I sobered up and sat up straight in my chair, looking around the room with a new awareness.

"I can, and I did. And if you would like to keep this digit in tact," the bronze guy pulled back on the reporter's thumb and the reporter grimaced in pain, "I suggest you turn around, grab your photographer friend over there."

I turned to find the photographer this guy was referring to--a man with a camera dangling at his waist, in a deep argument with a waiter and the manager.

"And leave the premises."

He let the guy go. The reporter yanked away, tucked his disheveled shirt back into his slacks, brushed his tousled curls off his forehead and walked away. The bronze guy stood there until they left the building. He turned and faced me. His face softened as he stared into my eyes.

"Mademoiselle, I do apologize for the depravity you just witnessed." He nodded.

I nodded in return. I couldn't help but be stirred by this handsome man. He looked good, smelled good, and spoke with an accent that was smooth and sexy. "But when I observed that the two were reporters, I had to intervene. I hope I didn't overstep my boundaries."

"No, no. Thank you. I didn't realize . . ." I smiled sheepishly.

"The pleasure was all mine." The golden Adonis smiled.

I acknowledged to myself that I was buzzed, but couldn't determine if it was the alcohol that made his teeth seem so sparkly white, or if a human being could actually have such beautiful, perfect teeth?

"Please, have a seat." I pointed to the seat he had just cleared. "Let me buy you a drink to thank you for your chivalry."

As I waved for the waiter's attention, he pulled out the chair and sat. Then, he gently pulled my hand down.

"I'm fine, thank you."

"Yes darlin', you are . . . that's the real reason I'm buying you a drink," I said. I downed the last of my martini and raised my glass toward the bartender.

Mr. Beautiful blushed, then said, "It appears as if you may have reached your limit at The George." He motioned toward the bartender who shook his head. I lay back against the pillar and soaked in this handsome man before me. A sultry smile slowly covered my face.

"Are you okay?" Mr. Beautiful looked at the empty martini

glasses, then back at me.

I dismissed his look with a wave. "No, I am not okay. Hence the drunken stupor." I forced a half smile.

Mr. Beautiful sat back in his seat and looked deeply into my eyes as if he were staring at something familiar. "Is there anything I can do to help you?"

I paused for half a second before replying, "Unless your tongue has stamina and you don't mind burying your head between my thighs all night—I'ma have to say nope!"

We locked eyes for a long time, then, I watched Mr. Beautiful push back his chair and stand. He extended his hand to me.

A huge smile covered my face. I took his hand, wobbling a bit. But he stabilized me. I grabbed my purse and Mr. Beautiful grabbed the billfold and we walked out of the bar together, my arm around his waist, his around my shoulder—looking like a happy couple.

Mr. Beautiful handed the waiter the billfold with five crisp one hundred dollar bills inside as he passed her in the walkway. "Thank you!" she called behind him.

At the elevator, he pressed the UP button. I leaned in close, absorbing the manly smell. Everything about him was masculine. His hair, his hands, his suit . . . and right now, all I wanted was to forget about my day. The alcohol had failed--perhaps some clitoral stimuli might do the trick.

We entered the elevator and he pushed PH. I slid in front of him and slowly ground my butt into his midsection. He smiled.

"Third floor." The white lady's voice came from the speaker above in what I thought was the sexiest elevator voice I'd ever heard. I laughed out loud.

The elevator stopped and an older couple stepped inside. Mr. Beautiful pulled me in close and slid his right hand underneath my suit jacket. He expertly found his way inside both my blouse and bra and I couldn't control a gasp. The old lady looked in my direction.

Mr. Beautiful gently rubbed my nipple between his index finger and thumb. I smiled, leaned my head back on his chest and applied more pressure to his now bulging erection. Not to be undone, he slid his left hand underneath my suit jacket and inside the top of my skirt. After two attempts, he found his way inside my panties and slid two fingers inside my warm lips. I buckled.

The old woman turned and glared at me. Mr. Beautiful quickly propped me back up. The woman gave us a menacing look.

"Fifth floor," the white lady cooed overhead.

He massaged my pulsating clit, moving slowly and rubbing ever so softly. I dropped my head and bit my bottom lip.

"*Ninth floor,*" the white lady taunted.

The older couple stepped off the elevator, but before the doors closed the old lady turned with a scowl plastered across her face. "For heaven's sake, you couldn't wait till you got to your room?" The doors closed and we burst into laughter.

"You heathen," I said facing Mr. Beautiful.

"You tart," he said, covering my mouth with his.

I wrapped my arms around his neck and leaned into his chest. Mr. Beautiful grabbed my ass and pulled me in close. He slid his tongue into my mouth, slowly and passionately kissing me.

"*Penthouse,*" the white lady announced.

We continued kissing as we entered what I assumed to be Mr. Beautiful's penthouse suite. I pulled off his jacket and started to unbutton his shirt, but he grabbed my hands and led me to the bedroom.

The wall behind the white leather headboard was covered with 18th century script—some piece George Washington had inked during his Presidency. But I couldn't decipher it as I passed the four white ink & quill sets perfectly spaced apart, resting in the enclave in the wall.

He led me to the suede espresso colored couch, then gently ran his fingers across my cheek as he stared into my eyes. He removed my jacket, then my blouse. He turned me around, kissing the nape of my neck as he unzipped my skirt. Mr. Beautiful reached around and gently grabbed my breasts. I leaned back into his chest, breathing deeply. He adorned my spine with feather light kisses. I shivered.

Mr. Beautiful pulled me down on the couch kissing me long and hard. I returned the intensity—sucking his tongue deep inside my mouth.

"Ouch!" He looked down into my mischievous grin. "Careful, you don't want to damage this tongue," he said as he removed my panties and pulled me to the edge of the couch. "You said you wanted it between your thighs all night, remember?"

I spread my legs.

"I remem—Ooh!" I said as his tongue slid expertly inside, parting my lips. "Yes . . ."

He shoved the ottoman to the side, got on his knees, slid his hands up under my butt and pulled me up to his face. I grabbed the arm of the couch with my left hand and the pillow with my right hand. "Fuck!" I screamed.

He took my clit inside his mouth, licking it over and over at a steady gentle pace for what felt like forever. My breathing grew deeper and deeper. My legs started to quiver. I felt the shaking start mid-calf; it became more intense as it surged up my legs, through her thighs "Oh shit! Oh shit!" I screamed. My body exploded into an intense convulsion. He held on to my waist as I shook, holding his tongue firmly on my clit the entire time.

I started to growl. "Mmmh. Mmmh. Yes! Yes!" I said in a deep husky voice, I did not recognize.

Mr. Beautiful slid two fingers inside my wet vagina, moving in and out as he sucked on my clit. I grabbed his hair, stroking it, pulling it, using it to pull him deeper inside me. I moved his head so his nose rubbed up against my clit while his tongue lapped my labia. "O-O-H-

H!" I screamed, pulling his head back and forth until I came again.

Mr. Beautiful came up for air; his face was covered in my juices. I turned and sat up, then fell back onto the couch.

"My god you have an amazing tongue!"

Mr. Beautiful smiled. "Well, I received explicit marching orders, and I aim to please."

"Where have you been all of my life?" I said staring softly into his eyes.

"Encontrar meu caminho para voce, meu amor," he said.

"I don't know what you said, but it sounded sexy as hell." I smiled.

He slid his hands underneath me and pulled me up into his arms. "You asked where have I been all of your life and I said I was finding my way to you…my love."

I swooned as he lifted me up. "Ooh, careful. I ain't no itty bitty woman." My feet were dangling in the air.

Mr. Beautiful said, "I don't know why you continue to question me." He carried me across the room. I nuzzled my face into his neck.

"I don't either." I whispered, taking in the masculine fragrance.

"Then stop. And trust me." I laughed.

"I don't even know you."

"You know me." the gorgeous man said looking into my eyes.

I kissed him slowly, over and over. He laid me gently on the bed. He stood, admiring my body.

I looked at Mr. Beautiful and knew with his good looks, his swag, and that damned sexy ass accent, that he had been with more women than I could probably count on both hands and feet, but in that moment he looked at me like he'd never seen a woman more beautiful than the woman lying naked before him.

He kissed my breasts, then the curves of my hips. He rolled me over and kissed every inch of my butt.

I lay quietly enjoying the feel of this man's loving touch. I smiled. *What feels like love. What love must feel like.* It had been so long, I couldn't remember anymore. I stared off into space, then closed my eyes as the beautiful Latin lover slid his face in between my legs.

✊ ✊ ✊

Adrian

Bzzz. Bzzz. Bzzzz.

I woke to my cell buzzing somewhere near my head. Disoriented, I reached out and fumbled around in the area of the buzzing, knocking over the cup and knocking the handle of the landline off the base.

"Shut up, dammit!" I screamed. "I can't find you." I reached over and felt the vibration in my hand.

"Hello?"

"Well got damn bitch, finally!" a male voice shouted in my ear. I pulled the phone away and sat up, trying to focus. I looked around, then down. I was naked, lying in an amazing suite—somewhere.

The room was modern chic, accessorized in white and dark brown giving it a very masculine feel. I reached over to the nightstand where my phone had been and picked up a note pad. *The George Hotel.*

George Hotel. George Washington. Washington, DC. The Senate Hearing.

"I assumed it didn't go well since I didn't hear from yo ass?" he said. "I figured I'd give you a couple of hours to throw back a few, but assumed you'd call me and give me details. But seriously? What the fuck, bitch?"

"JR. Shut up, will you? It's too early in the damn morning for all this bitching, and I haven't had my coffee--"

The elevator to the penthouse opened. I pulled the sheet up over my chest as the most beautiful man I had ever seen in my life walked through the door holding two cups of coffee and pastries.

I set up in the bed, mouth open.

"Bom dia Precioso!" he said beaming.

I sat there, staring at this amazingly handsome man, completely unsure as to whether I was dreaming or if he really just walked into the room.

"We're going to have to teach you Portuguese. I just said 'Good morning, precious." He handed me a cup of the best smelling coffee I'd ever inhaled. He walked back over to the table and started pulling out sugar, cream, and stirrers.

"Who the fuck is that? Is that a man in the background?" JR's voice came through the phone.

"Stop yelling!" I responded, annoyed. "My head is pounding."

The handsome man looked over his shoulder in my direction.

"That's what five martinis will do to you." He grinned.

"Five martinis, bitch, you are a light weight. One . . . maybe two, if Jesus asked you to join Him. You had five fucking martinis? What the fuck happened at that hearing?—No, wait, fuck the hearing, you have a man in your room, what the fuck happened last night with him?"

"Hell if I know . . . but this is one drunken decision I'm going to have to say I do not regret," I whispered, adoring this fine specimen of a man. He had on a white short-sleeve shirt with tan colored linen pants and white and tan leather loafers; a pair of brown sunglasses nestled comfortably in a patch of waves on top of his head. He was a beautifully bronzed complexion, with gorgeous jet black hair. His eyes, though small, donned the longest, sexiest lashes.

"Whaaat? Like that? And you have no idea who he is?"

"None, friend. Not a clue."

"Well, what does he look like?"

The handsome man brought me cream and sugar for my coffee

along with a delectable looking croissant filled with cream. I took them and mouthed, "Thank you." He returned to the table and prepared his coffee.

"Um . . . do you know that character from the movie The Mummy?"

"Who? Brendan Fraser?"

"Is that the one with the tattoos?"

The handsome man glanced over at me with a puzzled expression. I smiled politely.

"No, the one with the tats is Ardeth Bay. He looks like fucking Oded Fehr?" JR squealed.

"JR! My head?" I said, sipping on the coffee. "Yes. That's exactly who he looks like."

"And you fucked him?" JR said.

I looked up under my sheets to my naked body.

"I am not one hundred percent but pretty certain. Listen, the Senate voted down the legislation. I'm fine. Let me call you back later, okay?"

"Are you kidding me?" JR said. "My straight-laced friend wakes up naked in a room with an Oded Fehr look alike and I have to wait for breaking news at eight?"

I hung up the phone.

The handsome man walked over to the bed, took my coffee and handed me a drink. "Here, take this." He sat on the edge of the bed next to me. He tucked my hair behind my ears and looked at me adoringly.

"What is it?" I eyed the drink suspiciously. I didn't know this man.

"*Caipirinha.*" He laughed at my apprehension. "It's one of our most famous Brazilian drinks—actually, it's our national cocktail. It's a *batida* made with cachaça, sugar and lime, garlic and honey. It's a homemade recipe originally used for patients of Spanish flu. Drink it, it will make you feel much better."

I sipped the drink. He walked around to the other side of the bed

126

and lay across the covers, watching me.

"So," I said, smiling at him. "What's your name? And did we have sex all night?"

The Latin man laughed out loud. "Well if you have to ask, I suppose I did not provide you with a memorable performance."

"No, darlin', what it means is that I drank way beyond my limit. One is my cut off. I can't believe I drank five martinis?"

"Yep, five." He slid his hand underneath the covers and grabbed my feet. He gently massaged the sole of my right foot. I closed my eyes. If his foot massage was any indicator of his skills in other places, I was pissed I couldn't remember. I set my cup of coffee down on the nightstand so I could enjoy the massage.

"Damn, that feels good."

The handsome man laughed out loud. I opened my eyes and looked at him. "What's so funny?"

"Oh, you said that *a lot* last night."

He smirked. I blushed.

"Okay, so the sex was good, obviously. I'm disappointed I don't remember it."

"We did not have sex, I would never take advantage of you that way," he said.

I frowned. "Wait—what? Then what's with the 'you said that a lot last night' about?"

"You were at the bar when I noticed a reporter and his photographer a few tables away."

I watched his lips move as he described how it had gone down.

"And, well, let's just say that story will never surface."

I listened intently.

"But, to answer your question, when I asked if I could help you, your reply was, 'You can if you have a tongue with stamina and don't mind burying your head between my thighs all night.'"

I pulled the covers over my head. "I did not say that!"

The handsome man moved to the top of the bed and pulled back the covers. "Hey," he said.

I pulled the covers back over my face and turned my back to him. "Oh my god, I can't believe I said that."

"You said it because you were clear about what you wanted. And I wanted you . . ." He slid his arms around my waist and spoke into my tousled hair.

"So if we didn't have sex, what felt so good?"

The handsome man pulled me into him. He covered my neck with tender kisses. He slid his right hand underneath my arm and gently caressed my breast, then massaged my nipple. I closed my eyes, enjoying the tingling sensation growing in my midsection.

He slid his left hand between my thighs, moving up to softly to rub my triangle of hair. I responded by spreading my legs. He moved his fingers in and out of my warm vagina. I moaned with each stroke. He increased his pace to meet my grinding motions. After only a few minutes, his hands were drenched in my juices.

He threw the covers off, and slid in between my legs, vigorously licking me until I, clutching the sheets on both sides of me, screamed in ecstasy.

"Ohhhhh, my . . . Oh Lawd, Jeesus!" I screamed, and shook. My Latin lover never let up. He licked my clit until I lay motionless, drained from all the orgasms.

He finally lifted his face from between my thighs. I opened my eyes and looked down at him. He smiled a slow sensuous smile. I sighed.

"We didn't have sex," he said. "I buried my face between these beautiful thighs all night."

I blushed. "You did this all night?" I said.

"Sim meu precioso." He kissed the inside of my thighs. I shivered in pleasure. "What did you just say?"

"Yes, my precious."

I pulled him up toward me. We kissed slowly and passionately. I shifted underneath him, grabbing at his zipper. He kissed me deeply then rolled over and positioned himself behind me. Once again, he pulled me in close and kissed my neck.

I frowned. "You don't want to have sex with me?"

"No. I do not." He spoke into my hair.

I flipped around. "Excuse me?"

The handsome man smiled an easy smile. "No. I do not." We locked eyes. I turned my face away from him. He turned me back to face him. He stared as if he were looking at every freckle on my face, as if he were assigning each one a name.

With the tip of his finger, he followed the slope of my nose from my forehead down the bridge to the pointy tip. Then he softly followed the outline of my lips. I lay still watching the fascination in his eyes. He pulled my chin up and kissed me, his tongue expertly navigating my mouth in a sensual sweeping motion.

"The first time I am inside you, I want to make love to you."

I paused. "So you're assuming you're going to see me again?"

He paused. "I certainly hope so."

I turned my back to him. We lay spooning quietly. I closed my eyes.

"So, what is your name?"

We laughed a longtime at that question.

"Chico."

I turned to look him in the eyes.

"Like Chico and the Man?"

"Who is Chico and the Man?"

"It's a TV show from back in the late 70's, I think."

He shrugged and shook his head.

"I don't really know American television that well. Was it very popular?"

I laughed. *It felt foreign.* I thought for a moment, *when was the last time I laughed?* I couldn't remember. Surely it was prior to JJ's death.

Chico ran his fingers through my hair.

"Come to Brazil with me."

"What's in Brazil?" I said.

"Well me, of course."

He grinned. I laughed. He was a fine man. Just, absolutely beautiful. "It's my home, and I'd like to show it to you."

"I know after us being so intimate all night and morning, this is going to sound odd—but again, I don't know you . . . Chico."

He nodded.

I said, "I don't know you, darling. And so, jetting off to another country doesn't sound, how can I say it? The smartest, safest thing to do."

"And sleeping with a complete stranger is?" He whispered. "I could have been a mass murderer." His right eyebrow went up. "And if I were, I would have chopped your body up already." He tickled me.

I pushed his hand away. "Stop it!" I laughed. "I'm serious! You want me to travel how many thousands of miles?"

"I serious, too. It's fifty-five hundred miles, give or take," Chico said. "And any way. What do you have keeping your here?" He stroked my face, watching my brain process his invitation. "Come for two weeks. Let me show you my country, take you away from this vile country for just a little while." He held up the Boy Scout sign. "I promise you will have an amazing time."

I pondered. After yesterday's hearing, I was emotionally drained. I'd been on the circuit for a month, hitting every radio show, television show and community event that would have me, trying to drum up enough support to get this bill passed—only to have it rejected, again.

Chico was right. What *did* I have keeping me here?

Yes, I had my job. But, I wasn't lacking for money. There were my friends. But they had their own lives. They weren't relationships that would need or miss me for two weeks.

"Okay," I said tentatively.

"Great! I'll make the arrangements," Chico said. "How soon can you leave?"

I slid out of bed and walked to the nightstand to grab my cell. I scanned through my calendar for a few minutes.

"Tomorrow after two p.m."

Chico propped his face up on his elbow. "That's perfect. Shall we leave from here or do you need to return to Los Angeles?"

I felt a rush of fear. What was I doing? I really didn't know this man. What if he was a mass murderer? And just wanted to get me to his country and chop me up there, where nobody would find my body?

I stood naked holding my phone. I watched him watching me. He looked at me with complete adoration. It made me blush.

"You tell me." I placed my hand on my hip. "Can we get tickets to Brazil in less than twenty-four hours? I'm sure that will be pretty expensive."

Chico stood and walked over to me. He pulled me in close and stared at me.

"What?"

"You are the most beautiful woman I have ever laid eyes on."

I couldn't help but blush. No one had spoken to me like that since Brandon. Brandon always said the most beautiful words to me.

"Thank you. That's so sweet." I placed my head on his chest. He smelled so good. He wrapped his arms around me.

"Don't worry about the transportation. I will arrange everything. And if you're okay with it, let's leave from Dulles airport." He took my phone and keyed in his telephone number, then typed his name.

He opened his phone. "Give me your number, and I'll text you tonight with the time and gate information. Shall I send a driver for you?"

I smiled. "No, I can manage." I actually started to feel excited. It was like an adventure. A mini get away – a distraction.

"You won't change your mind, will you?" Chico said.

"Not with that tongue to look forward to. No way Jose." I

laughed.

This time he blushed.

*   *   *

"You're going where, with whom?" Linda asked. "Wait, back up. You had a one-night stand with some Rico Suave, now you're going to South America for two weeks?" She paused long enough to take a quick breath. "Who is this, and what have you done with my prude, up tight, follow the rules Polly Anna friend, Adrian Jackson?" Linda said.

"Forget you, Lindy Lu!" I laughed.

I was packing the last of my toiletries. "I already told Reggie and JR. Honestly, that's pretty much it. My circle of friends has dwindled down to a dot."

"Okay, so what do you know about this man? Shall I run a background check on him?" Linda said. "I mean, besides the fact that he's fine as fuck and has a golden tongue."

"Yeah, I don't know much else. And, right now, Lin—I don't need it to be more complicated than that. I'm not flying to South America to meet his parents and spend the rest of my life with him. I'm going to get away. To forget about the Senate, the hearing, the bill, and crappy U.S. of A."

"Okay, okay!" Linda backed down. "Well good for you. You deserve some pampering and a little adventure. I hope you come back walking bow legged like a cowboy from all the delicious sex! I hear the Latin lovers are the best."

"You hear, or you're speaking from experience?"

"Why do you always have to make me out for a whore, AJ? It really bothers me that you have this low opinion of my virtue," Linda said.

I burst into laughter.

"Ok, my friend. How about this. 'I appreciate your support'"

"Much better. Thank you!"

Francisco

"Thiago, my friend, I need you to reach out to the coordinator of transportation in the U.S. and arrange a charter flight for two back to Brazil, please sir."

"Sim , mas é claro . And for the manifesto? Who shall I say is accompanying you?"

"Annette English" Francisco replied. Thiago paused.

"Yes, of course. Senor, I will arrange it. And madam moiselle's accommodations in Brazil?"

"Thiago, please prepare the flat in Terra da Garoa."

"Yes, of course. When shall I expect you?"

"Schedule the flight for tomorrow at 6:00 p.m. US time."

"Putting you in Sao Paulo at 5 am with the time difference. I will make the necessary arrangements and confirm with you in less than three hours."

"Thank you, Thiago."

"My pleasure."

 Charter Flight Confirmation: zh10828
 (2) Passenger(s): Francisco Monsserate; Annette English
 Origination: Dulles, Washington DC
 Destination: Terra da Garoa
 Time: 6:00 pm

Antoinette started to delete the encrypted message until she saw the names. Francisco Monserrate and Annette English. Francisco? Was he coming back to the business? He had long since retired, so she thought. Was it a cover? She had obviously gotten the transcript by mistake. Antoinette dialed the command post.

"Antoinette Machado—MQ4726LH03
 Transcript: ZH10828
 Confirming Receipt."

Antoinette swiped her phone closed. Confirming receipt meant she'd remain on the notifications and alerts. *'What are you up to, Francisco? And who is this American you are transporting to Brazil?"*

Like Thiago, Antoinette knew the passenger name Annette English was the code name used for an American female to prevent authorities from being able to track her on the manifest.

Antoinette looked at her watch. She had less than three hours to make it to Dulles airport.

Antoinette

I watched Francisco waiting nervously at the gate. He checked his watch every five minutes. He looked handsome in tan linen slacks, a white linen shirt, and loafers. His hair was neatly pulled back by a pair of Ray Ban sunglasses. He lit up the moment he saw the tall American in the god-awful warm up suit approaching. She had an easy, purposeful stride, exuding strength, confidence and, even wearing warm ups, class. I grunted out loud.

Francisco greeted her with a sensuous embrace. She smiled and wrapped her arms around his neck, and they kissed, an easy, intimate kiss. Not too long, but long enough to let you know they were lovers. Long enough to see a teasing chemistry between them.

He grabbed her bag and they walked, talking and laughing, toward the gateway. On the tarmac, Francisco handed the pilot the woman's luggage, then took her hand and led her up the stairs into the private jet.

I watched the plane taxi down the runway, then watched as it ascended easily into the sky. I stood watching the plane until it became a tiny spec in the blue vastness.

"Bem," I said, as I placed my sunglasses over my eyes. "Isso e interessante."

11 AN EDUCATION, OF SORTS . . .

On the plane, Chico removed my sneakers and gently massaged my feet. I lay back and soaked in the delicious pampering.

"Is this how it's going to be the entire trip?" I asked, eyes closed. "Are you going to pamper me the entire time?"

"Yes. I am going to show you the time of your life, which means you will want for nothing."

I opened one eye. "What is your end game, Chico? Why are you doing all of this? What's your goal?"

He smiled. "Would it scare you if I said I wanted you to leave the United States and be with me?"

I opened both eyes. "Yes."

"Then, my end game is for you to simply enjoy two weeks of pure pleasure before you return home to the hell and misery you've been enduring for the past eleven months."

I watched his face for a moment. "Have you been checking into my background?" I pulled my feet away.

Chico grinned. "It's not like you're a recluse. Your face is plastered all over the news precioso." He grabbed my foot and tenderly massaged it. "I'm not a psycho. I'm not a stalker. I am here just to make you happy. Why is that so difficult to believe?"

"People don't do things just to do them, Chico. They always want something in return."

"Oh, I want something in return. But I want you to give it, freely and willingly."

I squinted my eyes, looking him over suspiciously.

Chico chuckled. "Americans are so untrusting. What a horrible life to live."

"What is your nationality? And what type of work do you do?"

Suddenly I felt nervous about this spontaneous decision. Although he had given me the information where I would be staying, and I'd given it to Linda and JR, I still felt foolish for jumping on a plane and flying to South America with a complete stranger.

"I am Brazilian. My home is Sao Paulo." He took my other foot and began gently massaging it.

"What are you, some kind of gigolo? Because if you've done your research you've discovered I'm not rich, by any stretch of the imagination."

"I have my own money." He pointed to the plane. "I was in private security for years and did exceptionally well. I have retired and don't really live a very lavish life, so I live very comfortably."

"A private jet is not lavish?" I said.

"I like to travel in a certain style. So I have some of the . . . extravagant amenities afforded to me by my previous career." Chico paused with a smile. "And I like nice clothes, and nice restaurants. But generally speaking, I live a very simple life."

"Do you always pick up women at bars?"

"I do not," Chico said. "I usually pay for company. It keeps things, easier."

A blank expression covered his face and I knew he went somewhere else, but I didn't probe.

"Surely it's not because you have to. You could probably have any woman you want."

"And I have slept with so many women--all nationalities, ethnicities, shapes, sizes, ages," he said quietly. "After a while, it doesn't matter. It's just empty sex. So, when I have the need. I take care the need. But, I don't exude too much energy outside of those moments."

Usually I was the one being deftly honest, offending those who wanted to play games and tap dance around the truth. But this guy was *not* American. There were so many things that pointed to it, including this conversation.

"Okay, all chivalry aside, what made you come to my rescue?"

"I hate scum," Chico said.

"Okay, and what made you take me up on my offer?"

"I think you are the most beautiful woman I have ever seen." Chico said.

"Which says a lot, I guess, since you've been with so many?" I rolled my eyes.

He laughed. "Your American humor is taxing." He sat back in his seat. "Those women have nothing to do with you."

I didn't think twice when Chico mentioned that he paid for sex. I understood that paying for affection and release kept life simple. I prided myself on avoiding unnecessary complications.

I understood the need for human touch, without the side effect of human drama. Paying for sex did keep things simple.

"So, you were saying?"

"I wasn't."

"Yes you were. You were telling me about your life—because your adulthood was summed up in three sentences." I gave him a dry smirk.

Chico laughed. "There's not really much to say. At ten years of age I became an orphan. My father's best friend took me in, raised me, trained me in the area of security and weaponry, and that's pretty much all she wrote. As you Americans would say."

"Oh no you don't," I said. "An orphan at ten and that's it? What happened?"

Chico looked to the right out the small window. "The sky was clear and blue, and the clouds danced around the sky. I remembered the day my life changed forever. I was outside playing with friends," he said.

"It was a military intervention by the dictatorship to eliminate '*The Araguaia Guerilla*'," he said. "That's what they called them. But they were really just college students and self-employed workers." Chico played with his fingers as he talked, the he looked up and into my eyes. "The long and short of it, was that my father was killed in battle in the jungle in 1972. Then they connected him to my mother, arrested and tortured her and her brother, then executed them in 1973 and 1974."

"Oh my goodness, Chico." I clutched my throat, trying to imagine life as an abandoned ten-year-old knowing my parents had been brutally murdered. "And your father's best friend took you in and raised you?"

Chico smiled and nodded.
"Yes." He paused for a long moment, then looked back out the window. He was silent before he turned to look at me.

"Oh, Chico," I said. "I am so sorry. You lost your family at such an early age." I watched his face turn somber and thought how generous and sweet he turned out despite his circumstances. He could have been bitter and angry for the rest of his life. It would have been justifiable.

I thought about how he came to my rescue and he didn't even know me. And how now, he was taking me away to forget about my pain. What an exceptional person to be able to put aside his hard childhood losses and grow up to be such a caring individual.

Francisco

I didn't tell Adrian that upon completion of my training with Atilla, my very first kill was the judge who made that ruling.

It was a good kill. I practiced all the *Tecnicas de Tortura* with great precision and skill.

"It was a challenging childhood. My adolescence was a period of learning. And as an adult, I have come to know many things," I said in a somber whisper.

"What have you come to know Mr. Chico?" She said.

"What I've come to know is that life is fleeting. You must enjoy all that it has to offer while the petals are open. For when the season changes, so does the posture of the flower. Some will close. Some will lose their petals altogether."

Adrian

I nodded, thinking about the past fourteen months of my life. I knew all too well just how fleeting life could be.

I watched him watching me and felt uneasy. It was as if his eyes were burning into my soul. I turned and looked out into the beautiful blue sky. *What are you doing, Adrian Jackson? Are you running from your life? Trying to escape the pain? Do you have a death wish? What are you doing, woman?*

As the plane tilted forty-five degrees, I thought again about how this was nothing I would ever normally do. Meet a man in a bar. Have sex, and then forty-eight hours later, take off with him to a foreign country.

No. I was Type A, by the books. Follow the rules: Perform and deliver. I was comfortable with making plans and seeing them through to the end—the almost certain end, because I'd planned every step, meticulously.

This—this trip, was *not* me. *Maybe this is what I need to get back on track with my life? Or, to figure out what's next in my life, or . . .*

"Stop thinking so much." Chico nudged me.

I left my mind and focused on this beautiful man sitting across from me. I smiled. "Easier said than done."

"It's very easy. Just do it."

"Just do it, huh?"

"Yes, just do it. Focus on something else. Something relaxing, something that will make you smile."

I sat for a minute, eyes closed. A mischievous smile crossed my face. I peeked out my right eye to see Chico watching with intrigue.

I slowly parted my legs. "Can you guess what I'm thinking about?"

Chico smiled. He pulled off my sweat pants and panties and slowly slid his fingers inside me. I closed my eyes and turned my head to the right as he gently stroked my clit. My hips began to move in time with his strokes. I grabbed the armrests, slid down in my seat, moving down harder on Chico's hand.

"Oh . . . um . . yes."

I gyrated, lifting myself up off the seat.

"Yes, it feels so good. You feel sooo good," I panted.

He moved at the same pace I moved. He watched me please myself on his hands. I moved fast and hard, over and over, over and over, until I reached my climax.

"Oh! Oh! Yes. Oh. My. Oh. Yesss." I fell into my seat, panting and closed my legs. I could feel the throbbing between my legs, in my chest, and in my head.

I looked at Chico, who was leaning on the edge of my seat, rubbing my thigh and butt. Adoring my light brown skin. He kissed my thighs.

"I like the way you think."

✊ ✊ ✊

After Chico made me cum, I dozed off for a four-hour nap. When I woke, Chico was staring out the window.

"Penny for your thoughts?"

He shifted in his seat. "You wouldn't get rich off of my thoughts." He placed a blanket over my shoulders and I snuggled beneath it.

"Ok." I said. "Then tell me how you became the retired jet-setter that we see today?"

"I'm not a jet-setter," he said. "I didn't have a childhood, really. I had to grow up pretty quickly, in order to survive.

"Do you think you're too serious?" I said.

Chico looked at me with a curious smirk. "Do I think I'm too serious?" He laughed. "I whisk you off on a private jet to another continent and you have the gall to ask me that."

"Yes. The question is still on the table."

"No, I don't think I'm too serious. I know when I need to be serious, like, in matters of work. But mostly, I am carefree and easy going. Unlike a certain someone I know." He looked over at me.

"Yes, I have been accused *publicly no less* of being too serious," I said.

"So why don't you loosen up?"

"I can't."

"Of course you can. Just do it," he said. I smirked.

"It's not that easy, Chico. Trust me."

"I do trust you, but I don't understand. Why is it so complicated?"

I paused for a moment. "I'm a black woman."

Chico waited. "Okay, *and?*"

"There is no *and.* I'm serious because I am a black woman."

"Surely your ethnicity has nothing to do with your disposition. I don't understand."

"I know. I told you it's complicated."

"I am trying to understand. But I can only understand if I have perspective. I'm sure you must tire of explaining yourself over and over. I see it on the television shows. But, I must say, answers like these do not help your cause."

"That's just it. I don't have a cause. I am a human being. That's it. But a black woman in America can't just be *that.* We have this . . . stigma. On the one hand, we're strong. Historically, we've had to be. When the slave masters ripped our families apart, the onus was placed on the woman to keep the family together.

"The men were shipped off to other plantations, made to procreate with women they didn't know like some breeding mill, no humanity whatsoever—the women were left to raise children in the most horrific circumstances.

"We couldn't protect our daughters who were victimized and taken at will by vile and abusive slave owners. We couldn't protect our sons, who were brutally killed, constantly emasculated, and always the target of deranged and unjustified hatred." I looked straight through Chico, off into the distance.

"How do you deal with that? No control of your future, your body, not able to protect the children you gave birth to, or be with the man you love? Made to have sex with men you don't know, who don't respect you, or love you—half the time they hate you.

"And if you fight . . . if you fight for your right as a *human being* to choose who you give *your* body to, you are beaten. The skin ripped off your body. Hung from a tree, for depraved people to sit and watch and cheer as they rip you limb from limb.

"How do you live day after day in an environment so cruel? How do you smile, or laugh. How do you believe in a God?"

"American slavery is by far the most cruel and inhumane demonstration of hatred in the history of the world," Chico said somberly. "But that was over a hundred years ago. What does that have to do with your happiness now? Why does what happened to your ancestors --in a time where there were no rights and privileges—affect you so much when you have them now?"

I smiled. I couldn't count on my hands how many times white people have made the same statement, have asked me the same question.

"Your father's best friend?" I said. Chico nodded. "He was a good marksman?"

"An expert, yes." He smiled.

"And he taught you everything you know?"

"Yes, I am a skilled marksman, probably only second to my

mentor."

"What makes you so skilled, Chico? Better question, what was it about your training that makes you who you are as a marksman?"

He thought for a moment. "I learned discipline, and how to take control of any situation. How to look at things from a variety of perspectives so that I can maintain control of the outcome."

I nodded. "You learned to think, act, and see life through the same lens as your mentor?" I said.

Chico nodded. "Yes. It was the only way to become the best. I had to think, act, respond, and yes, virtually mirror the thought processes of my mentor."

"Right. And so, it always amuses me when people ask *me* why does what happened to my ancestors affect me now? The fact remains that racism in America never went away. It just became covert and institutionalized. But the hatred is still passed down from generation to generation.

"White men teach their sons to hate like the redneck they are. They teach their sons to see black people through their lens: less than, sexual, threatening.

"White women teach their daughters to see black people through their lens: powerful, unworthy, unsophisticated. You can use whatever adjectives you want for the lens, as long as they are denigrating they work.

"But the point is this: these people still think and feel the same way about us. 1815 or 2015, it doesn't matter. They learned to be that way from their parents, and those people learned to think and feel that way from their parents, and it goes back generations – but people want to act like the Civil Rights Act stopped people from thinking.

"You hear them disrespect my President. He is the President of the United States! But they do it because they believe he is unworthy. He runs circles around C- average Yale-graduate, George W.

"My President earned his JD degree from Harvard. Are you

kidding me? Have you heard George W's speeches? By far, hands down, no comparison to my President's oratory skills.

"Yet, they call him monkey, and Mr. Obama, and do whatever they can to discredit him—and it's all because he's a black man. Nothing else. It's pure and simple, taught and learned hate.

"And as a black woman, I am still contending with that. The people who were taught and believe that I am less than hold positions of power.

"I don't have the leisure of being silly, or carefree. I don't have the time to slack or bring less than my A game. Not if I'm serious about my career. Not if I have any chance of being successful.

"I don't get the same passes as the next non-black person. They are waiting for me to slip, to make a mistake so they can say, 'See! She can't cut it.' So, I choose to be successful over lighthearted or carefree. I value what little achievements I am able to garner."

"Wow," Chico said. "I am . . . I."

"Right." I rolled my eyes. "Then they say, 'Why are you so serious?' as if I really have a choice. My least favorite stupid question is 'Why are you so angry?' The Angry Black Woman stigma," I said.

"*You* try growing up in a society that says your skin is too dark, your body too thick, your hair too kinky, and your voice too strong. *You* try finding love with a man that looks like you, who cherishes you, respects you, and supports you and all of your accomplishments in this day and time.

"*You* try and raise your sons to be good, decent, and accomplished—only to have them gunned down by officers sworn to protect them, and their deaths blown off, like their lives . . . the lives you've given birth to, aren't worth a penny on the street.

"*You* try to be *happy* knowing that the world sees you as this robot, with no right to feel, express, want or need *anything*—yet blame you for everything wrong in the black community.

"*You* try living through all of that without being angry, and then come ask me that question. But until then, I don't even dignify those ignorant, coined, catch-phrases with a reply."

Chico blinked and shook his head.

I snickered. "Yeah. And that's just the tip of the iceberg, baby."

✊ ✊ ✊

Adrian

The jet touched down in San Paolo near Congonhas Airport. I was excited.

"San Paolo is the financial and economic capital of Brazil. It is one of the largest cities in the world with a population of almost twenty million," Chico said. "Where we're going, the Terra da Garoa, doesn't sleep. There is never-ending entertainment day or night. With the tenth highest GDP in the world, San Paolo is synonymous to luxury and wealth."

I heard the pride in his tone. I grabbed his hand as we walked across the tarmac and into a waiting town car.

"Boa noite Sir Monserrate. Espero que o seu voo foi mais agradavel?" a very distinguished looking older man said over the half drawn partition.

"Indeed the flight was great, my good friend, Thiago," he glanced in my direction. "Indeed it was."

I blushed.

I was in Brazil! I had decided once I left the states I was going to have the most amazing time.

I knew when I returned back home, I would have lots of work to do—so I vowed not to spend a moment worrying about that task, rather spend each day taking in all that South America and Brazil had to offer. I took in the night lights of a booming city as Thiago darted in and out of traffic in Vila Nova Conceicao.

Chico owned an amazing villa that was built in 2012. It came with twenty-four-hour security, spa, gym and a cinema. We drove up the long winding private road to a modern looking pristine white and sand paper colored building.

It was a mansion on a hill. The four-bedroom villa was 9,688 sq. ft. of luxury.

Chico gave me the full tour, including the wooden deck outside with pool, heated spa, chromotherapy and six massage jets.

"And who keeps this museum up?" I said, walking through the gardens.

"I have a staff." He nodded across the walkway to a separate home where I gathered his employees stayed. There was a basement and six parking spaces for visitors.

"Modest lifestyle?" I said to him. "That's what you said on the plane, right?"

He laughed, took my hand and led me into the fabulous Monserrate Villa.

"And you've obtained all this through private security?" I looked up at the vaulted ceiling "I obviously went into the wrong business."

The first two days, Chico ensured that I got plenty of rest. He made me breakfast in bed and insisted that I lounged and enjoyed the many features of his remarkable home.

Day three, I was ready to hit the town and soak in all the richness and culture of Chico's hometown. For the first time besides the tangled "morning after" mess, Chico saw me with my hair down.

"Wow!" He gawked. "You look stunning!"

I'd spent hours trying to look nice and was pleased with his response. My hair fell to the middle of my back. I pulled it to the right, so that the front cascaded over my right eye, while the left side showcased make up I normally never wore.

Eye shadow, mascara, eyeliner, pink lipstick! I even stepped out in an eye-catching fuchsia split-back lace top and lace shorts topped off with nude strappy sandals that I picked up in D.C.

Chico wore gray slacks and a short sleeved chartreuse shirt. His hair was wild and wavy.

Sao Paulo was a cosmopolitan city. As we walked the streets, Chico pointed out descendants from Italian, Portuguese, Spanish, Lebanese, Arabic and Japanese immigrants living in harmony.

"Wow," I marveled. "This is amazing." I had heard plenty of Europeans and Canadians speak to how foreign the prevalence of race in American culture was to them.

Chico took me for a night out in the Vila Olimpia district where we visited the most traditional bars in Madalena. We danced and ate and drank and picked up random conversations with random people about the most obscure topics. On the walk home Francisco turned to me.

"Why do you think there's so much focus on race in your

country?"

I could sense the conversation on the plane stuck with him. I thought about my answer for a while before answering. "I think it's because as country, we refuse to authentically address it."

"What's there to address? You're different, and the same." I smiled. "Oh, but if it were just that simple."

"The cultural aspects of who you are make you different, which means you bring your thoughts, your insights, your beliefs, and your uniqueness to a situation. The human—the humane aspects of who you are make you the same, which means you have the same wants, needs and aspirations." Chico looked at me as if the answer was there, plain and simple, and that no one ever had thought to express those words in such a way that the solution could be so simple.

I nodded my head.

"The issue with America is that those who run the country and benefit most from having that power, refuse to acknowledge the value of being different. Instead, they use it to establish control. They refute the sameness, because in that space they would have to own their injustice," I said. "Those in power continue to put legislation in place that benefits those with wealth. It's a sick and sadistic way to run a country, but it's prevalent all over the world, isn't it? America just hides behind propaganda to make it appear as if it's so different. It's the same, it's just not as bold as the third world countries."

Chico squeezed my hand. Every time I talked about America and all of its problems, I tensed up.

"Seems to me you should be looking for another country to live. This one doesn't sound like it suits you very well."

"I'm well-traveled. Trust me when I tell you there are worse places to live! America is nowhere near perfect, but truth be told, I probably would have been stoned or shot already in another country."

We laughed.

"You have one week left in my country. Let's try and make it enjoyable, why don't we?"

I stopped and placed my hands on my hips.

"No *you* didn't just say to me 'let's try and make my trip enjoyable' when *you* just asked me that question?"

"Well, yes. I did ask the question--but I'm recalibrating. No more sad talk about dreary America. I won't initiate it. And neither will you?"

"I haven't so far. Have I?" I rolled my eyes.

Chico pulled me into him. "Okay. *I* keep asking the America questions! I will stop." I looked up into his eyes.

"Alright then. Own it!"

"I'm owning, I'm owning!"

Antoinette

I watched as Francisco pulled the tall woman into him. He kissed her, smiling and laughing. He dipped her and twirled her around, then they strolled happily down the street.

I grew increasingly annoyed. How dare he taunt me with this . . . corpulent . . . American--in *my* home country. I slid down my shades and continued to follow them.

The rest of the week was a whirlwind. Chico hit all the touristy venues: a concert in the municipal theater in the center, the MASP museum on Avenida Paulista, and because he knew I was a fashion lover, we spent an entire day at the renowned Oscar Freire boutiques in the wealthy district of Jardins.

The second half of the trip we attended a Formula 1 race in the racetrack of Interlagos, we watched one of the "Paulistanos" derbies in the Morumbi stadium and one in the brand new Arena Palestra Italia and Arena do Corinthians.

"Are you having a good time?" Francisco asked me two days before I was to leave Brazil.

"I am spoiled to death. How can I not?" I laughed. "I am truly having the best time of my life." I sat lounging in front of the calming water feature in the center of his backyard. The sun was warm and enveloping. I had several manila folders in my lap and some were strewn across the chaise.

"What's this?" Chico inquired.

"This, is reality." I placed my hands over my eyes to block the sun as I looked up at him. "I have several speaking engagements lined up upon my return, and I need to get back in the groove. So I'm brushing up on some cases and memorizing statistics that support my positions."

Chico looked disappointed. He sat down next to me and browsed through a few folders. *Unarmed People of Color, Killed by Police 1999-2014.*

On Wednesday, after the announcement that NYPD Officer Daniel Pantaleo would not be indicted for killing Eric Garner, the NAACP's Legal Defense Fund Twitter posted a series of tweets naming 76 men and women who were killed in police custody since the 1999 death of Amadou Diallo in New York.

Chico read the detailed accounts.

Tamir Rice, 12, Cleveland, Ohio—Nov. 22, 2014
Officer Tim Loehmann shot and killed Rice, who was holding a BB gun, seconds after spotting him at a park. **Aftermath:** *Rice's family has filed a wrongful death lawsuit against Cleveland.*

Ezell Ford, 25, Los Angeles, Calif.—August 12, 2014
Ford was shot by police who were conducting "an investigative stop." " A struggle ensued," read the LAPD's news release. Ford's family members say he was lying down when shot. **Aftermath:** *The LAPD, which hasn't closed the investigation into Ford's death, put an indefinite "investigative hold" on the coroner's autopsy report to prevent witness testimony from being tainted.*

Michael Brown, 18, Ferguson, Mo.—August 9, 2014
Shot by Officer Scott Wilson after an altercation that happened inside Wilson's car. Wilson reported that Brown "looked like a demon." **Aftermath:** *Wilson was not indicted by a grand jury. He resigned from the Ferguson police force. The family greatly wanted to have the killer of their unarmed son held accountable.*

Tyree Woodson, 38, Baltimore, Md.—August 2, 2014
Police say Woodson's fatal gunshot wound was self-inflicted. That would mean that he smuggled his gun into a police station after police brought him there for having several open warrants. "Things don't seem quite right here," said Baltimore Councilman Carl Stokes. "This person could have a gun, a high caliber gun, that could be used against other officers and then he allegedly kills himself." **Aftermath:** *Pending.*

Yvette Rasmussen, 47, Bastrop, Texas—February 16, 2014

Officers responding to a domestic disturbance call shot after she opened her front door to them. Initially, police claimed that Rasmussen had a firearm, but the sheriff's office retracted this the next day. **Aftermath**: *Deputy Daniel Willis, who shot Rasmussen, was indicted on a murder charge. Her family is asking for $5 million in a wrongful death suit.*

McKenzie Cochran, 25, Southfield, Mich.—January 28, 2014

Cochran died of "position compression asphyxia" during struggle with mall security. Cochran told them, " I can't breathe." His death ruled an accident by medical examiner. **Aftermath**: *No indictments for the security guards.*

Ramarley Graham, 18, New York, N.Y.—February 2, 2012

Graham was shot and killed by police in the Bronx, who chased him into his home without a warrant. He was unarmed. **Aftermath**: *The officer, Richard Haste, was initially indicted in 2012, but the case was later overturned. A second grand jury decided not indict Haste. Graham's mother said just last month that the Justice Department will proceed with its own investigation.*

Chico put the folders down. He barely made it through the first two pages . . . there were still another four to go. He rubbed his forehead and looked at me as I continued combing over my documents.

"Adrian. How can you sit and read these for hours on end?" He said, "No wonder you stay so somber, so . . ."

"Angry?" I waited for him to answer and when he didn't, I continued, "I have to look at them. I have to read their stories, memorize the details. If there are pictures, I look into their eyes. I try to feel their souls and imagine their last moments on this earth."

"That is torture." He rubbed my leg. "Why are you doing this to yourself?"

"I'm not doing this to *myself*. The police are doing this to me and every mother out there whose child's life they took as if they had the right."

"I understand, but--"

"If you understand you better not say *but*!" I said. "The minute you say but, you negate everything that precedes it.

"So *if* you understand, stop right there. And if you don't understand--then just keep it to yourself." I turned my attention back to my papers. But after a couple of seconds, I couldn't help it. "I'm sick and tired of explaining *why* I fight for Black lives!" I screamed. "They matter! They fucking matter! Okay?" Tears streamed down my face."

I held up the folders in my hands. "I bet you if white boys all of a sudden started turning up dead, the country would be in an uproar!" I threw the folders to the floor. "I want this damned country to feel for the lives that were taken! I want this country to grieve. I want this country to know that every life matters, not just white peoples'. Black lives matter too, Chico. That's why I do it. Okay?   Because every one of these people's lives matters." I got up from the chaise lounge and walked down the paved path up the stairs to the villa.

Francisco

I left my villa. Inside the garage, I started my car.

"You've become so desperate you're reverting to fat black Americans?" Antoinette leaned forward in between my two front seats. "And you're slipping. If you were still actively working, there's no way you would have missed me in your vehicle. Your sedentary life is making you lento e despreparados!" She climbed into the front seat as I put the car in reverse and pulled out of my parking structure.

"So slow that I didn't see you at Dulles, or on my estate last week, or vila Olimpia in Madalena? I saw you. Every time. I just didn't care that you were spending your days watching me. Lembrar-me do novo que esta desperdicando sua vida?"

"I am not wasting my life. But look at you. You call hanging with some fake American social activist a life?"

"My life is none of your business," I replied.

Antoinette sat stoically in the passenger seat. "You don't have a life," she berated. "You fuck ugly Americans and live like a ninety year old retired man."

I pulled the car over. "Get out, Machado," I said, looking straight ahead.

"Please, no terms of endearment. Your sweet talk is sour to my ears."

"Yet here you are, in my vehicle—uninvited."

"I'm here because despite you being the asshole that you are, I still care for you." Antoinette turned to look at me.

I looked straight ahead. "What do you want Ahn-tone-ett?"

"You know what I want, Francis." She slid her hand over mine.

"Ahn-tone-ette."

"Fuck you." She jumped out the car and disappeared.

I turned back on the road and sped off to my destination. I saw Antoinette in my rear view mirror watch me speed off in the dark as she stood on the side of the road.

✊ ✊ ✊

Antoinette

Five years, two days, seven hours, and six minutes ago, Francisco Monserrate ripped my heart out. He betrayed my love, the love of all time, and shattered my heart into a million—no, a trillion pieces. He told me, to my face, that he didn't love me, never had, and never could.

Who does that? Who says that? Yes, only an asshole. Only a beautiful, magnificent, charming *asshole*.

Francisco and I had been lovers for years. We met in class, during Phase III training. We were the top of our class and had to compete against each other for the title of General.

I was much better than Francisco. But I loved him the first day I met him at age twelve. He was a scrawny looking boy. But his eyes were so deep set into his forehead, and when he smiled, oh my! That smile could melt a frozen snowcap. And it had.

There was no stone, nor metal or, organ more cold and impenetrable than Antoinette Marie Machado's heart. That was, until I laid eyes on Francisco that Thursday, April 28, 1976. From that day forward, he would own my heart.

As I moved up in rank and skill, so did Francisco. When it came down to the final examination, Francisco would take the title. Or, as only I knew--been given it. That's how much I loved him.

I knew I had the worst reputation among assassins. And I loved it. They called me cold and heartless. I didn't understand how you could be an assassin and be anything else? What? Because I took contracts other assassins refused: religious leaders, women, children? Or because I was a woman who could be as ruthless as a man? I made it a point to let everyone know I could run with the boys. I garnered respect for showing no fear.

I was given the name Hatchet. One reason was because my last name translated *meant* hatchet, but primarily because I was like a psycho maniac who kills his victims with a hatchet.

All of my kills were clean, never messy or botched—the reference had nothing to do with my style or service, but everything to do with my personality.

I'd heard the rumors. *I did not to have a soul, a conscience, or a heart.* Maybe so. As a female assassin I set the standard for badass. And I thoroughly enjoyed my reputation--did everything I could to maintain it.

Including having two signature shots. One was my *Kill Shot*. It's the one I used for the majority of my targets. It was executioner style: One Soft Tip bullet to the head. Clean, final. This was the shot under classmates called my compassion shot because the bullet had a tendency to flatten the projectile when it hit a target, the bullet didn't open up like hollow point rounds so the shot was quick, clean, and the victim never knew what hit him. I didn't particularly care for it being called "compassionate".

My other shot was the *Rim Shot*. This shot was reserved for hits that involved personal vendettas. I used a ballistic tip bullet which had an exaggerated opening in the tipoff the copper jacket that caused the bullet to expand upon impact making a loud cracking sound to the skull.

Francisco and I became lovers at nineteen years old. We were on assignment in Istanbul for six weeks when it happened.

It was convenient, as we always worked closely together. It was simple, in that we both lived a life we understood. And it worked, primarily because we both could detach at the drop of a dime. That was, until the Montelban case.

Pilar Montelban was Francisco's first defensive detail. Up until then, he was always on the offensive. The Comandante was training us to work both sides in order to capitalize on all aspects of the market. Pilar was the daughter of Archbishop Corleon Montelban, the successor to the newly established Guatemalan regime.

Seven attempts had been made on his life. Francisco was to ensure Pilar's safety until after the rebellion. He was with her 24/7 for six months.

It was during this time that Francisco and Pilar fell madly in love, and I fell into deep dark rage.

I watched that weak, sniveling bitch work her way into my lover's heart. And then, into his bed.

I watched them make love on the veranda. I watched them make love in the library. I watched them smile at each other across the room, speaking a non-verbal language with their eyes that Francisco and I used to speak, but now he barely acknowledged me.

As hard as I tried, I could not win back his love. In between my panicked rage and depression I approached the Comandante.

"You need to speak to Francis."

"I need to?" He looked at me over his black horn rimmed glasses. "That sounded a lot like a command."

"He's compromising the assignment. He's too close to the target. He's losing perspective."

The Comandante eyed me up and down. "Is it he who is losing perspective?"

I stormed out of the Comandante's office.

Two weeks later, after six months of successful protection, Pilar was found dead, floating face down, drowned in her bathtub.

Francisco wanted to quit, but the Comandante said that was unacceptable. "Quem pode encerrar sus familia? No one can ever quit their family."

Francisco was in such a bad way, even Atilla spoke to the Comandante about his disposition.

"A broken heart never fares well in war. It makes a man weak and vulnerable. You put him and the rest of the team at grave risk."

The Comandante called Francisco in and told him to go away for forty-five days; then upon his return he should be healed, hard, and ready for work.

I went stir crazy when I learned that Francisco was leaving for six weeks. I confronted him.

"Where will you go?" I asked.

"Where you are not," He replied.

"I can go with you."

"You can get out of my face."

"You used to love me."

Francisco stared into my eyes. I had hoped he see the love that filled every crack and crevice of my being. The love that superseded his betrayal and would forgive him if he would just come back to it.

"That was then."

"And now?" I whispered.

Francisco grabbed his backpack and walked past me. I grabbed his arm. Francisco stopped, never turning to face me.

"And now, you're dead to me."

On day forty-five, Francisco returned to headquarters a different man. He was cold and distant, but never more on his game than then.

Francisco

"Comandante." I hugged my mentor.

"Francisco! My son, how are you?" The corners of the Comandante's mouth inched up forming a half-moon.

"I am well."

The Comandante turned one chair around to face the other and pointed for me to sit.

"This is good news. I was concerned. It's not like you to visit during the evening unless there is something pressing." The Comandante sat back in his chair and searched my face. "Is something pressing, my son?"

I smiled. Alberto Cavalcanti knew it touched my heart when he referred to me as son. I adored and respected him immensely.

"There is." I shifted in my seat, "I have come to apologize for my behavior during our last meeting and ask for your forgiveness."

The Comandante nodded. "Of course, Francisco. Of course." He smiled, pleased. "Does this mean that you have reconsidered my request?"

"Si Sinhor."

"Ah! This is wonderful news!" He leaned in and slapped my shoulder. "Wonderful news indeed. When would you like for Geovanne to begin?"

"I need to conference with him tonight," I said. "We will begin training first thing Monday morning."

"Yes. Yes of course." The Comandante stood and pressed the intercom. "Vitoria, summons Geovanne to the library immediately."

I shook my head. The Comandante winked at me.

Francisco

"Sinhor Monserrate." Geovanne entered the library.

He was not an exceptionally handsome young man. Although neat, in his tan slacks, white button down shirt, navy blue jacket, and tan suede loafers with red soles, there was nothing distinctive about him. He was from Porto Velho in Northern Brazil. Like a large portion of the natives from the upper region of the continent, Geovanne was light complexioned with blonde hair and blue eyes.

Geovanne stood 5'11" but carried himself as if he were 6'3". *Atilla's student.* I could tell right away under whose tutelage each cadet studied. Each trainer had their own etymology, a specific set of standards, characteristics and sway that identified their training ethos.

Under the Comandante, you were stealth, lethal, unheard and unseen—you blended in with your environment. Your strength was always the element of surprise.

Under Atilla you were cold, bold, and ruthless—you dominated by fear, force, and agility. Your strength was always your ability to level your enemy—complete control, dominance and destruction.

Much like traditional middle education, each cadet studied under each commander, learning all the required techniques and styles; however because each cadet spent his/her final phase of training being mentored by the Master Trainer, their influence was prevalent.

Antoinette studied under Atilla. Because she was the first female to make it to Captain, he was exceptionally hard on her. While she never buckled, I always believed it had a profound effect on the way she navigated the world. I was trained by the Comandante. There was something to be said about Alberto Cavalcanti's pathway.

There was a part of me that believed it was much more ruthless than Atilla's because at least with that style, you were allowed to be freely destructive.

The Comandante took pride in the appearance of civility: *The*

Gentleman's Way. But in that space cadets had a tendency to become more sinister. It was like all the civility in appearance caused them to go extra dark and do the most vile and debased things to their targets behind closed doors.

I turned my back to Geovanne.

"Permission to speak, Sinhor Monsserate?" Geovanne said.

I nodded slightly.

"Sinhor, it is an honor and a privilege to receive instruction under the great General Monserrate o Invincible." He stood, eyes fixed to the back of my head, motionless, breath shallow. If it weren't for the mirror hanging on the wall, allowing me to watch him, I wouldn't have known he was there. I smiled.

"Geovanne?" I said.

"Yes sir?" Geovanne replied.

"What is it that you would most like to learn?"

Geovanne paused thoughtfully. "Sir, my goal is to become the very best. To earn your respect and to demonstrate to Sinhor Comandante that he did not make a mistake by allowing me into La Familia." He lowered his eyes. "I apologize, but I do not know what I most need to learn in order to directly answer your question, but those are my goals."

"Those are lofty goals, cadet."

"Yessir, and I am up for the challenge. I will not disappoint you."

"Is that a promise?" I turned to face Geovanne and looked him directly in the eyes, as is customary with a Gentleman's Bond.

Geovanne returned the stare. "Yes sir, on my word or my life that is my promise."

I nodded.

As I walked passed him, and out the library, I handed him a black notebook.

"Monday. 0:500 hrs. Aeroportocongonhas."

Geovanne nodded. "I'll be at the airport."

I returned to the villa to find Adrian and Thiago snuggled up in the theater watching one of Thiago's favorite movies. Adrian was wiping tears from her cheeks and Thiago was bravely fighting back his.

They sat holding hands as if they were long-time friends or lovers. Adrian was covered in Thiago's coveted cinema blanket.

I chuckled.

Thiago jumped up. "Sinhor Monserrate!"

Adrian looked confused.

I waved my hand, instructing Thiago to sit, but he quietly and quickly disappeared from the room. Adrian watched and turned to face me.

"What was that? Why did you make Senor Thiago leave?" She stood and placed her hands on her hips. "What are you, some elitist snob or something? You don't consort with the help?"

I made my way down the long aisle and into the row where Adrian stood.

"Hold up!" I laughed. Hands up in defense. "Before you take off my head. No I am not an elitist. And I motioned for him to stay. It's just a cultural practice . . . nothing else. Calm down." I slid my arms around Adrian's waist and looked into her sparkling green eyes. Something stirred deep inside me.

She wrapped her arms around my neck and looked up into mine.

"Are you still angry with me from earlier this evening? I am very sorry I upset you. I can see my ignorance with regard to your pain and plight as an African American woman in America is very frustrating. Truly, that is not my intention. Please, forgive me."

"Okay, you're forgiven." She leaned in and kissed me very slowly. "Chico, I have enjoyed my time with you these past two weeks. Thank you so much. And if this is all that we can ever be, I want you to know that you have made this trip the most amazing adventure I've ever experienced."

"What are you saying? Are you saying goodbye? Was my transgression that insulting?"

"I think it's probably best. We come from different worlds. I have so much to accomplish, I don't have time to educate people, or make them feel okay, and I definitely am not seeking anyone's approval for what I'm doing." She pulled away.

"I understand. And I'm sorry you feel that way," I said. "But tonight is your last night in Brazil." I kissed her. "Can you forget that you've dismissed me for a couple of hours? I would like to give you a proper goodbye."

I gave her the most sensual look I could muster. It was sincere, but it was my intention to be close to her the last night in Brazil.

The corners of her mouth slowly curved up into the most devilish smile.

"Well, I guess I can do that. For a couple of hours."

✊ ✊ ✊

On the flight back to America, I brought Geovanne. I introduced him as a colleague in the security business. He and Adrian exchanged pleasantries and he sat quietly in the back of the jet.

I shared that I was the young man's mentor and was helping him with growing his business internationally. And, while in America, I would be introducing him to some of my former clients to help him make connections.

"Well that's nice." Adrian said.

"Yes, well, I'm a nice guy," I replied.

Adrian chuckled.

"Yes, that's true. You are a very nice guy." she said.

Adrian stared out the window, closed her eyes and slowly crossed her legs. I couldn't help but think she was remembering how I moved my tongue between them just a few short weeks ago as we flew into Brazil.

Last night, I made love to Adrian again, tenderly, and adoringly—but to her dismay, once again I would not penetrate, leaving her obviously dissatisfied—even though I had brought her to climax over a dozen times.

"Make love to me." Adrian whispered in my ear.

"When you've allowed your heart to love me, then I will make love to you like no man has ever done before." I replied.

She was furious. "What? Are you some freak? Is your penis little? Do you have erectile dysfunction?" She snapped.

I pulled her in close. I knew my rejection caused her to feel insecure. Women, especially American women, believed their bodies were the Holy Grail that sex defined their womanhood. A rejection of both was the fastest way to disintegrate their confidence in their desirability.

"I am none of those." I kissed the top of her head. "I told you . . . I pay for sex. I can have it anytime I want. I do not want to have sex with you, Adrian. You mean more to me than that. When I am intimate with you it will be because you love me. And then, we will make love."

Adrian's body slumped in rejection. She turned her back to me the rest of the night. In the morning, she was quiet. And on the plane, she studied the portfolios of the unarmed victims of the police.

I placed Adrian's luggage in the trunk of the town car.

I leaned in through the window and kissed her goodbye. I looked into the same sad eyes I had seen in the newspaper a few weeks ago.

I made a silent vow to take her away from this god forsaken place. I knew it would not be before she accomplished her goals and avenged her son's death. But I was a patient man.

"You have my number, Adrian," I said stepping back from the car. "Call me, if you need anything."

Adrian smiled. She mouthed, *Thank You* as the car pulled away.

She couldn't say the words out loud. She was visibly too choked up to speak. The tears poured down her face as she made her way back to her reality.

12 THE SHIT'S ABOUT TO HIT THE FAN

"Hey woman!" Linda said, picking up my call. "How was it having Brazilian dick up in you for two weeks straight?"

"Oh my god, Lindy Lu. Can you get any more crude?"

"Yes I can. How was--"

"Stop it! Just stop it, please."

We laughed.

"Well shit did not stop because the lovely and talented Adrian Jackson left the country."

"I know. I'm just disgusted. Another child killed at the hands of the police!"

"Did you see the latest news coverage? Apparently, they made three stops on the way to the station. Eyewitnesses say Eric was begging for his inhaler. That's just criminal."

"It is absolutely criminal. As a *law enforcement* agent, you need to ensure the safety of your passengers, not do things to cause their death!"

"Right? It's just horrible. And then, these assholes must really think somebody is stupid. To say he inflicted the injuries that caused his own death? Seriously. Did you see all that footage that showed the police tying him up like a pretzel?"

"My God. Have you spoken to his mom yet?"

"I have. She definitely wants to speak with you."

"Okay great. Let's you and I meet tomorrow to talk strategy. I think we should capitalize on the rioting going on in Baltimore over this."

"Absolutely."

"We need to crystalize the messaging. Right now all Fox News is showing are the ignorant people who all over the board and aren't speaking to the issues.

"We need to get in there and bring back the focus, otherwise this propaganda is going to kill us in the Fall when the bill comes back up for a vote."

✊ ✊ ✊

Francisco

I sat across from Geovanne as he laid dozens of maps, photos and background reports across the table. He had GPS coordinates, safe house locations, escape routes, and contingency plans, letting me know he had been up all night working on his assignment.

"Sinhor Monserrate?" Geovanne said. "May I show you the plan?"

"First, explain the goal. The best plans Geovanne, are those with?"

"Clear goals."

I nodded.

"The plan is to annihilate the target without being detected by the United States CIA and FBI. The target has three tiers:

High Priority - Tier I: Sons of white police officers who have killed unarmed African Americans.

Priority - Tier II: Sons of white police officers.

Casualties of War - Tier III: Sons of non-African American police officers.

"There are 236 white police officers who have killed unarmed African Americans from 1999-2015. Of those, 60% have sons. Of those 70% have sons that are 100% white, 30% are of mixed ethnicities. I have four months to remove Tier I targets."

"By month six, US Intelligence Agencies need to make the connection." I listened. "By month nine the country will know and be in a state of panic. And by month twelve, the plan will conclude with the desired outcome. The passing of legislation that ends racial profiling in America."

Geovanne and I spent six hours mapping out the course of action. We read each story; I looked into the eyes of each potential victim, and created a chronological timeline of each murder.

"We will target the oldest to the youngest," Geovanne said, posting the pictures of the police officers across the wall.

"How many for each region?" I stood back and scanned the photos.

"No sir, for the deaths to go undetected and for us to be able to completely annihilate the entire Tier, we will have to zig zag across the country." Geovanne posted a map up on the white wall with pins on the locations of the targets.

"In particular, high incident states such as New York, Missouri, Los Angeles, Miami, Maryland, Mississippi, and North Carolina will require special consideration in order to remain under the radar," Geovanne replied.

"What do you recommend as the course of action, Geovanne?" I challenged. "Your goal is to eliminate the Tier One priorities, but doing so places your entire plan in jeopardy because the majority of your targets are in densely populated regions."

Geovanne stared at the screen. "Well sir, since the goal is to go undetected for four months, I would suggest that those deaths be made to look like accidents, natural deaths, and acts of nature."

I paced back and forth. "Then how will you instill panic? Those assassinations will not be included in the profile, and therefore will extend the amount of time it will take the US government to make the correlation."

Geovanne nodded. He stared at the screen.

"We will have to zig zag across the country, randomly removing targets in a disjointed, highly irregular pattern."

"I need you to spend some time with this. And think of it from this lens, Geovanne: What is the best way to infiltrate the enemy camp?"

✊ ✊ ✊

Francisco

"Ola Precioso." I said into the phone.

"Chico. Hello. How are you?" Adrian said. I was happy to hear the smile in her voice.

"I am well." I said. "I miss you?"

"I miss you too. Are you calling to tell me I'm going to see you soon?" Adrian cooed.

"No Precioso, quite the opposite. I'm calling to tell you that I will be out of touch for some time. I am working on a project with Geovanne."

"Oh. I see." Adrian replied. "That's perfect timing actually. I'm about to launch a speaking tour—the schedule's looking pretty full. I need to ramp up some more visibility before this bill comes up for vote."

"Sim, eu entendo." I said. "I am sure your hard work and diligence will pay off. I will call you as soon as I return, if that is ok?"

"Yes. It's fine." Adrian said. "Be safe."

Adrian

"Hey mama!" JR said.

"Hello precious. How are you? I miss you." My voice was distant and hollow.

"I miss you more. I am good, just worried about my girl. What's up? What can I do to help?"

"JR, I really need some Intel on that Senate committee. Can you find out who's behind the kibosh? I know Senator Franks is the ringleader, but I need to know who else has their hand in the pot."

"That shouldn't be too hard. Let me give my boy Ralph a call. I'll hit you back in a few."

"Thanks, babe. What would I do without you?"

"Good thing you'll never have to find out."

Geovanne

The first hit was complicated.

Four New York police officers had been acquitted in the fatal shooting of an unarmed African American man. Only two of the officers had sons. Of the two, one officer had three sons.

"Sinhor Monserrate, I am at the location of the officer with three sons. Sir, permission to proceed with the plan as discussed?"

"Permission granted."

I watched the house for three hours. My recon revealed that the police officer worked graveyard shifts, the Gang and Drug Units.

The wife was a stay at home mom and a drunk. She had been to the hospital seven times in the past year for major bruises, swollen eyes, broken ribs, a collapsed lung, and a deviated septum.

At 2:00 pm, she'd assemble the children 15, 11, and 7 in the minivan and take them to the YMCA, she'd come back and drink for four hours and then drive and pick them up.

I entered the house at six thirty, after the kids had been in the house for a half hour and chlorophylled the wife.

I entered the fifteen-year-old's room, who was watching porn with Dr. Dre's Beats headphones on. I stabbed him twice in the neck, leaving him drooped over his keyboard.

I then entered the room of the eleven-year-old who was playing video games and stabbed him in the chest three times.

I smothered the seven year old.

I staged the home to look like a robbery. I broke the back door glass and tracked mud into the house. I removed all valuables— jewelry, video games, flat screen TVs, I even took the headphones off the oldest son.

The officer would come home to an unconscious wife and three murdered sons. The news the next day reported: "Home invasion, Triple Homicide."

I text'd Francisco. "1 of 246."

✊ ✊ ✊

Francisco

I followed Brett down to the beach in Pensacola.

The young man was tall, about 6'2", blonde hair, light brown eyes, and tan. Brett walked up to a guy sitting at the base of a lifeguard station wearing bright green board shorts and a neon pink t-shirt. They shook hands and exchanged commodities.

Brett walked down the white sandy beach to a group of guys hanging out nearby. They congregated for a few minutes, then walked along the shore until they reached the boardwalk. They filed in under the worn wooden posts, looking behind them as they entered.

Thirty minutes later, three of them staggered out, high and disoriented. They made their way to the downtown area. Five minutes later, two more guys stumbled out. One was holding onto the post being pummeled by the rising tide.

"Brett!" the short guy slurred. "Bro, let's go." The two waited a few minutes.

"Yo, B?" the taller guy screamed. "Dude, what the fuck?"

The short guy looked back.

"He's fuckin' wasted, Bro!" They laughed, "Fuck it. Let's go."

"Yo, Brett. Fuck bitch, let's go, dude." The tall guy started to walk in Brett's direction, but the short guy grabbed his arm.

"Mikey, he's totally fucked up."

"Right, which is why we need to fucking wake him up and make him come with us, dude. What the fuck?"

"Bitch, we're supposed to meet Katie and Wendy in fucking fifteen minutes." He pulled the taller guy. "You know if Brett shows up, you won't be getting any play from Katie." The tall guy paused for a minute.

"Bro, let's go meet the girls. Then come back for his ass. Let him sleep off his speedball coma. You know we won't be able to wake him up anyway."

"But the tide?"

"Bro, he's way in the back. Twenty minutes! We'll be back in twenty minutes."

"Fuck it. Okay." They stumbled up the beach and to the boardwalk.

I stood over Brett's heroin and cocaine homeostasis body. I removed all of his clothes and jewelry, pulled out a .38 revolver, attached the Supertrapp 3" silencer and shot him twice in the chest. I shoved the clothes in a backpack that I tossed over my shoulder and walked off down the beach. I pulled out my cell and text'd Geovanne. "15 of 246."

The 6:00 news flashed Brett's All Star football photo with the caption: "Football Hopeful Robbed, Killed in Broad Daylight at Pensacola Beach."

A reporter interviewed the two friends who left Brett behind. They were in tears.

"We had just seen him, right Mikey?" the short guy said to his friend, shifting from one foot to the other and running his hands through his hair.

Mike just stood there, staring off into the direction where they had gotten high. He wiped the tears from his face with the back of his hand. "We just saw him earlier in the day and he was fine. Brett was a cool guy. You know? He was . . . he was cool."

The short guy turned away from the camera, bent over and placed his hands on his knees, his body jerked forward as a stream of green chunky mass shot from his mouth.

"The family is asking for time to grieve. No doubt the investigation will be handled efficiently as Brett Dickenson is the only son of Detective Jim Dickenson, a twenty year veteran on the force," said the reporter as they cut to the B-roll of paramedics wheeling the body bag up the beach.

Geovanne

Francisco had just returned from a trip up to the Bay Area. He'd taken the train and killed two there.

One, he pushed in front of the train in the subway.

The other he stabbed during a rave.

Every target had to be killed, so that when the CIA and FBI put together the pattern, they would come back and investigate those murders and realize that they were a part of the killing spree.
It was barely the first month and already we had eliminated 15 of the 70 targets. *At this rate, we will clear the first Tier well under the four-month target date.* Completing this task before the deadline was my personal goal.

I was due to meet with Francisco in forty-eight hours. I wanted to terminate at least twenty targets by the time we met.

I looked at my watch. I handed the bus driver my ticket. I would hit two in New Orleans and one in Memphis. If all went well, I planned on hitting two in Ohio on my way back to Los Angeles.

Francisco

I drove to Arizona to take out one target by asphyxiation. The boy's father had killed a twenty-one-year-old African American with the chokehold, so I killed his son by choking him to death.

They would find his limp body with a crushed trachea face down in a shower. I wanted to make it clear that there was no way they could come to the conclusion that this young man had killed himself--even though that *was* the finding for the twenty-one year old who died in the back of then Sergeant Winston's cruiser.

Next, I took a helicopter to Las Vegas where I decapitated another target.

I left the head sitting on the boy's chest; his eyes were wide open. He couldn't have been more than sixteen years old. That one was brutal.

The cops who killed the man in Las Vegas claimed they 'found' him hanging from his cell, an apparent suicide.

It was time to up the ante. I needed to start bringing attention to the homicides. It was time for widespread panic across this god-forsaken country.

I hadn't had much one on one time with Geovanne, but the Comandante was right, he was a natural. Or should I say, an instinctual killer.

I was impressed so far with the conception and execution of the plan. It was going off without a hitch. I made a mental note to check in and provide him with feedback.

Learning only happens through trial and error. Though Geovanne had not made any errors so far, I wanted to provide him with direction and feedback in order to enhance his strategic planning moving forward.

Geovanne had come up with a brilliant work around for New York, which held the bulk of the targets. He ran an algorithm to determine the distance between each location—which in some cases was the same location, as the police department was the last place the victim was seen alive.

New York, Los Angeles and Ferguson had shown that despite all attempts to stagger, zigzag, and otherwise spread out the assassinations—it would virtually be impossible to accomplish without drawing immediate attention to the murders.

So he decided New York, Los Angeles and Ferguson would be the tipping points for setting off the mass hysteria.

Geovanne would obliterate the targets in New York while I annihilated the targets in Los Angeles, whoever was finished first would take on Ferguson. We had a gentleman's wager on who it would be.

< Linda: AJ, Barbara Walters wants an exclusive.
< Adrian: So does Diane Sawyer.
< Linda: As does Oprah.
< Adrian: Tell Oprah she gets the exclusive after the bill is
             passed. Right now, I need to fan some flames.
             Let's go with Barbara, she has a larger primetime
             demographic.

"Sixty-one percent of Americans now say race relations in the United States are bad, the highest percentage since 1992, according to a recent new York Times poll, which finds that majorities of both whites and blacks now view race relations negatively," Barbara Walters said into the camera.

"Meanwhile, 79 percent of African Americans think police are more likely to use deadly force against a black person than a white person, but 53 percent of whites say race does not play a role in such instances.

"In the wake of the death of Freddie Gray in Baltimore and the unrest that followed, Americans' views on race relations in the U.S. have grown significantly more pessimistic.

"Tonight I have with me, Adrian Jackson. Thank you for joining me tonight," Barbara said.

We met in a beautiful hotel suite in The Plaza Hotel in Manhattan near the ABC Studios.

"Thank you for having me," I replied.

"You heard the recent report, what are your thoughts on race relations in the U.S. today?"

I smiled. "My thoughts are that America has no relation to race. You're either black and experiencing racism in America. Or, you're white, denying its existence.

"There is no real discussion about the problem, or, for that matter, solutions--but there's a lot of postulating about the symptoms."

"And when you say there's no real discussion, you mean that black and white America can't seem to agree on viable solutions?"

"I'm saying you can't get to viable solutions until you first agree that there is a problem. Currently, which is why you see the jump in the statistics you quoted, America is seeing that racism does in fact exist.

"For years, white America has contended that it doesn't. It's just been black people being lazy, wanting handouts. Or thugs disobeying the law and wanting to skirt punishment.

"There's the reference to family values, because, of course, the black family doesn't mirror the nuclear make-up of the white family and so, obviously they have no family values.

"And what I'm saying, Barbara, is that until recently, with this coverage—be it videos taped by bystanders at the scene, or leaked facts from law enforcement agencies, or just hard evidence discovered from the truth—America is being forced to admit that, oh my, there *is* racism in America."

"I see. And you don't think America believed it before this proliferation of videos?"

"I think white America had the great fortune of controlling the stories that were featured on the news, and therefore shaping the attitudes and perceptions of African Americans. So that it could justify the institutionalized and systemic racism that exists.

"But now that all of the story is being shown, and not just pieces and clips—all of America, including the white America that is so quick to repeat the sound bites that have historically justified racism, now has to take a closer look at the facts."

"And what would those facts reveal?" Barbara said.

"They would show that by far, racism exists, it never went away. It just became more sinister, more covert."

"And can you define for us what racism in America looks like?"

I paused. "No."

Barbara's right eyebrow inched up. "No, you can't define--"

"No, I *won't* define it. Of course *I can*. But I'm not here to fix America's race issues. That's not my job, my purpose, my task," I said.

"What I will define for you tonight is the reason for the riots in Baltimore, and Ferguson, Los Angeles and New York.

"People have been bashing the Americans who have dared to stand up against the racist police brutality that is prevalent in law enforcement agencies across the country. They are called thugs, and rioters, vandals, looters and every other derogatory name you can think of."

"Are you saying that the people who are looting are justified? Property damage to innocent store owners have been estimated at--"

"And how much have black lives been estimated at?" I said. "Because I'm not hearing that number at all." I looked around as if someone would throw out a number.

"How much? These people are protesting against the taking of *human* lives. And here is where I say racism is alive and thriving—in micro-aggressions like that statement. Statements that insinuate property is more important than the fight for black lives."

"No one is saying human life is not important--"

"That's exactly what you're saying when you continue to focus on the loss of property . . . when the response to us screaming black lives matter is all lives matter."

"Well, don't all lives matter?"

"Well are *all* lives being threatened? We're screaming black lives matter, we're tearing down buildings, and throwing rocks at the perpetrators *because* black and brown lives are being taken at the hands of those paid to protect them. All lives aren't in that situation every day. Black people are Americans, too, Barbara."

"Who said they weren't?"

"Those who refer to us as thugs and vandals. It's their way of dehumanizing people."

"But some would say that they are opportunists, and give African Americans a bad name."

"All of this explaining. All of this justifying. It's just exhausting. We are Americans. We are human beings." I threw my hands up. "At what point will white America just accept that?" I looked into the camera.

"I am just sick and tired of having to explain why we're mad as hell and not going to hold peaceful non-violent protests—dammit, we're saying no more, loudly, violently—so that you know we care that black lives matter. It's obvious that we can't right these wrongs in the criminal court system. Hell, half the time we can't get an indictment." I turned to face Barbara.

"So, stop asking us to lie down and take this mass genocide by the officers sworn to protect and serve their constituents. If they can't do it, then dammit—fire them, and hire people who can.

"We're done with this hypocrisy. We're done with this institutionalized and systemic racism. And we're done with asking for permission just to live." Tears streamed down my face. "We're done."

Barbara said, "And we're done with this segment this evening. Adrian Jackson, thank you for your candor, your passion, and speaking with me tonight."

Ring. Ring. Ring.
"Hello?"
"We're not going to just let you niggers take over this country.
We'll kill you all before that happens. Every one of you Sambo,
Aunt Jemima--"

I hung up the phone.

✊ ✊ ✊

"Oh my Lawd!" JR said. "The social media outlets are on fire with 'Adrian Jackson said this', and 'Adrian Jackson said that.' Girl! You have hit a nerve in good ol' America!"

"Boy, I ain't thinking about any of that right now." I massaged my temples.

"Really, then what are you thinking about?"

"I have two more talk shows, a radio interview with KJLH, and a town hall I have to prep for. And I am seriously exhausted."

"Then stop. Rest," JR whispered.

"I can't, JR. You know the bill will be coming back up for a vote again. This time I need for them to feel the pressure."

"Them cracker ass crackers don't give a damn about us."

"And that's exactly why I can't stop. What information do you have for me, JR?"

"Girl, so not only is Walsh blocking this bill, but apparently Franks and Kolbane are all making calls and asking other Senators to vote it down as well!"

I paused. "Damn. And do you know if they've been successful?"

"According to Ralph, they have more than three fourth's of the vote."

Tears came from nowhere and flooded my face. Angry tears. Frustrated tears. Sad tears. I couldn't believe this. All this work over the past three months and this bill was still going to get buried?

"What are you going to do, mama?"

"I guess I'll have to move to Plan B. I can't let JJ down now." I sighed.

Senator Walsh's aid played back the podcast of Adrian's radio station interview.

Senator Walsh clicked off the TV, picked up the phone, and dialed a number.

"Hey Jerry. I think we may have a problem that needs fixing. Get over here." The Senator stared out the window. Less than a half hour later there was a rap on his chamber door.

"Jerry." The Senator didn't look up, missing the annoyed look on Guillermo Rivera's face.

He finally looked up as he handed him a manila folder. "We have a problem that needs to go away."

Guillermo nodded. He quickly flipped through the dossier.

"This is a not a professional. So one Vicar is suitable," Guillermo said.

"No, not a professional. A civilian. It should be clean and easy. Just make sure it's done. And make it look like a hate crime. A skin head or KKK."

Guillermo nodded.

He pulled out his phone on the way out. "Marco, I have a small job for you."

Adrian

I pulled out of the parking structure of Dietrich, made a right, and was merging into the center lane when two patrol cars pulled up to both sides of me, sandwiching me in.

I looked to my right and the police officer glared at me through the passenger window. I returned the glare. We pulled up to the intersection and I turned to my right to see the driver of the cruiser almost snarling at me.

I laughed out loud.

As the light turned from red to green, and I inched forward, the cop in the passenger seat brought his right index finger to his lips and made a motion, like he was blowing the barrel of a smoking gun, then smiled and slowly looked my way.

I rolled my eyes in disgust and looked to my right to find the driver of that cruiser making the same gesture.

I shook my head and smiled. As I gassed my vehicle, I threw up both of my middle fingers, letting them know it would take more than those cowardly threats to scare me.

Chief Bollinger

"Chief! I can't believe this shit!" James burst into my office. I looked up at him over my steel rimmed reading glasses. I didn't bother to ask *what* because I knew he was going to tell me regardless.

"The FBI wants us to put a detail on Adrian Jackson?" James said.

"Oh that. Yes, she's been getting more death threats than the President lately." I sat back in my chair and crossed my arms over my chest.

"As well she should!" he screamed. "Have you heard the inflammatory shit she's been saying about law enforcement?"

"Of course I have. But it doesn't matter. We have to protect her."

"And you think she'll be safe with us protecting her?" James said.

I looked over my glasses at James. "She better well damned be. I will not have Adrian Jackson's death, on top of all the other shit, on this department's head."

"Yeah, well, good luck with that." James walked out my office, slamming my door behind him.

"What are you talking about?" Adrian said to me when I called her into my office for an update. "I thought this was an update on Jared's case, or at the very least, some good news about a piece of legislation."

"I'm talking about your safety." I sat on the edge of my desk. I was in full uniform today. I'd be acting in an official capacity in a ceremony later.

Adrian shook her head. "No thank you, Chief Bollinger. But I appreciate the offer."

"You don't understand. I am acting in an official capacity here. The FBI has issued an order for us to bring you into protective custody. You don't have a choice."

She stood up. "Darlin', I always have a choice." She looked at me and headed toward the door.

"You know you're basically signing your death warrant if you walk out that door."

She turned to face me, paused for a minute, looking at me with – I couldn't quite tell if it was contempt, sympathy, or apathy.

"I'm not afraid of death or dying. All that I had to live for on this earth is gone. There is absolutely nothing anyone can do to me that would cause me an iota of fear." She swung her purse over her shoulder and walked out the door.

All I could think at that moment was, *Now that's a dangerous woman. No fear, and a personal vendetta to score?* She had just raised the stakes. But I didn't know if she realized how high.

Adrian

"What the fuck, AJ? The FBI said you have to be in protective custody?" Linda said. "Then this shit must be bad."

"Probably," I said, distracted. I was reviewing my power point, preparing for tomorrow's SNH. "What do you think about this graph on slide six?"

"Adrian Jackson?" Linda said.

"Yes, Linda Lewis."

"This is serious. People are threatening your life. They want to kill you."

"People have been threatening my life for months. They are cowards," I said. "They just want to scare me so I'll stop talking."

"Then maybe you should. This is not worth your life."

I paused for half a second. "Then what is it worth?"

"The time, energy, the change you could make in the world. But it's not worth your life. Fuck that. Call that detective now."

"What do you think about that graph on slide six?"

Francisco

"Sinhor, Monserrate," Thiago said over the phone.

"Yes, Thiago, what's going on?" Thiago never phoned me on the burner.

"Sir. Mademoiselle Annette English?"

I froze. "Yes?"

"There is a ticket out for her."

"Who is the originator?"

"I—there--there is a broker," Thiago stammered. "Once it came across the interceptor, I just thought I should call you. I will find out who the originator is immediately."

"No, of course. You were absolutely right to call me, Thiago, my good friend. Get the information to me as soon as you know, please."

"Yes, of course."

I hung up the phone. I sat in silence for thirty seconds, then punched in Adrian's number.

"Hello?"

"Hello, my precious."

"Francisco!" Adrian said. I was happy to hear the joy in her voice. But I needed to remain focused, her life was in grave danger. "You're back?"

"Yes." I said. "I have been thinking about you and called as soon as I landed."

Adrian chuckled. "Would you consider it crude to tell you that I miss the delicious taste of your sweet nectar on my tongue?" I said. I was walking fast paced to my car, Geovanne close on my heels.

"Um, considering what I said to you during our initial conversation, I'm going to have to say nothing you can ever say could be crude."

I forced out a fake a chuckle. Inside the car, I quickly backed out the stall and pulled out the underground parking structure. Geovanne entered information into a GPS tracking device. In seconds a red dot started flashing. I raced off to the address flashed on the screen.

"Muito bem," I said, weaving in and out of traffic.

"English," Adrian said.

"Very good," I said. "As I am trying desperately to stay in your life, I wouldn't want something as trite as a misconstrued compliment to be the reason that I am kept out of it."

"Are you trying desperately? Nothing about you conveys desperation; It has been weeks since I've spoken to you. I'm afraid you will have to try harder."

I genuinely laughed out loud at that statement. "Well, then I shall." I paused. "Thank you so much for taking my call. It was a gift from the gods to hear your voice. Let's talk again soon."

"Let's," Adrian replied. "Ate entao, adeus."

"Portuguese!" I said. "Very good. I am . . . pleasantly surprised, and deeply touched. You speak it so naturally."

"Thank you. Just my way of letting you know I am trying to do the same over here," she whispered. "Let's talk again soon. Adeus." She hung up the phone.

Adrian

I winked at Linda as I walked up to the table. She threw me back an inquisitive look and mouthed 'Who is that?' I mouthed back 'Chico,' right before ending the call.

I closed the case of the phone, shoved it inside my purse and turned to greet Linda who, was already seated and nursing a drink.

"Hey woman!" I said, leaning over to kiss her.

"Hey you." Linda hugged me.

"I miss you." I held on to her a little longer than normal. Linda pulled back.

"What's wrong?" she asked, looking concerned.

I socked her shoulder. "Shut up!" I screamed. Linda motioned for the waiter to come by. "What, I can't miss you?"

"No, of course you can. And you should. But the fact that you do has me worried. AJ doesn't want or need anyone."

I rolled my eyes. "That's the strong black woman stereotype again."

"Uh, no, bitch. That's the truth. I've been your friend for over fifteen years."

We laughed.

"Yes ma'am? How may I help you?" the waiter asked.

"May I have a margarita on the rocks, with grand marnier, please-- and salt?"

"Yes, right away."

"So, you were cup caking with your Brazilian lover, were you?"

"His name is Chico, and technically he is not my lover. A lover actually makes love to you."

"What the fuck does that mean?" Linda stopped drinking mid-sip.

"That means, he has the tongue of a god, but I couldn't tell you anything about his penis."

"Oh my!" Linda took a long gulp. "There's something rotten in Denmark Marcellus."

"Yeah, who you telling?"

"You finally decide to tip over to the wild side and get the only fucking asexual Brazilian around? Only you, Adrian Jackson!"

"He's not asexual. And why are you so quick to blame me? Hell, I was ready to go buck wild. I don't get any credit for that? You're such a Negative Betty!"

"You were with a man for two weeks and he never stuck his dick inside you? He's either asexual or gay. I thought I'd spare your little feelings, honey and go with door number one." I threw her a mean stare.

"*Actually*, he doesn't want to have sex. He wants our first time to be us making love."

Linda spit out her drink. "How old is he?" Linda screamed. I looked around the restaurant.

"Be quiet, you're so damned loud. Anyway, he's fifty-two, why?"

"Because that's some bullshit if I ever heard any. A woman is throwing herself at a man and he refuses? His ass is gay."

"First of all, I wasn't throwing myself at anyone--"

"Okay, you spread your legs, right? You pushed up against his dick at some point, rubbed it, grabbed it---you did something to let him *know* you wanted to feel his penis inside your vagina, right?"

"Oh my gawd, Lindy Lu! Stop it already."

Francisco

I pulled into the restaurant parking lot. I quickly scanned it and spotted Adrian's car. I nodded toward Geovanne who stepped out the car.

I took in the entire area. I saw a couple unloading their kids from a minivan, two teenagers getting inside a convertible Solara at the end of the row I was walking down, and a large party walking into the restaurant. I jogged a couple of feet and merged in with the family.

I searched the restaurant for Adrian. I located her and another female in the middle of the dining area. I turned to see a waiter walking toward their table.

I scanned him from head to toe. He was an older Italian man with straight black hair combed back into a long ponytail. He was dressed in all black, with a long apron tied around his waist.

I turned to look for Geovanne who appeared at the opposite end of the restaurant facing me. We made eye contact. I pointed to the waiter's shiny black dress shoes, then to Adrian. Geovanne nodded and quickly moved into action.

The waiter had both drinks on a tray and was about to grab them when Geovanne slid on a baseball cap and sunglasses, placed his cell up to his ear and started talking loudly.

"What do you mean my account is closed? I have over $6,000 in that account. I need to speak to a manager!" He bumped into the waiter, knocking over the drinks. "Ah shit! What the fuck, dude?" Geovanne said, but kept walking past, brushing the drinks off his jacket. "No, I'm not talking to you! Some jerk waiter just dumped drinks all over me. Jesus, fucking Christ!"

The waiter picked up the glasses, set them on a nearby counter and quickly exited the door leading to the patio. I watched Adrian and Linda turn to watch the waiter leave the restaurant. I quickly scanned the room and noticed to his left, a German man standing near a partition. He pulled a pen out of his pocket.

I quickly darted behind two waiters and over to the stocky man. Just as he pulled the pen up to his mouth I jammed my hand into his throat.

The German jutted forward, but not before the dart was launched. I quickly turned to see Adrian still looking over at the door where the first assassin exited. When she turned back around Linda was slumped over to the side clutching her chest.

"Linda!" Adrian screamed. She jumped out of her seat and ran over to Linda and pulled her up right. "Somebody call 9-1-1!" The waitress closest to her ran to the back. "Linda. Linda. Honey, can you hear me?" Adrian's eyes filled quickly with tears. The lady in the booth behind her slid out of her seat.

"She's probably having a heart attack. Let's pull her out of this cramped booth and lay her down so she can get some air." She helped Adrian get her down on the floor.

I snapped the German's neck and slid him into the bathroom. I propped him up in the stall and quietly snuck out of the restaurant unnoticed.

I did a quick inventory of the surrounding parameters looking for more hired guns. I saw Geovanne through the window coming out from the dumpster. Geovanne closed the iron gates and headed in the direction of my car.

I moved in the opposite direction. I checked one last time to ensure the restaurant did not hold contingency number three, and to make sure Adrian was fine.

Besides being visibly shaken up over her friend lying on the floor, Adrian was fine. The ambulance pulled up just as I turned and headed back to my car.

"The police are going to investigate those two *pistoleiros*," Geovanne said.

"What was your solution?" I asked, looking into the rear view mirror.

"A bullet between the eyes."

I nodded. "A snapped neck and bullet between the eyes . . . this is an affluent neighborhood. They will try and bury this story as quickly as possible. It's bad for business and for the police—makes them look like they aren't protecting the rich."

I dialed Thiago. "It was a double hit. Who is the originator?"

"Sinhor Monserrate, the originator is a Senator Walsh."

I hung up the phone.

✊ ✊ ✊

Adrian

"AJ, I don't know how you're still standing, honey," JR said. "How is Linda? How are you?"

I sipped a glass of wine. "Who says I'm standing?" I lay stretched across my bed, wine glass in one hand, wine bottle in the other. "Linda is in a medically induced coma. They don't know if she's going to make it, JR. They're saying she had a heart attack followed by a stroke. They induced the coma to give her body time to rest."

"Dietrich ain't no joke. They will stress you out. That's why a brotha had to bounce."

"A brotha bounced because he got a hefty salary increase and a title."

"Well, there is that."

"Oh my God, JR, shut up!" I chuckled a little. "You know Linda thrived off that pressure." I shook my head. My nose started to become congested. "I don't think it was stress."

"It had to be. What else is going to cause you to clutch your chest in the middle of a restaurant and fall over on the table?"

"I guess. It's just so . . . messed up."

"It is." JR sat quietly listening to me think on the other end of the phone. It's what I did. If you were in my inner circle, you learned quickly to be at peace with holding the space.

I let out a deep sigh. "JR, were you able to find out who the Senators are who are blocking this legislation?"

"Yes. Senator Franks, of course. Senator Walsh. And Senator Fairbanks."

"Fairbanks?" I sat up. "Are you serious? That spineless little weasel. He's always acting like he's so progressive."

"Girl, they're all politicians. That means they bend whichever way the wind blows."

"Yeah, but still . . . okay. I don't know what to do now that Linda is . . ." I closed my eyes. "JR, I just can't deal with another--"

"You won't have to. Linda is a bitch. Bitches don't die. They spit down the throat of death, and yank off its balls while they're fucking it in the ass."

"Ouch."

"I was trying to encourage you."

"Yeah. Okay. That wasn't that though, son. I'd be good with *She's Strong*."

Guillermo never received confirmation from Marco or Amott. He sent Ricardo out to find out what happened.

"Marco was shot between the eyes. Amott's esophagus was crushed." Ricardo said.

"Professionals?"

"Looks like it."

"She has a protection detail?"

"She has something. She's in perfect health. The friend got the sumo cocktail."

"Is the friend dead?"

"Yeah, she'll never be more than a vegetable."

"Great. They killed the wrong one." Guillermo shook his head. "Look Ricardo, we've got to eliminate that girl. The Senator has been calling asking if it's done. I need it done."

"Consider it done then."

"Text me when it is."

Geovanne

Francisco and I sat in the restaurant re-working our strategy.

"This changes everything," Francisco said.

"How so?"

"I can't leave her out there unprotected, Geovanne. The plan is pointless if Adrian is dead."

I watched Francisco sit in deep thought. The pieces were falling into place now. Francisco was doing all of this for this woman.

After we neutralized the operatives in the restaurant, I went online and read up on Adrian Jackson.

While I didn't understand the situation in its totality—people being killed for their race—I knew I only had this opportunity because Francisco loved this woman. Therefore, I would do everything in my power to ensure I did a stellar job on this assignment.

This was personal for Sr. Monserrate. Master Atilla always said *Personal Ties are the Strongest Ties*. This was a perfect opportunity to gain some extra momentum--some favor, or at the very least, a few points.

Sr. Monserrate had a reputation for being very hard on his cadets. If I could use this situation to my advantage, then I certainly would.

"Excuse me, gentlemen," the waitress interrupted our silence. "Can I get your drinks started?"

I looked up and paused for half a second—a half second too long. Francisco immediately turned to look at the waitress.

At first glance she had a striking resemblance to Adrian. She was tall, light complexioned with long dark hair. Her nose was a bit wider and she had brown eyes, not green like Adrian's. She had full breasts, a small waist and a full round rear. She could definitely pass for her sister.

"Yes, please," Francisco said, turning back around in his seat. "I'll have a Manhattan please."

"I'll have a rum and coke. Thank you," I finally replied.

"No problem, gentlemen." The waitress jotted down our orders. "Our specials for the day are Chilean Sea Bass with a mango chimichurri sauce, and a savory shrimp and Langostino lobster linguine at market price. I'll be right back with your drinks and to take your orders."

"You broke," Francisco said looking into my eyes as soon as the waitress was out of hearing distance. "That one little pause could have gotten me killed if she had been a trained assassin."

I admonished myself internally. I knew Francisco was right. I knew it the minute I turned to face the waitress.

"Yes sir," I replied.

Francisco turned to watch the waitress. "She looks so much like Adrian, though. I understand what happened." Francisco smirked.

"In these cases, when you feel your body instinctively responding, go inside and physically bring that area under control."

I listened closely.

"Think back to Track Training," Francisco said. "Focus. Control."

I closed my eyes and nodded. "Reimagine seeing the waitress. Now register recognition. What sensory glands are you feeling?"

"Movement in the optic nerve," I replied.

"Good. Now Focus. Now control the sensation," he said.

I was attempting to focus, but it was creating tension instead of relaxation.

"Relaxation is the key to control."

I finally stabilized my breathing. My chest was barely rising. But I still felt the tension.

"Your frequency is too high. Try visualizing the waitress. Look at her eyes. Her nose. Now her lips. Imagine kissing her lips, feather kisses."

I focused on laying light kisses on the waitress's lips.

"Now give her a name. Good. Now say her name as you lay those kisses gently on her lips."

Francisco watched as I began to focus. My forehead softened. My jowl relaxed.

The waitress approached. "Okay, I have a Manhattan for you." I heard the drink on the table in front of Francisco. "And a rum and--" She paused mid-sentence. "*Coke. For him.*" She whispered, and said, "*Sorry*" to Francisco. The waitress hurried off to the next table. I remained stable.

"Much better," Francisco said. "What's her name?" Francisco asked, sipping his drink.

"Sinhor?" I opened my eyes.

"What is the name you gave the Adrian look-alike?"

"Adrianna."

Francisco laughed. I smiled. I'd never seen the General smile. As quickly as it came, it disappeared.

"Thiago gave me the name of the originator. I will handle him. I need you to protect Adrian."

"Of course, *Geral.* It would be my honor." I knew the gravity of this request. It was worse than the Capstone Test. At least if you failed that, you remained a First Classmen. If I failed this test—and I knew very well it was a test—my career would be over.

Francisco

"Precioso, eu preciso ve-lo imediatamente," I said into the phone.

"I got the Precious, and then after that it's all womp, womp, womp," Adrian said.

"I need to see you right away."

"I'm sorry, Chico, I can't. I'm at the hospital with my friend Linda. She--"

"Had a heart attack," I said with her.

"Yes." Adrian paused. "Is it on social media? That's not possible, she has protected status."

"I know because I am in private security," I said. I looked over at Geovanne who was mapping her coordinates. The machine flashed "Cedars Sinai" and I made a "U" turn and headed that way.

"Do you trust me?" I asked.

"I don't know you," Adrian replied.

"Do you know me well enough to believe that I wouldn't lie to you?"

"No. Every man lies," Adrian said.

"Do you trust me enough to believe that I care for you, and do not want harm to come to you?"

"Yes."

"Good. Your life is in danger." I said.

Adrian paused. I heard her heels clicking on the tiled floor. She was pacing.

"What have you heard?"

"It's not what I've heard, Precioso. It's what I know."

Adrian gasped. "What do you know?"

"That I cannot have this conversation over the phone. I need to see you. Can you meet me downstairs--" I looked over to Geovanne who handed me a piece of paper with the name of the café inside the hospital. "Inside Plaza Café in twenty minutes?"

"You're here?" Her phone went dead.

I had Geovanne try and reconnect the call, hoping it was just a dropped call. But everything inside me knew.

"Nothing," Geovanne said.

I banged on the steering wheel. "Call Thiago. Have him search the airwaves."

Adrian

I woke up to a blurry room. *This shit is happening way too often,* I said to myself. But, when I got my bearings I realized I wasn't held up in a room with a sexy Brazilian between my legs. I was lying across a couch in a room with five men in dark black suits staring at me. I sat up.

"What's going on here? Who are you? And where am I?"

"Good afternoon, Mrs. Jackson. My name is Special Agent George Anderson." He opened his jacket and flashed a badge on his hip. "I am with the FBI."

I looked him up and down. He was a tall dark chocolate brother. Broad shoulders, long thick legs. He had a nice athletic build. He was bald with a goatee. In another circumstance, he definitely would have caught my *love for chocolate* eye.

"I take that back—I don't give a damn who you are. What's going on, and where am I?" I stood.

The other three men reached for their weapons. Special Agent Anderson raised his right hand and the men moved their hands away from their waists. I watched carefully.

"No need to get upset, Mrs. Jackson."

"Really? I've been kidnapped by the FBI, but there's no need to get upset?" I rolled my eyes.

The Agent smiled. "We haven't kidnapped you. We've secured your safety."

"Oh, is that what you call kidnapping these days?" I eyed the other three men up and down suspiciously. "Last time I read the Constitution, I do believe it said I still had some civil rights—one of them being the right that protects me from the powers of the national government in areas not enumerated."

I met eyes with Special Agent Anderson who was smiling at my quote form the Constitution.

"They told me you were smart--"

"And you doubted them, did you?" I replied. I turned to look for my purse and noticed my suitcase in the corner. "So, am I being held against my will—and I hope you have a damned good lawyer if that answer is anything other than, 'No ma'am you are not'."

"If you would calm down for just one second," Special Agent Anderson said. "My god, woman. I am not the enemy here." He held his hands up in surrender.

"Well of course you are. You've retained me without my permission." I placed my hands on my hips.

Special Agent Anderson shook his head. "Mrs. Jackson, we were asked specifically by the President to secure your safety. His words specifically to me was 'Get to California and keep Adrian safe, please.'"

I softened. I had only met the President that one time. I was moved that he would send the FBI to protect me. At the same time, it hit me. *Oh shit, I must really be in danger for the President to send FBI agents.*

I sat on the edge of the bed. It all became real to me in that instant. I had talked a good game about not being afraid to die, but for the first time since Jared was killed, I thought about being dead. It frightened me.

Special Agent Anderson watched as I went through a myriad of emotions. I guess he sensed that I was going through something personal right then, so he motioned for the other agents to leave the room.

"Ma'am, are you okay?"

"The President sent the FBI to protect me from--" I waved my hand over my head "Whomever is trying to kill me." I looked up at the brother. "Should I be okay?" I wiped tears escaping the corner of my right eye.

Special Agent walked over to the desk and grabbed some Kleenex and handed it to me.

"Thank you."

"Absolutely," he replied. "You should feel very special, for one. And then, safe. Which, honestly—you're not. Your life is in grave danger."

Those were the words Chico said to me before—"Where's my cell?"

"It's been dislodged," Special Agent Anderson replied.

"Dislodged?"

"Chip removed, destroyed. No tracking device that could lead potential killers to you."

I flinched. "What?"

"I told you. Your life is in grave danger. You think we were playing?"

I sat quietly for a moment. "How can I make a call? I need to make a call."

"I'm sorry, ma'am, I can't allow that. A call would breach security."

"Then how am I supposed to let me friends and family know I'm okay? People will worry, you know?"

"Yes, ma'am. According to our reports," Special Agent Anderson pulled out a black note pad from his jacket breast pocket, "you have two friends, a James Richardson and a Linda Lewis. Mr. Richardson was notified at 17:30 hours that you were under the protective custody of the Federal Bureau of Investigations, and that there would be no contact for the foreseeable future until your safety and security were assured." He flipped the page.

"And Mrs. Lewis was defused forty-eight hours ago by a dart laced with traces of potassium causing what outwardly appeared to be acute myocardial infarction, but is actually decorticate posturing which will lead to inevitable brain death."

I stared at Special Agent Anderson, processing his cold glib prognosis of Linda's . . . I placed my face inside my palms, but the Agent never noticed.

"In terms of family, there is a one Reginald McAllister, First Lieutenant in the United States Army. Currently stationed at Camp Darby, located in the Province of Pisa. Records indicate a consistent monthly call, and therefore--" Special Agent Anderson went to look at his calendar and noticed Adrian sobbing quietly.

"Oh ma'am . . . what's wrong?" He looked around the room, then back at Adrian.

"You just told me my best friend is brain dead. You think I should be laughing right now, Special Agent Rocks-For-Brains. Can you just get out, please?"

Agent Anderson paused, then turned and walked out the hotel room.

Geovanne

"Sim Geovanne?" Francisco said.

"Sinhor Monserrate," I said. "I have located Senhora Jackson." I made a left into the parking lot of II Grano Restaurant in West L.A."

"Where is she?"

"She is in protective custody with the FBI at the Standard Hotel Downtown L.A." I entered the restaurant and quickly scanned the room. "I will meet you there in twenty minutes."

"Muito bom, Geovanne, muita bom. Adeus"

Francisco

I text'd Geovanne when I arrived. We met outside on the rooftop at the fire pit. I was surprised to see the waitress sitting next to Geovanne.

"Good evening," I said with an authentically huge smile.

"Good evening," the waitress replied.

"Good evening, Sir." Geovanne stood and shook my hand.

"Sinhor Monserrate, please allow me to introduce you to Miss Candace Fontaine."

I nodded.

"The pleasure is mine." Candace smiled.

"Miss Fontaine is an aspiring actress."

"I am, and I'm serious about my craft. When Vaughn asked me if I would be interested in this gig, I was like, 'Hell yeah!' because you never know when opportunity knocks. And I'm the type of sistah who is gone always be ready, if you know what I mean."

I smiled and looked at Geovanne who gave me a reassured look. "Yes, I do know what you mean." Candace could pass for Adrian's twin at first glance, but the minute she opened her mouth, all bets were off.

Adrian was stylish and polished and . . . classy. Although Candace was about ten years younger than Adrian, she looked like she had lived a hard life.

Geovanne would share with me later that she was a single mom of a seven-year-old son. She had to drop out of college because she was in an abusive relationship and left Texas to get away from her husband.

She was a junior at Rice, majoring in Marketing and Communications before she left. Candace was currently working as a waitress and actress to support her son.

Geovanne laid blueprints down on the edge of the fire pit.

"They have Senhora on the tenth floor, in room 1024. The Standard has twelve floors."

I leaned in and listened to Geovanne's plan.

Geovanne listened for four hours until the FBI agents ordered their meals. He pointed to me and I slid on the waiter's jacket. He nudged Candace who was asleep on the queen size bed.

"Let's go. You're on!" I said to Candace.

She smiled, ran to the bathroom and applied her lipstick. "Is everything in place?"

Geovanne listened carefully to the conversation of the FBI agents. He gave me the thumbs up.

The Agents patted me down, checking in my sleeves and socks. They checked the food before it entered the room. There were two agents stationed outside. When I rolled the cart into the room Adrian was laying on the bed reviewing a stack of documents.

"Your dinner is here, ma'am," the FBI agent said.

Adrian didn't look up.

"Go ahead and set up over there at the table."

"Yessir," I said.

The agent closed the door. I stood staring at Adrian for a few minutes. She was absolutely gorgeous. Even in her jeans and t-shirt, she looked beautiful. "Ola, linda, eu missued voce."

Adrian looked up I put my finger up to my lips. She sprang from the bed and ran into my arms. We kissed long.

"How did you find me?"

There was a thump on the food cart. Adrian jumped. I moved over to the cart and removed the food. I lifted the tabletop and Candace stood up. Adrian grabbed her chest. "What the?"

"Hurry. Take off your clothes." I pointed to Adrian.

"What?" she said, stepping back.

"She's going to put on your clothes. You're going to go in the cart and I'm going to take you out."

"Oh. Okay." Adrian stripped down to her underwear. When she handed Candace the clothes, she grabbed Adrian and hugged her.

"Thank you, Mrs. Jackson for all you're doing to protect our sons. I have a son, Tyler. He's seven, and I worry about him every day," Candace said. "Thank you." She slid on Adrian's clothes.

Adrian was taken aback by the young woman's words, and by the fact that she looked so much like her. She kept staring.

"Hurry!" I said. "We've got to go."

Adrian crawled into the tiny space. I replaced the cover and knocked on the door. As I wheeled the cart out, the agent walked inside the room and looked around.

Candace didn't look up from the folders. But if she had, the agent would have stared into green eyes, the magic of opaque colored contacts.

"How was the meal, Mrs. Jackson?" the Agent asked.

Candace looked over at the food. "I don't know. I didn't touch it."

The Agent shrugged and walked out. Candace smiled.

Francisco

I wheeled the cart down the hall and onto the elevator. I pressed the button for the ninth floor and pushed the cart to 914. Inside the room, I removed the cover. Adrian jumped out and into my arms.

"How did you find me?" she said after a long kiss.

"I told you, I'm in security."

"Okay, what kind of security are you in that you can get past the

FBI?" Adrian sat on the edge of the bed and waited patiently.

I sat next to Adrian and stared into her sparkling green eyes.

"The kind that will make sure that you're always safe." I pulled the scrunchy off her pony tail. Adrian's hair cascaded down her back. I ran my fingers through her curly black mane.

"Pretty soon Adrian, some information will be hitting the airwaves that is going to shake up America forever," I said.

"Shake it up how?" Adrian ran her hand through her hair. I grabbed her hand. "Do you remember at the villa when you were preparing for your speaking engagements? Do you remember when you said 'If all of a sudden white boys started getting killed, the country would be in an uproar?'"

I stared at Adrian.

"Yes. I remember saying that."

"They're going to start . . . turning up dead."

Adrian pulled her hand back from mine. "What do you mean?"

"I mean. This country is about to break out into a major panic. Dead white bodies are about to be discovered all over the country.

"And in no time, they are going to figure out that there is a pattern." I knew my next words could scare Adrian into never seeing me again. She might think I was some type of psycho or serial killer.

"Wait. What do you mean? What are you saying, Chico?"

"I'm saying that pretty soon the FBI and CIA will put together that at least 100 young white men were brutally murdered over the past couple of months."

"They will look for a connection, a pattern, so that they can create a profile of the killer. They will find that they are all sons of white police officers who killed an unarmed African American."

Adrian sat staring at me, trying to take in all that I was saying.

"What . . . what have you done, Chico?" Adrian asked.

"I have just leveled the playing ground," I said. "Do you want your bill passed?"

"Yes, of course. That's what this is all about."

"I know. That's why I'm telling you, by the time we're done with this crusade, your bill will pass," I said. "Otherwise, you'll be at this forever."

"Because you killed innocent white boys?" She shook her head. Adrian turned to face me. "You're not in security, are you?" Before I could answer, she asked, "Who are you? Is your name even Chico?"

I could sense Adrian's tension, hear her fear.

"I was in security . . . a specific kind, but I'm retired now," I said. "And my name is Francisco Monserrate. My family calls me Chico."

Adrian looked me up and down, then into my eyes.

"Wait, so you've been on a?"

"Crusade."

"Across the country. Killing the sons of the white racist cops who have killed unarmed African American men?" Adrian said it like she needed to hear it again in order for her to believe what I was saying was real.

"Yes. That's right." I said.

Adrian

I walked to the window and stared outside. Chico remained sitting on the edge of the bed. He watched me struggling with processing what he'd just told me.

I turned and looked at him. *I should have known he was too damn good to be true. I messed up and hooked up with a psycho serial killer-- a fine psycho killer, with a bomb tongue.*

"Are you an assassin?" I said. "Is that how you were able to get past the FBI?"

"Those keystone cops? Any minor league person can get by the FBI."

"Answer my question Chico—Francisco?"

"Technically, no. I'm not an assassin," Francisco said. "I am retired."

I looked at him from head to toe. Even in the polyester waiter uniform, this man was fine. I tried to wrap my head around what he was telling me.

"You're a retired assassin, I'm sorry." I threw my hand up. "And you killed those . . . you killed the sons of the white police officers for me?"

"Absolutely. It was a brilliant idea." He smiled.

I shook my head. "It wasn't an idea. It was just an . . . an off the cuff rant."

"It's going to work, though. You'll see."

"What do you think is going to happen?" I said.

"That bill is going to pass. That I know."

"Because you . . . killed those boys?" I stared at him.

"Because your government will want to stop the mass hysteria that is about to unfold," Chico said.

I just stood there. Glued to the floor.

"Adrian? Are you okay? Do you want me to leave?"

I focused on Francisco. I couldn't make sense of it, but as much as I tried to will myself to be terrified, I was not. This man had just told me that he basically went on a killing spree, for me—my cause, and I was not freaking out.

I wasn't feeling fear. I was feeling an odd sense of, gratitude? No not gratitude. Appreciation? No. For the first time, in a long time, I didn't feel like it was me against the world. I didn't feel—alone.

There was someone else invested, someone else who cared enough to do *something*. I didn't know if this was the right something, but I felt a huge sense of relief knowing he had my back. I looked deep into Chico's eyes. I didn't see psycho. I saw assurance.

I couldn't put my finger on it, but I knew I didn't want this man to leave.

I walked over to Chico and slid on his lap. I looked into his eyes and leaned in and kissed him long and hard. He grabbed my waist and returned the kiss. It was passionate and hungry.

He flipped me over and slid on top of me slowly grinding. I responded by spreading my legs and pushing up on the hardness growing inside his pants.

He kissed my neck and shoulder. He pulled the shirt over my head and removed my bra. He took my breasts into his mouth, sucking one, then the other. I closed my eyes and melted into the moment. I grabbed the back of his head and ran my fingers through his thick wavy hair.

Chico pulled off my pants. He removed his shirt and pants. I smiled. I motioned for him to come to me. He pulled off my panties and lifted me up to his mouth.

"Damn, I love your tongue," I whimpered.

Chico looked up. "What else do you love?" he said, slowly caressing my clit.

My body responded by going into orgasmic convulsions. Chico licked and licked until my body went limp. He released my waste and I fell down onto the bed. I slid up on the mattress and watched him. He smiled at me.

"Que pensamentos surpreendentes estao dancando em torno de que a mente brilhante de seu?"

I smiled. I loved the way he spoke Portuguese to me as if I understood what he was saying. As if we were on the same frequency. There was something kind of sexy about it.

"What amazing thoughts are dancing around in that brilliant mind of yours?" Chico translated. He slid behind me and wrapped his arms around my waist. He buried his face deep inside my hair. I smiled and lay quietly for a moment.

"I was thinking about how happy I was to see you this afternoon." It was almost a whisper. "And, it kind of scared me."

"Why did it scare you, Precioso?"

I didn't respond right away. I didn't really know, honestly. I probed my mind as he gently kissed my shoulder.

"I think . . . because before today, I didn't have anything to be happy about." I turned to face him. He had the same adoring look that he had the first time I lay naked wrapped in his arms.

"You know, I've been so . . . detached. So focused on saving our babies' lives, fighting against the hatred, strategizing . . ." I looked down. Chico kissed my eyelids. I began to cry.

"What's wrong?" he said.

"I don't know who I am anymore. I don't know what drives me outside of this damned bill." Chico wiped my tears. "And, when I saw you today, and I was happy—it scared me because, I didn't expect it. and I don't know what to do with it . . . or what to do with what you've shared with me right now."

"What do you want to do with it?"

"I want to place it all in a nice little box and make everything fit. I want it all to make sense."

"What about how you feel doesn't make sense?" Chico propped himself up on his elbow.

I did the same.

"So much. Up until ten minutes ago I didn't even know your last name. And apparently your real first name. I didn't know you were a . . . retired? *Retired right?* Assassin?" I rolled my eyes. "That's . . . just, well crazy! I've had the face of a professional killer between my legs. On multiple occasions!"

Chico chuckled a bit, grabbed my hand and kissed my palm. "None of it makes sense!"

Chico sighed. "So let me ask you this. Does your son being murdered in front of you make sense?"

I dropped my head. He gently lifted my chin so I would meet eyes with his.

"No."

"Does it make sense, that one human being gets to decide if another lives simply because he wears a badge made of pewter?"

"No."

"Does it make sense that despite all your efforts, the logic of human rights, and all the proof that has been provided to show how basic human rights are being violated—your elected officials still refuse to pass a law simply stating that no one is above the law?"

"No."

"Then why are you having such a hard time trying to figure out why your heart," Chico placed his hand over my heart, "wants to find safe harbor in a world that is so dark and hateful?"

I thought about it. "My heart doesn't work, Chi—Francisco. I think, I'd just heard the news that my best friend had been killed and . . . I was being held captive against my will . . . and then I just saw a familiar face."

"Oh really," he replied. "Then what was the happy stuff all about?"

"I was happy to see a familiar face."

Chico got up out of the bed. I watched as he started to dress.

"What are you doing?"

"What does it look like I'm doing?"

"Why are you getting dressed?"

Chico stopped dressing. "Adrian. I am old enough to know you can't change a person. They are who they are. And, I respect that. I think I fell in love with you the moment I laid eyes on you—and it wasn't the night I met you at the bar.

"I can't explain it. And I can't fight it. It's just how I feel and who I am. I've never tried to make you love me —but, I'm old enough to also know that a one-sided relationship is not a situation I want to be in." He sat on the edge of the bed and slid on his shoe.

I slid behind Chico and wrapped my legs around his waist. I wrapped my arms around his chest. "It's not one sided," I whispered.

Chico sighed.

"Please. Don't go." He turned around and I didn't blink. I didn't laugh. I just stared back at him.

"I don't know what it is I feel for you exactly, Chi—Francisco." I paused. "I'm going to have to get used to that."

"Don't. Call me Chico. I told you, it's what my family called me."

"Chico, I don't know what it is I feel for you. But, I do feel something."

✊ ✊ ✊

Francisco

I stood for a moment, watching her. Staring into those green eyes, looking at the freckles that covered her nose and cheeks. I looked at her lips, how perfectly they fit her face. And I smiled.

Adrian extended her hands out to me and I took them as I slid in between her legs on the bed. She pulled me down into her and we kissed over and over.

Adrian pulled my shirt over my head and tossed it. She kissed every inch of my chest. She flipped me over and slid on top and slid her tongue inside my mouth. I knew she felt me rising underneath her.

She sat up and unbuckled my belt. She unbuttoned my pants. Adrian watched as I allowed her to pull down my pants revealing a huge bulge in my black boxer briefs. She slid down to the edge of the

218

bed, positioning herself directly over my hardness and kissed it gently.

She kissed each side, the top, over and over. With each kiss, it grew harder and harder. My heart was racing. I watched her as she reached inside my underwear and freed the eager rod—it was steel hard.

I closed my eyes as Adrian threw her leg over my waist and straddled me. She tilted forward on her knees and guided me inside her with her right hand.

"Mmmm," I moaned. Adrian moved up and down slowly over the tip of my dick. "Ooh," I whispered.

Adrian lowered herself slowly down my shaft. "Oh my," she said. "Damn, baby." Her eyes were closed.

I watched, intrigued as she moved up and down, up and down – each stroke faster than the last, every pound of her ass on my pelvis, harder than the last.

She was holding on to the back of the headboard, steadying her pace, bouncing up and down.

She was so wet, her juices made a smacking noise every time she popped up. It was like a sexual symphony. And I watched the maestro as she orchestrated the score.

"God . . . you feel so good," Adrian said. She placed her hands on my chest and pumped quickly back and forth, grinding downward as she moved. I was startled at the growl that escaped my precioso's mouth. "Gerrrrrrrrrrrrrrr," she growled. "Mmmmmmm," she moaned. "You feel so good."

Beads of sweat covered Adrian's top lip, sweat was streaming from her forehead and down her chest. I was covered in sweat and didn't know if it was mine or hers.

My back was drenched, my legs were drenched. We were covered in hot sticky sweat. Adrian froze. She reached for my hands and I grabbed hers, interlocking my fingers into hers.

She squeezed them tightly as she shook and shook . . . I did not move until Adrian fell over on the bed next to me. She lay on her stomach, facing me, breathing deeply. I lay watching her.

"Do you realize that you stare a lot?" Adrian said.

I smiled and wiped sweat from Adrian's lip.

"No seriously. It's creepy sometimes. You, just staring at me. Not saying anything. It's not normal, *Francisco*."

"I'm not normal," I said. I crawled on top of her and kissed her neck. I pulled her hips up and spread her legs. I slowly slid inside her tight warm wet walls. "I thought you knew that by now."

Adrian

Chico closed his eyes and plunged slowly and deeply inside me. It felt like a slow surge of electricity was consuming my body. His strokes were long—it felt as if his shaft ignited every sexual sensor in my vaginal canal. It was so intense, I could barely stand it.

My head was filled with a noise I couldn't recognize—a humming? No, a buzzing? No—what was that filling the cavity of my brain?

I felt, drunk, high—this was crazy. I had never felt anything like this before! I tried to loose myself free from underneath Chico. But the more I struggled, the deeper he would plunge.

Chico stretched his legs out behind him, laying on top of me. His face nuzzled in my neck. His chest on my back. He slid his hands underneath my stomach and with his left hand he parted my lips and with his right hand he found my clit and gently started to massage it.

A bolt of lightning shot through me.

"Whoa!" I screamed. I started pumping at the same pace as his stroked my clit. He slid his index finger and middle finger across my clit over and over while he plunged deep inside me.

"Oh my god! Oh my god!" I panted. My nipples tingled, my toes tingled. Every nerve in my body was tingling. I tried to move, but Chico plunged deeper. "Ohhhh!" I screamed into the pillow.

"Oh! Oh! Oh!" I whimpered. "What . . is that? What are you doing?" I pushed back into Chico's pelvis, taking all of him in as he hit my spot, over, and over again. I climaxed so hard . . . so deeply . . . the room went silent. Francisco pumped and pumped and just as I was rounding off my orgasm, he released his.

"Mm. mm. uh. uh. ahhhhhhh." Chico stiffened. He grabbed my shoulders. He grunted several times. Then fell on top of me. We lay there sticky, sweaty, and exhausted. After a few minutes, Chico rolled off of me and lay on his back staring up at the ceiling. I lay on my stomach watching him.

"You're staring at me. That's creepy," Chico said.

I grabbed a pillow and whacked him across the face. We laughed.

I slid into his arms and lay across his chest. Chico lay rubbing my arm "You finally had sex with me."

Chico looked down into my face, then kissed me tenderly.

"No, Precioso, I finally made love to you."

Adrian

I slept, for the first time in months. I woke up to Chico staring at me adoringly.

"There's that creepy staring shit again," I mumbled.

Chico laughed. He pulled my hair out of my face. "Just admiring your beauty."

"I'm not beautiful at this time in the morning," I moaned.

Chico smiled then became very serious. "Wow?" I said. "What just happened? Your face went from happy to serious in a matter of seconds."

"Adrian, your life is in danger and I need you to be safe."

"I know, that's why I'm being guarded by the FBI."

Chico rolled his eyes. "Those idiots don't even know that you're gone. I need you to be safe." He paused. "Come to Brazil with me. I will keep you safe."

"If I move to Brazil, I probably wouldn't be in danger anymore. The threat, whoever it is, is here in America."

"You're right about that. So leave America," Chico said. "There's nothing here for you anymore, is there?"

I thought for a moment. There really wasn't. Linda was gone, Reggie was stationed in Europe, and JR wasn't safe as long as he was around me. "No, there isn't," I conceded.

"Then, let's go. Tell me what you want packed and we'll have Thiago take care of everything. If you don't want to bring any of this stuff, we'll buy you all new things when you get to Brazil. Whatever you want."

I stroked the stubble on Francisco's chin. "I can't. I have to finish this—for JJ."

"JJ would want you to be safe; the only way you can be safe is by going off the grid. Please, won't you reconsider?"

"No, I have to see this through," I whispered. "And what's going off the grid?"

"Going off the grid is the same as riding under the radar—it's basically disappearing. There's nothing to connect or track you. You'd close out your bank accounts, credit cards, any outstanding debt or bills and you'd disappear," he explained.

"How would I do that?"

"We'd change your identity. Severe ties with friends and family. Only use cash for transactions. Plan very carefully and keep you out of photos and videos, off emails and the internet for at least three years," Chico said. He pulled me in close and kissed me tenderly.

"What do you think about the name Isobela?"

"Well, it wouldn't be a huge stretch seeing as my middle name *is* Isabelle."

Chico smiled. "I know that." He kissed my nose. "

"You'll be alive. And safe. And with me."

I paused. I stood and paced the room. "I can't begin to think about that, Francisco. I have to get this bill passed."

"Even at the cost of your life?"

"If that's what it takes. Then yes," I said. "I'm not afraid to die."

"Well, brava!" He clapped. "You're not afraid to die. Has it ever occurred to you that *I* may not be ready for you to die?"

"Um, actually, no. It never occurred to me," I said.

Francisco shook his head. He looked down at his watch. "We have to go." Francisco pulled the cover off of us. I grabbed the covers and pulled them over my head. "Adrian. We have to get you back into the room before they notice Candace is not you." He pulled the covers back.

I let out a loud moan. "Okaaaay!" I rolled over and got out of the bed. I grabbed my clothes and started getting dressed. "What's the plan?"

"We return you to the FBI. The 'shit should hit the fan' as you Americans say in a few days. It's important you're in their custody when it does so that they don't view you as a suspect."

I listened. Francisco put on the uniform and dialed Geovanne.

"Everything ready? Okay. Yes, got it." Francisco walked over and moved in to kiss me.

"Eew!" I pushed him away. "I have the dragon. That's gross."

"The dragon?" Francisco looked at me, confused. "What is that?"

"Morning breath." I laughed. "Um. How can I explain? Oh, okay—dragon breath is hot, it singes—like morning breath."

Francisco shook his head and laughed out loud.

"Americans. You're so dramatic."

"I am not kissing you without brushing my teeth. You can call that dramatic if you want. I call it good hygiene."

Geovanne brought the breakfast cart. Francisco helped me get back in. This time Geovanne took the cart to "Adrian." Candace and I switched clothes, hugged and traded places.

I walked over to Geovanne and gave him a tender hug. "Thank you. Thank you so much for all of this. All you're doing."

Geovanne looked down. "You're welcome, Senhora."

I sat on the bed, picked up the folders and nodded. Geovanne knocked on the door and the agent opened it. He walked in and scanned the room.

"All clear." he said into his sleeve.

Francisco

"Geovanne. I need you to keep an eye on Adrian," I said. I had showered and was wearing a pair of dark black jeans and a black silk shirt with black sued loafers.

"Of course."

"I need to get the contract on Adrian terminated." I grabbed my car keys. "And I don't trust the FBI. They can't keep anyone safe."

Geovanne nodded.

"I will protect Senhora Adrian, Geral.". "I'm sure they've learned of the two we neutralized. They should be sending the second wave," Geovanne said.

It was standard practice. The broker would keep sending assassins until the hit was made. Each assassin would be more skilled than the previous—and cost more.

If the first assassin had been able to take her out, the broker would have received more money. But because he had to advance to the next level, it was tapping into his bottom line.
I nodded and walked out the hotel room. I dialed Thiago.

"Are my contacts in place?"

"Yessir. You are scheduled to meet Oswaldo in the service elevator Sunday morning at 10:00 am."

"Perfect. I will fly out tonight. Thank you very much, my friend."

"My pleasure." Thiago hesitated. "Senhor Monserrate, please take care of Senhora Jackson. I have grown fond of her."

I smiled. Thiago disapproved of everyone.

"I will."

🤛 🤛 🤛

Francisco

I arrived at Reagan Airport at 6:00 pm. I took a flight out of LAX after confirming my meeting with Thiago.

I had hotel reservations so I could sleep, and then meet Oswaldo the next morning at the rendezvous point. But I never checked in. I was too anxious to sleep.

Instead, I sat outside across the street from *Senate Square*, two redbrick towers in Capitol Hill. These luxury apartments were a mix between classic and contemporary.

I watched my target leave the building. I exited my car and followed him as he jumped on the new Street Car Line. He exited at McPherson Square that let out to the "H" Street Corridor.

The Corridor included a visual and performing arts scene, hipster bars, music venues, and a boom of high-end condos and apartments.

The target walked four blocks to 14th Street, and then two more blocks to Green Ct. He ducked behind a building and down an alley. I followed him easily unnoticed.

At the end of the alley, he entered into a seedy looking bar, called *The Green Lantern*. I walked in to find strobe lights flashing on everyone on the dance floor, which was not packed, but was pretty crowded.

A performer was on stage doing Karaoke while stripping off

a costume layer by layer. There was a big guy roaming around in a green wig. I took this in, all in a matter of seconds, as I kept my eye on the target.

I walked upstairs to a dance floor that was a madhouse, including the hardcore porn that played on wide-screen monitors behind the bar.

The target found a seat at the bar next to a 20ish year old with blonde hair. He looked young enough to be his son. I watched as the target made small conversation with the blonde boy. After about ten minutes, they walked to the back of the club. I followed them into the restroom.

On the way, several men grabbed my hand, or tried to pull me to the dance floor. I was polite, but firm, and never lost sight of my target. One drunk guy tried to grab me and kiss me and ended up in a fetal position on the floor. I hit him so quick and hard, no one knew what happened.

I entered the restroom full of patrons doing everything *but* going to the restroom. I moved past men on their knees, men bent over, men in a corner kissing . . . I spotted the target and the blonde boy in a corner near a urinal. The boy was standing, the target was sitting in a urinal with his mouth on the boy's large dick sucking eagerly.

The boy threw his head back, grabbed the back of the target's head and pumped faster until he reached an orgasm. I watched as the target slurped, gulped and swallowed what appeared to be a mouthful of a load.

The target smiled, wiping remnants from around his mouth with his shirt sleeve. He handed the blonde boy money and passed me as I turned my back to him once he stood.

The target returned to the bar and the restroom three times with three different young boys in their twenties before he left the establishment. He jumped back on the trolley and returned to his apartment.

I checked my watch. I had four hours before I was to meet Oswaldo. I returned to my car, reclined the seat and dozed off.

When the sun rose, so did I. I reached back into my travel bag and grabbed a clean shirt. The one I had on in the club reeked of stale, dank funk. I changed and exited the car. On the way to the apartment, I dropped the $300 Armani shirt I'd worn into the trash.

The Senate Club featured luxury amenities including a state of the art screening room, a full-service business center, a kitchen and bar for special occasions with friends or neighbors to lounge by the fire or shoot a game of billiards.

There was a 24 hour rooftop dog park, complete with an agility course, an onsite fitness center with first-rate equipment, and extra space for yoga and stretching as well as a rooftop pool.

Inside the eclectic lobby, I walked across the beautiful cherry wood hardwood floor, past the large cream and brown leather chairs and through the French doors on the far right to the service elevator where my contact waited.

"Good morning, Senhor Monserrate." Oswaldo grabbed my hand and shook it.

"Bom die meu amigo. Tem sido muito longo." I embraced the tall, lanky man. His hair was pitch black, the same dark color as his large eyes. He had broad shoulders, making him look even thinner. He wore a porter's burgundy and tan colored uniform.

"Yessir, it's been too long. Six years to be exact."

"A familia estava animado ao ouvir de seu retorno."

I thanked him for his enthusiasm, but I quickly told him that I was not returning to the family. This was just a special assignment.

Oswaldo smiled. "Sometimes a special assignment is enough to help you remember all that you walked away from."

"And sometimes it is enough to remind you of why you left."

The elevator stopped at the fifteenth floor. Oswaldo handed me a key card. "You will have two uninterrupted hours."

"I won't need that much time. But thank you." I hugged him and exited the service elevator. I used the key card to enter the apartment.

It was an open layout with high ceilings and oversized windows that showcased a dynamic city view. I walked across the natural oak floor past the custom designed kitchen with granite countertops and stainless steel appliances, then down the long hallway to the master bedroom. The room was dark. Black out curtains blocked the golden rays that welcomed the District of Columbia's midmorning.

I yanked back the curtains. The screeching of the metal grommets against the metal curtain rods startled the target out of his sleep, and the bright sun instantly disoriented him. I walked over to the bed and punched the target in his nose.

"Ow! Fuck!" he screamed, grabbing his face. His hands filled with blood. I grabbed him by the crown of his head and dragged him by a patch of hair to the chaise near the window.

"What the fuck?" he screamed again, trying to free his hair from my fist.

I plopped his naked body on the apple green Wayfair leather chaise. I pulled my Glock 19 semiautomatic pistol from my waist, shoved the magazine into the butt of the gun, yanked the man's head back and jammed the four inch barrel so deep into his mouth, he gagged.

"Regurgitate on me and I will make you lick every drop of it up," I said easily.

The target forced the bile back down his throat. His eyes registered fear, his heart rate was erratic, and his breathing short and shallow. He watched me click the safety off the revolver. His red eyes filled with tears, his face turned crimson red, and his pupils dilated three times the normal size.

"Terminate the contract on Adrian Jackson." I said. I drug him five feet over to the desk. I slammed him down in the chair, the gun still lodged in his mouth. The target flinched. I handed him the cell phone off the desk. The target tried to speak, but gagged. I removed the gun.

"I don't know what you're talking about."

I slammed the butt of the gun on his nose.

"Aahhh!" he screamed. "Fuck you!"

I pulled out my cell, swirled the chair around, swiped the phone and shoved it in his face.

"I believe I would be too old for you, right Senator Walsh? You seem to like young blonde *boys* with huge testicles full of semen." I flipped through each compromising picture. The Senator was clearly identifiable in each photo. His face registered complete fear.

"I. I. Can't. The broker . . . he doesn't honor cancellations."

I pulled out a bottle of bactine, flipped the cap open, pulled back Senator Walsh's head and sprayed a hefty dose of the benzalkonium chloride and lidocaine up his nasal cavity.

"Aahhhhhh!" Senator Walsh screamed, which was immediately squashed by the choking and coughing.

A pink foam bubbled out of his nose and down his face and tears poured down his cheeks as he fought desperately to free himself from my hold.

I returned the gun to his mouth. I shoved it so deep down the Senator's throat he gagged. I quickly turned the Senator's head to the right, seconds before the vomit hit the massive windowpane. He struggled for air and started to turn blue.

I stood over him and watched unemotionally until he was able to catch his breath, and gather enough air in his lungs to return his face back to pink.

"Here's what's going to happen. I'm going to give you two minutes to end this contract. If you don't, then I will kill you. I will choke you to death, put you in a leopard bra and pink panties, red lipstick and blue eye shadow, and a pair of chandelier earrings.

"I will position your ass up with a huge black dildo sticking out of it. I will take photos and send them to every news outlet across the country. And then I will follow those emails up with time stamped pictures of you sitting in a urinal with your mouth around three different cocks in a gay bar."

Senator Walsh crumbled. "Wait! Wait!" he cried. "Please, don't. I have a wife and two kids."

"A daughter and a son," I said as I looked at him without a bit of emotion. The Senator was covered in dried blood and vomit. He was rank.

"Yes! A daughter and a son who need me," he pleaded.

"No, they don't need you. You're a liar and a disgrace. You pretend to be someone you're not. And then you act like other people are beneath you. You don't do your job and ensure every citizen's rights are protected. Instead you block them--just because you can."

Senator Walsh's head snapped back. "You're a nigger lover?" he said in between gasps.

I stood, grabbed the patch of hair on Senator Walsh's head and banged his face on the desk.

"Aahhh fuckin' shit! Fuck, fuck!"

"The second thing you're going to do is pass the Anti-Profiling Bill."

"I will do no such--"

I grabbed the patch of hair. Senator Walsh held up both of his hands. "Okay, okay! Don't – please." Senator Walsh's once beak-like nose had swollen into a Karl Malden nose, except the bridge was mush, swollen and purple.

"You will do it. Or, I will kill you, then release the urinal pictures." I handed him the cell phone. "Now, pay the broker."

"What?"

"Pay the broker. It will fulfill the contract. All the broker wants is payment. Complete task or not, it's all about the money. Pay him the money."

Senator Walsh paused. I watched as he processed his options. He picked up the phone and transferred the money. I took the phone after he completed the transaction and called Thiago.

"Verify the transaction and confirm the fulfillment."

"Yessir," Thiago said.

I turned back to the Senator. I needed him alive so he could pass this bill. I knew Adrian wouldn't rest until that bill got passed.

"I can always get to you," I said to him. "But, don't do what I've instructed, and I will kill your family." I paused, looking the Senator in his eyes. "Do you think I'm lying?"

Senator Walsh's eyes filled with tears. He shook his head.

"Good." I stood and started to walk off. "Because I hate racists." I turned back to Senator Walsh. "There's nothing I enjoy more than ridding the world of debase and vile creatures. And their offspring." I smiled.

Thiago's text came through. *Transaction verified. Fulfillment confirmed.*

13 THE SINS OF THE FATHER

'The Lord is slow to anger and abounding in steadfast love, forgiving iniquity and transgression, but he will by no means clear the guilty, visiting the iniquity of the fathers on the children, to the third and the fourth generation.'

Numbers 14:18 ESV

Geovanne

Francisco flew back to Los Angeles and we met up.

"How was the trip, sir?"

"Outstanding," he replied. "How are we coming with the plan, Geovanne?"

"We're on point," I said, reviewing my notes. "We're ready for Phase II."

He smiled. He had been waiting patiently for this part of the plan.

"Excellent. What's going on with Adrian?" His smile turned into a serious expression.

"I have been keeping her under close surveillance. So far, nothing."

"Okay. This situation is about to get volatile. We won't have any room for errors."

"Understood," I said. "Senhora Jackson is back on the speaking circuit. She was on the radio this morning. I am surprised the FBI allowed her to make the appearance."

"I'm sure they didn't have much choice. When Adrian makes up her mind, that's pretty much all there is to it." He chuckled. "Can you secure the itinerary for her upcoming public appearances?"

I handed him two pieces of paper. "Senhora's itinerary for the next two months, sir."

He nodded. I watched Francisco's eyes dart from one line to the next. I watched how he squinted just slightly when he saw a potential problem. And, I watched how he leaned back in his chair when he went into deep thought mode.

"These places are very public. But it's the transportation routes, and the in between places like the hallways, and green rooms, and holding rooms that I'm concerned about. The FBI will do a sweep, but if an assassin is out there, then he will be ten steps ahead of them."

"Senhor, I have developed several contingency plans for the next three public appearances. Would you like to review them?" I handed him my hand held tracking device.

He nodded as he reviewed each plan. "Very good. And what about the rooftop access?"

"I have Charlemain covering that." I replied.

"Charlemain, from Atilla's third command station?"

"Yessir."

"He is pretty high ranking. How were you able to manage that?"

"He was my Captain, sir."

The corners of Francisco's mouth edged up, just slightly. Enough for me to know I had done well with securing Charlemain for the job.

"Very well. These look good, Geovanne." Francisco patted me on the shoulder. "Then, I'm off. And you?"

"Headed for New York tonight."

"It's time," Francisco said.

"Yes sir. It's time."

Francisco

I slipped into a long blue jumper, placed the baseball cap over my hair, put on dark sunglasses, grabbed my tool box and jumped out the back of the van. I made my way up the circular drive way and rang the doorbell.

"Yes?"

"Good afternoon. Mr. Banton?"

"Yes."

"I have a repair request for your shower, sir. Apparently there is a clog?"

"Ah. No, I don't know anything about that?"

"Okay. Tell the Mrs. to call back and reschedule with the appointment desk," I said, grabbing my toolbox. "It probably won't be for another week or so, and she won't be able to get a time certain appointment—just a window next time. But we'll definitely get her back into the route. You have a nice day, sir!"

"Hey, wait!" Mr. Banton yelled. "Just because I don't know about it doesn't mean it wasn't made. C'mon in. The last thing I need is for my wife to be pissed at me for one more thing. I don't know why she left knowing she made an appointment. But that's neither here nor there, is it buddy?"

I followed Gerald into the living room. "No sir, not with the wives."

We chuckled.

"We have three bathrooms. Does the order say which one has the clog?"

"It says 'shower' suspects hair clog," I said, pretending to read the details on the order.

"Ah, then that would most likely be Amy's shower. This way." Gerald Banton took me down the hall, and to the right. I had studied the schematics of the house for hours." I knew every room of the house and exactly where each member of the family dwelled. Mr. Banton's study was in the front of the house, just to the right of the entrance.

"This looks right. Do you mind if I just take a look to make sure?"

"Sure, go right ahead. Do you need me for anything? I have a few reports I need to finish in my study, or--"

"No, sir. Go right ahead. It shouldn't take more than ten minutes to run the camera down the drain. If I don't see a clog, I'll come get you and perhaps you can show me the other bathroom. If I do see the clog, you're fine with me just snaking it and taking care of it?"

"Yeah, yeah. That sounds fine. I'll be in the study if you need me."

I placed the toolbox down on the bathroom floor. I text'd Geovanne, "Everything clear?"

Geovanne replied, "Yessir, good to go!"

Geovanne was posted outside, making sure no one entered the house unexpectedly. Amy was supposed to be in class, and Mrs. Banton was at the country club playing tennis. Afterward, she would have a drink with her girlfriend, Darlene, and then run over to Sprouts to shop for dinner.

I pulled on leather gloves, then grabbed the mini recorder, my .38 revolver, a huge plastic BBQ Rib Bib, and a pint of Jack Daniels, then walked toward the front of the house.

I walked purposefully toward the study, entering the room completely unnoticed. It wasn't until I was upon him, placing the pint of Jack Daniels on the desk that Gerald saw me.

"Whoa!" Gerald laughed nervously. "Buddy, you scared the shit out of me. What's this?"

I pulled the glock out and pointed it between his eyes. The man froze.

"Hey . . . what's going on here?"

I kept my arm nice and steady as I rounded the desk, opened the drawer and pulled out Gerald Banton's agency issued 17 glock. I placed it in my waistband and moved back around to the front of the desk.

"You're going to die today, Sergeant Banton," I stated. "But before you do. You're going to do something you should have done eighteen months ago: tell the truth."

I reached up on the bookshelf, pulled out a book, opened it and grabbed the silver .32 caliber revolver. Sergeant Banton watched as I cleaned the study of all his hidden firearms and weapons.

"I'm going to die today?" Sergeant Banton repeated.

"You are. But first, open that bottle and take a drink," I ordered. The officer did not move. I clicked off the safety to the glock. "So, you have two choices. You can be a bad ass cop, and get a bullet in the brain right now. But know this: when your wife comes home and finds your body slumped over your desk, that won't be the worst of her problems.

"She's going to panic and call the police, but before they arrive, a slew of reporters will get here. And what they're going to report is that the sergeant involved in the infamous Jared Jackson murder, who was never indicted, was a dirty cop all along. They will report that you had been killed over stolen evidence from a drug bust."

"What? I never--"

"Doesn't matter. The evidence has already been planted. Phone calls have been made from your phone. The stolen cocaine from the drug bust will be found on these premises. You will go down for being a dirty cop.

"Your wife and daughter will get nothing. No retirement, no insurance. They will be ostracized by the good ol' boys in blue . . . by the women in the country club. The girl in the private school. She will be shamed for the rest of her life."

The sergeant sat processing all that I was saying.

"So, as I said. You have two options. You can be a bad ass cop and take this bullet to your brain." I placed the mini recorder on the desk. "Or, you can tell the truth of what really happened that day and have your death look like the suicide of man who had a conscience.

"At least your family will have some dignity and will be able to collect some insurance money so they can maintain their lifestyle." I sat in the brown leather chair in front of the desk. "Which do you choose?"

We locked eyes. The sergeant blinked several times, either coming to terms with the gravity of the situation, or pushing back tears. I couldn't tell—and didn't care.

"I choose the latter."

"Good. Now drink." The officer picked up the bottle and took a long swig of the whiskey. My hand stayed steady. "Now, turn on the recorder and make your dying confession about what happened the day Jared Jackson was murdered."

Officer Banton

I sat there motionless for about two minutes. The truth of the matter was, I had to work to remember. I had spent the past year and a half telling the same lie over and over, I honestly almost forgot the truth.

Well, I never really forgot the truth. The truth was that Peter killed that young man. He killed him in cold blood for no reason other than he was black and he had pissed Peter off.

And I did nothing to stop him. And more than that, I went on record saying that an innocent person had provoked his own death—when nothing could be further from the truth.

The truth was that Peter Carpenter was every vile thing Adrian Jackson accused him of being. Sadly, it made me worse because I lied to protect Peter knowing exactly who he was.

I took another swig of the JD and rubbed my head. For months after the incident I remained inebriated. I kept seeing Pete shoot that kid in the face, and seeing his mom crumble in front of him. I couldn't take it.

At the station, the guys would pat me on the back, and tell me I was True Blue. I'd smile and nod, but it made me sick to my stomach. Every opportunity I got, I'd sneak and drink. I had Jack Daniels strategically stashed everywhere, in my locker, in my patrol car, at home—everywhere.

It had only been three months since I went through a detox program in Connecticut and got clean. And while my road to recovery was difficult, the best part was being able to talk about what really happened to someone objective. Someone I'd never see again, and who would never reveal my disgusting secret.

I grabbed the bottle again, but the guy with the gun snatched it away. "Before you get sloppy drunk," he pointed to the recorder, "speak" and make it sound like you're confessing to your wife . . . like you're apologizing for taking your life, but you want her know why."

I nodded. "But I'll say it to Amy. Lisa could care less about whether I'm dead or alive."

When I was going through the investigation, I tried to confide in my wife. But she was cold. She told me to *man up,* to play the game, and do whatever I needed to do to protect Pete. The last thing she wanted was to be ostracized from our social clubs. When I tried to tell her that Jared was innocent and he hadn't done anything to provoke Pete, she went off.

"Shut the fuck up, Jerry. He was a nigger! My God, you mean to tell me you're more concerned about some dead nigger who probably deserved it, than your partner, who would give up his life for you?

"Sure, maybe he was innocent this time. But what about all the things he'd done before and got away with? It probably just finally caught up with him. He got what he deserved. But you, you better get your morals straight."

Francisco

Sergeant Banton turned on the recorder.

"Amy, baby—daddy loves you. I love you more than life itself." He took another gulp and wiped his mouth. "That's why I can't go on this way. Living a lie."

He looked at me; I nodded.

"I want you to grow up to be a decent human being. A woman who loves and respects every human being for who they are, regardless of their race, social economic status, religion or sexual orientation.

"I've always tried to instill that in you," he whispered. "But I am a hypocrite. Daddy is a hypocrite and he just can't live with it anymore."

Officer Banton's eyes were glossy. I could see he was getting buzzed.

Gerald picked up the recorder and recounted the details of Jared's murder, play by play. He confirmed all the things Adrian said on the stand, and filled in the missing pieces that the jury never got to hear, but if they had, surely would have indicted and convicted Sergeant Carpenter—and probably Officer Banton for not intervening.

He told his daughter how much he loved her. He apologized for leaving her this way and said he had faith that she would be strong enough to grow into the amazing young woman he knew she could become.

He told her to follow her dreams and know that despite all of this, he loved her always. He was in complete tears by the time he finished his confession.

I looked at my watch. I had seven minutes before Sergeant Banton would pass out. I stared at him. I felt no sympathy. I saw him as a coward and couldn't see how his daughter would ever see him as anything else.

"I know," Officer Banton said. "I am pathetic. But you don't understand the pressure, the expectations of the force---there is a serious code."

"Then leave," I said evenly. "If you could no longer serve in your capacity in the manner in which you swore, then you should have walked away."

"And do what? Being a cop was all I knew. It was all I ever wanted to be," Officer Banton replied.

I sat silently for a moment. "And create what was next for you. Obviously you weren't being the cop you thought you were going to be. You weren't happy. You should have left and done something else."

"Easier said than done."

"No," I said. "It's not easy. But nothing worth anything in life is ever easy." I watched as the sedative I'd mixed in the liquor kicked in. The officer slipped into a quiet sleep.

I pulled out the BBQ Rib Bib and placed it over my jumper. I waited two additional minutes, then pulled out the officer's agency issued weapon.

I pushed him back into the chair so that he sat upright. I placed the gun in the same hand he used to grab the bottle of Jack Daniels, placed it under his chin, and pulled the trigger. I let the gun fall naturally from his hand onto the desk. Red and pink brain matter splattered across the wall behind him.

I pulled out a dubbing device from my toolbox. I connected the recorder to the dubbing device and copied the confession. I left the recorder on the desk and walked out of the front door and down the circular drive way.

I text'd Geovanne. "It is done."

For the next seven days, Geovanne brutally murdered sixty-five white males, who were the sons of officers who had killed unarmed African Americans, up and down the Eastern seaboard of the United States.

By day two, the news outlets had picked up the story.

"Ten white males have been brutally murdered. Police are calling it a serial killer."

Because the murders had taken place on the East coast, all the FBI/CIA/local Law Enforcement focus was placed on that region of the country.

By day three, Francisco started killing the white males on the West Coast. His first target: Chad Carpenter, the twenty-two year old son of Sergeant Peter Carpenter.

Chad Carpenter was a senior, majoring in Architecture at California Polytechnic State University, San Luis Obispo. His girlfriend found him slumped over his steering wheel in his carport, with a five bullets to the face.

Mass hysteria gripped the country. Every news outlet was covering the story.

"White Males Under Siege. Serial Killer on the Loose."

✊ ✊ ✊

Chief Bollinger

"Chief, have you heard the news?" James barged into my office.

"For Christ's sake, James, didn't your mother ever teach you to knock before entering a person's room?" I snapped.

Of course I'd heard the news. What the fuck did he think, he was the only fucking person watching television and getting updates from the FBI? In less than twenty-four hours, the rest of the world will know that not only were white males being targeted, but that they were the sons of police officers who'd killed unarmed African Americans and Latinos over the past twenty years.

James looked flustered for a moment. "Of course my mother did," he replied. "I just didn't know you were so particular about knocking protocol."

"Well I am, got dammit. From now on, knock!" I stood looking out of my window. Normally the cityscape would soothe my nerves. But for some reason today, it was suffocating me. I turned to face James who was sulking. "What is it?"

"News reporters are looking for a statement regarding the murder of Chad Carpenter, since he's the first known white male killed by the serial killer on the west coast, and the son of Sergeant Carpenter."

I ran my hands through my black and white hair. I'd just informed my rank and file of the serial killer and his targets.

All white officers with sons have been warned to keep their sons inside until further notice.

If they were away at school, they were to bring them home. If they lived on their own, they were to bring them home. If they weren't speaking to them for whatever reason, they were to get on the phone and get them home—every son of every white officer in blue was a target.

✊ ✊ ✊

I stood before flashing cameras in my fully decorated dress blues uniform, representing the rank and file.

"Ladies and gentlemen, it has been confirmed by the FBI/CIA and DOJ that indeed, we have a serial killer on our hands." The flashes lit up the room.

"And that in fact, this serial killer has made his primary target sons of white officers, who, as far as we can tell, have been involved in some shape, form, or fashion, with a murder involving an African American or Latino victim."

Reporters started hurling questions from all directions.

"Chief Bollinger, have there been any demands from this serial killer?"

"No, no demands have been made."

"Chief, how many deaths so far have been attributed to this serial killer?"

I took a deep breath; I knew the answer would cause complete panic and mayhem in my city.

"This is an ongoing investigation; therefore I'm not at liberty to provide that information at this time. We're looking to see if there have been any additional victims that law enforcement may have believed to be random or accidental.

"Once we have a better idea of the scope of this situation, we will share it with the public. For now, we are encouraging all white males to be extremely cautious.

"We have no solid evidence indicating that only males of sworn law enforcement agencies are the only targets, and until we capture this suspect—and citizens of Los Angeles, know that we will capture this maniac, and bring swift and hard justice in this case—we ask that everyone please, just exercise common sense and caution. Thank you. No more questions at this time."

"Chief Bollinger!" one reporter screamed, as the chief left the podium. "My sources say the number of deaths across the country total over one hundred-fifty, can you confirm that number?"

News reporters ate the statement up. Before midday that number had been quoted on every news station and media outlet across the country.

"An unidentified source has reported . . ."

"An unconfirmed number . . ."

"Allegedly the number of deaths total . . ."

The FBI and CIA had been inundated with calls from every high-powered executive requesting definitive information on the case. And every security company across the nation was receiving calls for quotes on beefing up home security systems, and estimates for body guards for their sons.

The airlines were inundated with calls on the safety measures being taken as their sons traveled, sometimes across the country, to return home to frantic mothers worried about keeping their babies safe. Air Marshals were assigned to aircraft with five or more white males traveling any leg of a flight.

Adrian

I sat at Linda's bedside watching the mayhem unfold on a local news station. I held her hand and wept silently, knowing the inevitable fate of my friend.

Atkins, Linda's husband of ten years, refused to give up hope or remove her from life support despite the neurosurgeon's emphatic prognosis that she would never advance beyond a vegetative state.

Clearly Linda had worn the pants in the family, because Atkins was a hot mess. Even when her parents pleaded with him to let her go, he refused. So, I visited her regularly. Often, those would be the only times Atkins would leave Linda's side, afraid her parents would sneak in and unplug her monitors.

"Look, Lindy Lu," I said to the shell of a body lying there. "Chico said this would happen. My God, I did not believe him." I looked on in intrigue at the coverage.

"My son's life is in danger!" one white woman screamed into the television. "He's a good kid. He's never done anything to anyone. This is not fair!"

I rolled my eyes. How many times had I heard those words from an African American mother after her son had been brutally murdered by a cop?

"Whoever you are! Our sons didn't have anything to do with those the cops who killed those innocent people. Those cops are responsible for their actions, not our sons—can't you see that?"

"Why are you taking out your rage and hatred for a group of people on innocent victims?" Another clip showed a woman holding up a picture of her son, playing rugby at age thirteen. He looked so sweet and innocent.

I took a deep breath.

"The shit is about to hit the fan now," I said out loud.

I kept my phone turned off during my visits. But I knew my voicemail would be full and I'd have dozens of requests to appear on shows when I left the hospital. I needed to think very strategically about my next steps. I turned to my friend.

"I miss you so much. I don't know what to do."

But in my heart, I knew exactly what I needed to do. I just didn't know if I had the courage to do it.

Francisco

I sent the audiotape to LAPD's Internal Affairs department, Chief Bollinger, and the District Attorney. By the end of the week when I hadn't heard anything on the news about the tape, I sent a copy to Adrian, TMZ, and the Los Angeles Board of Police Commissioners.

"In today's news, the gossip website *TMZ* released an audio tape in which Officer Banton, partner of the LAPD Sergeant Carpenter, is heard confessing to his daughter about what really transpired the day Jared Jackson was shot to death on the corner of 1st and Grand. According to point-by-point confession, Officer Banton corroborates the story as told by Adrian Jackson.

"Officer Banton was found by his wife, last week in his home, an apparent suicide—after confessing to his daughter that 'he could no longer live with himself knowing that he had lied on the stand about the murder of Jared Jackson,'" said Ingrid Robeson, anchor for Channel 7 News.

"The FBI isn't confirming the authenticity of the tape. But our sources in law enforcement have indicated that the audio is real. We're waiting to see if the District Attorney will file charges against Sergeant Carpenter, who will bury his son on Wednesday of next week at the Cathedral of Our Lady of the Angels."

"Ingrid," her co-anchor said. "Things are about to get heated in this city."

"Roger . . . I think this is bigger than the city. I think things are about to get heated around the country."

"Some ask, 'How could there be a God when tragedies like these happen to good people?' And to that I say, there is a God to love us and comfort us through tragedies like these, " Father Rasmussen said. He raised his hands. "Let us pray. Into your hands, we commend Chad's spirit, oh Lord."

✊ ✊ ✊

After the service, the family lined up at the church entrance to receive the visitors. Sergeant Carpenter thanked each person who shook his hand and expressed their condolences.

"Sergeant Carpenter, sir," a young rookie said. "I am deeply sorry for your loss. On behalf of the 52nd, sir, we would like to present you with a small donation." The rookie handed the officer an envelope.

"Thank you, brother," Sergeant Carpenter said. "And please let my brothers at the 52nd know how much I appreciate their support, will you?"

"Yes sir. I definitely will, sir." The rookie hugged Sergeant Carpenter and patted him on the back.

Sergeant Carpenter turned to greet the next person. She was dressed in an elegant black dress that landed right above her knee. She wore a small black pill hat with black netting that covered the top half of her face. All he could see were her lips, which were a ruby red. She extended her hand to the officer who took it inside his. She leaned in and whispered in his ear, "Officer Carpenter, how are you?"

"I'm good, thank you."

"You're more than good. You're alive and well. Breathing. But Chad's dead. Yeah, you might as well get over that."

Sergeant Carpenter snatched his hand away from hers.

"What the fuck?" he said.

His wife turned to face him.

"Peter?" she said, looking embarrassed.

But before he could fully register the statement, Adrian had walked away and was halfway down the stairs.

14 WHITE PRIVILEGE. BLACK BLAME

Adrian

The FBI ushered me into the back door of the studio. Special Agent Anderson met with the studio security to discuss the details of the taping. Since the arrest of Sergeant Carpenter two days after he buried his son, threats on my life had quadrupled. The trial had lasted for eleven days. With the jury in deliberation, tensions heightened, the FBI were taking extra precautions.

I waited in the green room with two agents stationed outside until it was time to take the stage.

"Excuse me, I'll need to see some ID," the tall agent said.

"What? I'm the makeup artist," the woman replied. She had on a black baseball cap, a black t-shirt with "The Talk" splashed across in white lettering, black pants and shoes. She carried a tower full of makeup and had a slew of brushes in what looked like a modified tool belt, tied to her waist.

"You know what?" She rolled her eyes, "I'm union, baby. I don't have to take this shit. But you're going to be the one answering to the producer when she gets on stage looking like a washed out chicken. I'm still gone get paid." The woman turned and walked away.

The tall agent looked at the short agent who shook his head.

"Hey," he called. The woman turned around, rolling her eyes. "My *name* is Vuh-Nessa."

"Vanessa. I apologize," the agent said. "Please, go do yo' thang, girl." He smiled.

Vanessa softened, batting her long lashes.

"You know I'm gone always do that." She pointed her finger at the agent. They laughed as she entered the room.

✊ ✊ ✊

Adrian

"Hello, Mrs. Jackson."

I turned—Candace put her finger up to her mouth. "My name is Vuh-Nessa. And I'm your makeup artist for this taping. So tell me, do you think you're a warm, sun kissed, or latte palate?" She clicked the door closed.

"I think I'm more of a sun kissed kind a gal!" I said running over to hug Candace. "Girl, you manage to always get into the most well-guarded places."

"Geovanne! It's that Geovanne, girl. I don't too much fuck around with FBI agents on a regular, if you know what I mean?" Candace smiled and opened the makeup case. She stuffed white tissue in my collar, pulled out primer and started applying the clear make up.

"Are you really going to do my make up?" I chuckled.

"I have to or else it will blow my cover!" Candace applied a thick matte foundation that covered my freckles flawlessly.   "Listen, after the taping, we're going to take you to a safe house. Francisco says he doesn't trust the FBI."

We both laughed.

"And he thinks he can protect me better than they can?"

"Oh yeah, girl. They got some secret agent espionage shit going on. You'll be safe. Don't worry about that. And Geovanne, girl, he's Type A! He's been over everything about a dozen times. Ain't nobody going to find you." Candace applied a thick coat of mascara to my lashes. "Just look for me, I'll give you the signal—you slip out the second double doors to the right of the stage."

"Got it. Second double doors," I said, looking up so Candace could apply the mascara.

"I like this suit you got on. Classy. But you're always stylish and classy. That's why these white folks can't stand you. They can't call you ghetto," she said.

I smiled.

"How many degrees do you have?"

"Two. Both in Marketing," I said. There was a knock on the door. "Everything okay in there?"

"Naw, I dropped my $100 case of eye shadow." They waited. No one entered. Candace winked and swirled me around in the chair. "I learned how to apply make up to cover up the bruises that asshole gave me. I wouldn't necessarily call it a skill." She removed the tissue from around my neck and smiled. "But it certainly came in handy today."

Adrian

"For six months, America has been under siege." The camera zoomed in close on Sharon Osbourne. "To date, over 150 white males have been brutally murdered by what law enforcement agencies believe to a coordinated effort by several individuals with an apparent vendetta against police officers who have been implicated in fatal cases involving unarmed African Americans." The camera panned out to include all the women sitting around the studio table.

"Today on *The Talk*, we have with us two mothers who have lost their sons to this tragedy. We have Adrian Jackson," the camera zoomed in on me, "mother of 21-year old, Jared Jackson—by all accounts a brilliant researcher." The screen went to a picture of Jared in his lab coat, flashing a beautiful smile.

"Also, joining us in the studio, is Liza Dickenson. Mother of twenty-two year old Brett Dickenson, high school football star and son of Pensacola Officer Jim Dickenson. Brett was one of the first victims of the notorious *Blue Blood* serial killer, responsible for the brutal murders of white males across the country.

"Ladies, welcome to the show." Sharon grabbed the hand of the women sitting on both sides of her. "It's a tragic time in our country, when our young men are gunned down for no reason at all."

The women nodded in agreement.

Sara Gilbert chimed in, "It has to be difficult for both of you. You're on opposite sides of this situation, Adrian—your son was killed by a police officer, and Liza—your son was killed by someone angry at police officers for killing Black youth.

"But what we're hoping to do is focus on those areas that we, as human beings . . . you know, like the fact that you're both mothers, that you both had amazing sons whose lives were tragically cut short at the hands of another human being --- we want to have a dialogue about what's next in the healing phase for us as Americans, and not fuel the flame of anger and hatred."

"That's not why I came on the show Sara," I said, shaking my head.

"Okay, but don't you think you could participate in a conversation that focuses on love and not hate."

"Now that white boys are being killed, all of a sudden we need to focus on how to end these senseless killings? Focus on love, not hate? I find that to be quite hilarious, *Sara*."

"I don't think one life is more important than the other, Adrian."

"Sure you do," I said. "The title of your show today is All Lives Matter."

"Yes, because they do."

"They do *now* that white lives are being taken," I said.

Liza burst into tears. "You know what? I believe these people started killing our sons because of you!"

"Mrs. Dickenson!" Aisha interrupted.

I put my hand up and nodded toward Liza to finish her statement.

"All of these protests, and statistics about police officers killing black people, it just agitated someone, and now they're killing our innocent sons!" Liza said.

"They're being killed in protest to black males being killed. You don't see that? So that attention is brought to this situation. So that women like you can feel the pain that black women feel about their sons."

"Our sons aren't any less precious than white women," I said. "We carried our sons for nine months. We gave birth. Black mothers want to see their children grow up and be happy."

"We don't want to fear for their lives every time they walk out the door. And when they do die, when they are killed—we have the right to be devastated, to be angry, to be hurt . . . Just like *you*. But you're missing that point, too, I see?"

"I don't understand why I have to hurt so that you can stop

hurting." Liza sobbed. "Are you a part of this? Are you giving instructions to these murderers? You tell him to stop! You tell him that these boys are innocent."

I paused, adjusted my blazer, and focused. "I am not giving anyone instructions to kill these young men. But I will tell you this. It's obvious that someone wants equity. Someone wants you to see how we feel. Someone wants police officers who look at our children as expendable and less than human beings to see how that feels." I took a deep breath and looked at Liza.

"I don't want you to hurt Liza. But guess what, your pain isn't any deeper, any more sacred, or any different than my pain. I want your husband to stop killing innocent black people. I want his fraternal organization to stop believing that they can kill our children, plant a weapon, and get away with it. It doesn't work like that."

"Adrian," Sheryl Underwood interrupted. "It seems to me that there is a disconnect. What can these mothers do to understand how black mothers feel?"

I looked at Sheryl like she was crazy. "I don't know."

Sheryl waited. I sat there. I didn't attempt to offer a solution.

"You mentioned that someone wanted them to know how black mothers feel, I'm asking you to share with them what that is so that they can understand and perhaps--"

"Oh, then clearly you misunderstood my statement." I smiled. "I could care less if any one of these women 'understand' how I feel. I don't need anyone to understand."

"But if they want help understanding, there's a great book by Marita Golden and Susan Richards Shreve called *Skin Deep*. They can read it and learn all about how white women and black women feel about race. I told you, that's not why I'm here." I turned to face the camera.

"I don't *understand* how it feels to get raped, to be homeless, to be forced into prostitution, or how it feels to have cancer—but I fight for those causes. Do you need to stamp your approval on the moral efficacy of something for you to know that it's wrong? *It is wrong for a person to die because another person hates them.* End of Story!

"But that's the main issue with white privilege. White privilege says, if I don't experience it, approve it, then it doesn't exist. Therefore it's not real. I'm not asking Liza or any other white woman to understand it. I'm telling them that they *will* accept it."

"Well, this is not how this conversation was supposed to go," Julie Chen said. "I'm not sure how we come to a happy medium here."

"I'll tell you. It's really simple, Julie." I looked directly at Liza. "Racist white supremacists need to own their bigotry." I pointed to my index finger. "You know you're racist. Stop acting like you're not. You are the problem, not the people you hate. Sharon, Sara—you want so badly for "us" to see the similarities and not the differences.

"That can't happen when you have bigots pretending to love and all the while they hate. They hate so much that they create systems and laws that keep the playing field at a disadvantage for those they hate.

"But then they're quick to say 'Earn your place at the table.' And even if we manage to overcome the institutional and systemic racism, and make it to the table, they still find ways to block the path for the people they hate to fairly compete.

"So, don't turn to me and ask me to hold her hand, to see the similarities in us, to focus on love when I'm not the one hating. I am simply demanding what's my right. I have a right to live."

I turned to Liza. "Or is that a white privilege, too?" I turned to Sharon. "I have the right to be proud of being black. Or is that a white privilege only?" I turned to Sara. "I have the right, not only as an American, but as a human being to want . . . to need, to hurt . . . to love—just like any other red-blooded American.

"So when I say black lives matter, when I protest, when I fight—don't you dare ask me to be non-violent. Don't you dare ask me to see the similarities, and focus on love. Don't you dare."

I looked into the camera. "Right your wrongs white America. Then come talk to me. But until then, we don't have anything to talk about. But you better believe, it's not business as usual. It's a new day in the USA."

The studio was a clusterfuck after the taping. Sharon was throwing vases and cursing. Sara was in tears. Sheryl was laughing hysterically. I waited for the signal from Candace and slipped into the women's restroom.

Five minutes later, Candace exited the lavatory wearing the same outfit I was wearing and the two agents followed her. I slipped out the second double doors and into the black Suburban Candace said would be waiting outside. I jumped into the back seat and the vehicle sped off.

"Ola Precioso," Francisco said, looking into the rear view mirror.

"Ola Morpheus." I laughed.

Francisco looked back.

"Who is Morpheus?" he said.

Candace walked back to the green room without making much eye contact with the FBI agents. Inside, she changed back into her make-up artist outfit. She text'd Geovanne.

Two minutes later, there was a loud boom! And Candace stuck her head out of the room long enough to see the two FBI agents turned to face the commotion.

She slipped quietly out the room and inconspicuously out of the studio where Geovanne sat waiting patiently in the running vehicle.

Adrian

We all met up in a plush home deep in Topanga Canyon.

"This is a safe house?" Candace said as she entered the beautiful home.

Geovanne smiled. "Yes. What did you expect?"

"Uh, I don't know. Some small cabin or two bedroom condo." She stood in the middle of the foyer and gazed up at the vaulted ceilings. "This, is a freakin' mansion."

Francisco smiled. "Make yourself at home, Candace. And let Geovanne know if you need anything special. We will have it delivered right away."

Candace smiled as she took a self-initiated tour of the five-bedroom home.

I slid comfortably into the plush couch in the living room. I removed my jacket and shoes and lay back in the corner of the dark brown leather sectional.

Francisco walked into the room carrying logs of wood. "I thought a fire might be nice."

"A fire would be perfect." I watched Francisco build a robust fire in the stone fireplace.

Geovanne entered a few minutes later carrying red wine and wine glasses. "Where's Candace?" I said.

"She's napping. She said all the excitement wore her out."

I smiled, accepting the glass from Geovanne. Francisco sat next to me. He grabbed my feet and massaged the soles. I slid down into the couch and closed my eyes. Within minutes I dozed off.

Francisco

"Senhor Monserrate," Geovanne said. "What are the reports from Senhor Thiago?"

I stared into the crackling fire. "Last count the Senate was almost at majority vote." I turned to face Geovanne. "We're almost there."

Geovanne

I left the safe house at 3:00 am the next morning. I flew to Cleveland where my operative had been on surveillance for fifty-six hours.

"Senhor Azevedo," Jon Pierre said. "There were thirteen officers in total. Twelve white, one Hispanic. They killed the two African Americans, one male, one female."

"How many bullets, Jon Pierre?" I reviewed the police reports.

"One hundred-thirty seven, Senhor."

"And the final report?"

"Unarmed. No weapons found along the nineteen mile route."

Jon Pierre handed me the dossier.

"Good job, my friend. Good job."

< Geovanne: How is Trey?
< Candace: My baby is good. I talked to him for 2 minutes, like you said.
< Geovanne: This will be over soon.
< Candace: I know. I'm not trippin'.
< Geovanne: I will see you in 4 days.
< Candace: Please be safe. Promise?
< Geovanne: I promise.
< Candace: <3
< Geovanne: What is that symbol?
< Candace: It's a heart you dork. Do you have one? I think you have stolen mine.
< Geovanne: ☺
< Candace: Oh my God, G! You can smile?!

I slid the cell phone in my pocket. I was smiling.

"Ladies and gentlemen, please. Calm down," Special Agent Creuzer said to the crowded room. "The sooner you quiet down, the sooner I can make my report."

"Unless the report says you've captured the Blue Blood Killers, we don't care to hear anything you have to say, Special Agent Cruezer," Arnold Winston said.

Arnold was a retired sergeant from the Cleveland Police Department.

"Mr. Winston, please, can you let us do our job?"

"Can you *do* your job?"

"Gentlemen!" the Mayor interjected. "Please. I know tensions are high, but this is not helping."

"What would help," said Sandy Goldstein, Deputy District Attorney, "is if our legislators would just pass this damned bill already. You know that's what they want."

"Who is *they*, Sandy?" Arnold screamed. "The thugs and criminals who want to run this damned country?"

"I think it's the unarmed black people who are sick and tired of being hunted." She rolled her eyes and threw him the bird.

"Whose side are you on, Goldstein?"

"Last I checked, it was justice."

"Ladies, ladies!" Cruezer said.

Arnold sneered.

"It's been two days of terror for the good citizens of Cleveland."

"You mean for the thirteen officers who executed the two unarmed African Americans in 2012?"

"Got dammit, Sandy!" Arnold yelled again. "Those are our boys being terrorized. Have some fucking respect."

"Oh, great. *Now* you want to talk about respect. What was it you said when the protestors called for respect of the two killed like caged animals in that ambush? Oh wait, you said *those were the breaks?*"

"You know Sandy, since you seem to love those niggers so much, why don't you go live in the gutter with them!" Patrick Winehold said.

Sandy smirked. "Patrick. Where's Matthew?"

"Why? So you can hand deliver the address to the goddamn killers yourself?"

"People. People. Really. This is not helping one bit," the Mayor said. "Please, can you let Special Agent Cruezer give his report? Special Agent?"

"Thank you, Mayor Brennen." Special Agent Cuezer cleared his throat. "As of zero-four hundred hours, two more victims have been claimed by the Blue Blood Serial Killers." The crowd gasped. "Bringing the total up to seven. Nationwide that's 226."

"He's not going to stop until he takes out the entire white race!" Patrick said, flailing his arms in the air.

Sandy rolled her eyes.

"We're confident it's more than one person. Murders have occurred simultaneously in various regions of the country. Our intel--"

"Your intel sucks!" Arnold waved him off as he stomped to the rear of the room.

"Our intel says they're international terrorists."

"Awe fuuuuck me!" Arnold shouted from the back of the room.

"Terrorists could give a rat's ass about cops' sons. It's those fuckin' Black Panther fucks." He pointed. "They're on the rise again. I'm telling you."

"International terrorists posing as American operatives."

The room went into a loud uproar.

"Well what are you doing to protect our sons?" Patrick said.

"These kids are innocent. And don't you say a word, Sandy

Goldstein! Do you hear me?"

Sandy smiled.

"We're moving the remaining five males to a safe house as we speak. They'll be protected by the FBI."

The black van rounded the curb doing 35 mph, hit the spikes and spun into a ditch. Geovanne and Jon Pierre walked across the street. Jon Pierre took out the two FBI agents in the front. Geovanne opened the back doors.

An agent lunged at Geovanne, but he grabbed his arm and tossed him to the ground. In one move he broke the FBI agent's neck.

Geovanne returned to the van and stood on the protruding bumper. He looked through the night detector scope and counted six bodies. Five were the police officers' sons, the other was the second FBI agent. Geovanne emptied one hundred-thirty seven rounds into the van.

Francisco

Day four, Geovanne returned to the safe house in Topanga Canyon. Candace greeted him at the door.

"Geovanne! Eu perdi seu rosto serio!"

He laughed out loud. "Do you know what you just said to me? You just said that you missed my serious face."

Candace smiled broadly. "You like that? Francisco has been giving me and Adrian Portuguese lessons. It's a lot like Spanish, only more complicated."

Geovanne walked passed Candace and into the foyer.

"How is Trey?" he asked.

Candace lit up.

"He says he misses me." She placed her hands over heart. "Isn't that the cutest?"

"Yes. He loves his mother."

"Yes. And his mother loves him." Candace followed Geovanne into the living area where I was leaning over a table of papers.

"Geovanne, eu tehno palavra do Comandante. Ele quer falar com voce. Chama-lo de imediato.".

Geovanne nodded. "I will call him right away," he said. Then excused himself.

"Francisco?" Adrian said over her shoulder.

"Si Precioso?" I did not look up.

"I need to go to L.A.. Is that possible?"

Now, I looked up. "Why do you need to go to L.A.?"

"Two reasons. One: I have to make a statement at Sergeant Carpenter's sentencing.." She smiled. "He was found guilty."

"Yes!" Candace said, clapping.

I walked across the room and kissed Adrian.

"This is amazing news, Precioso. Congratulations." I placed my hand on her shoulder. She placed her hand on top of my hand.

"Thank you. It is. It's just—I'm so thrilled."

"And the second reason?" I said.

"Two: I need to be able to call into this radio show because Senator Franks will be dialing in. And he's one of the reasons why this bill isn't being passed. I need to refute his lies."

"What time is the show?"

"It airs at 7:00 p.m. I could just dial in for that though."

I looked at my watch. It was 12:00 pm.

"No, we will need to leave the safe house to avoid having the coordinates of this location identified. It's one thing to access the internet. We have a firewall to encrypt transmissions. It's another to actually make a direct call. That could jeopardize our location."

"But you definitely cannot make an appearance at the sentencing Precioso. The FBI will be waiting to see if you show up so they can bring you back into custody.

Adrian paused. "Okay."

I saw the disappointment in her face.

"I will come up with a work around. Don't worry."

Geovanne returned to the room.

"Is everything okay?" Adrian said.

"Si Senhora. Everything is fine. Geovanne glanced in my direction.

"Adrian. We will leave in an hour. I will find a secure location for you to dial into. Is that okay?"

"That's perfect. Thank you. I'm going to go upstairs to change."

"Okay." I said.

"I'll go with you." Candace said. They trotted up the stairs.

Once they were of sight, Geovanne spoke.

"Antoinette," he said. "Comandante said she has gone stealth."

My jowls tightened. I looked in the direction of the staircase.

"You must keep an eye on her at all times."

"I have given you my word. I will keep her safe."

I nodded. My shoulders and face relaxed.

266

The corners of Geovanne's lips slightly curved up.

👊 👊 👊

Adrian

"TMZ's release of the confession by Officer Banton was a game changer. Today Adrian Jackson was awarded six million dollars in her wrongful death law suit against the City of Los Angeles." a news reporter announced.

"Right on the heels of a guilty verdict of Sergeant Carpenter, the officer who killed her son. Experts are saying the criminal conviction contributed to the large amount of the award in the civil case."

"Once again, TMZ breaks the story. The release of a taped statement by Adrian Jackson had been blowing up the airwaves all day."

"Today is a victory for truth." I said. "We know that this award only happened because a man had a conscience. If he had not, my son's murder would have gone unpunished. And a cold-blooded killer would still be under the protected shield of the Los Angeles Police Department."

"This *screams* volumes to the deep seeded, institutionalized racism prevalent in our criminal justice system. It is because of this entrenched bigotry and discriminatory practices that I am establishing a Human Rights & Justice Advocacy Fund, designated solely to fighting this disease in our law enforcement agencies across the country."

"Five million dollars of this settlement will be used to cover legal fees for the top criminal attorneys, to hire private investigators, appoint special prosecutors, and support advocacy and lobbying groups that ensure that the human rights of African Americans and Latinos are protected in the United States. This fund is specifically to fight racial profiling and discriminatory practices of racist police officers in America.

"You know, someone asked me if I feel justice was served with winning both the civil and criminal cases? Today is not about me and whether I feel good about winning.

"It's about Peter Carpenter being punished for murdering an innocent man, violating basic human rights, perjuring himself under oath, violating his code of ethics, and abusing his power as a sworn officer. So, yes, I feel justice has been served in that respect.

"I hope the judge sentences him to life in prison, so that he can live out the rest of his days in hell mourning the loss of his murdered son--just like so many of us are.

"I want him to have the same gaping hole in his heart that he gave me eighteen months ago when my son died in my arms."

✊ ✊ ✊

"Wow! Eighteen months ago Adrian Jackson was accused of being cold, unfeeling. Maybe then her grief was still new? She was struggling to cope with her loss. Today, she oozed feeling, emotion, loss." A reported said.

"We will see how this all unfolds, the jury should be coming back with Peter Carpenter's verdict any day now. In the meantime the FBI has no real leads on what's being called the Blue Blood Killers, responsible so far for over 250 deaths across the country.

"Racial tensions are high as minority communities protest the special protections provided to the sons of police officers, while--as they say, when their sons were being brutally murdered, the city sent in tanks and cops with riot gear."

Adrian

"Contrary to popular belief, America will not be held hostage by some rogue terrorist, some vigilante thug," Senator Walsh said.

"So in other words, you're digging in your heels and refusing to enforce the constitution and ensure that *every* American's civil rights are protected?" I replied.

"Those are not my words, Mrs. Jackson," Senator Franks said. "As you've stated, the constitution already provides for every American's civil rights, including those of the sworn officers who put their lives in danger every day to protect the *good* citizens of the United States.

"We will not jeopardize their safety and rights as law enforcement agents by giving criminals a 'Walk out of jail Free' card which is what this bill essentially does."

"How does it do that, Senator?" I said. "It specifically states that the bill is for real protection against abusive policing practices."

"Mrs. Jackson, once you start hacking away at our legal system, you tear away at the very fabric of our constitution."

"What does that even mean?" I said. "I asked a direct question sir, are you going to answer it."

"What I will not do is participate in your race-baiting, turning decent Americans against each other by using the race card."

"What are you talking about? Senator, I've been very clear about what my position is. And it's not divisive. If anything what the bill does is create equity, inclusiveness, and –quite frankly, builds a bridge towards harmony in this country, that's been a long time coming."

"So what are you, the next Martin Luther King? Do you want a statue in our Nation's capital?"

"Can you please, just stick to the facts? Do you know *how* to do that?" I said evenly.

"The facts are that this bill is unnecessary. It undermines the protections of our sworn officers, and it creates a slippery slope for criminals to bypass the judicial system."

"Senator Franks, I don't know what television you've been watching lately. But, those good citizens you're talking about are those courageous black folks and their allies who have been protesting across the country in Baltimore, Florida, Los Angeles, Missouri—calling for an end to centuries of structural racism and discriminatory policing. And do you know what they were met with? Excessive militarized violence by law enforcement."

"No Mrs. Jackson, what they were met with were law enforcement officers protecting the property and businesses of hardworking Americans. They're arresting the thugs, looters, and criminals who are smashing the windows of police cars and putting our officers lives in danger."

"No, Senator Franks. They are protesting the death of a human being, whose spine was severed by white racist cops. And instead of prosecuting these murders, and firing the other officers who subscribe to this racist culture, you're supporting a justice system that values property over black lives."

"There you go, race-baiting again."

"So, let me get this straight, Senator Franks; every time I tell the truth--truths you see every day on the news, then I'm race-baiting?

Senator 264 unarmed Americans have been killed by racist cops. That's not allegedly, that's fact."

"And as an elected official of the great state of Virginia, I will ensure that every American's civil right is protected under the laws governed by the United States constitution," Senator Franks said.

"We only have 15 seconds. Since we opened with Senator Franks, we'll close with Adrian Jackson. Mrs. Jackson?"

"Yes, what Senator Franks is saying loudly and clearly to black America is that he and his colleagues have no intention of protecting our civil rights. They are fighting to keep the laws, the laws that allow law enforcement agents to kill our black and brown youth—status quo.

"We must demand that President Obama sign an executive order strengthening Federal laws on racial profiling and enforcing them," I said.

"I'm Mark Green. And that does it for me. Join us here next week on *Both Sides*. Because there's never one side of a story. There's this side, and that side. Our promise, is to always give you Both Sides."

14 A DAY IN HISTORY

Adrian

Monday, April 16, 2016, the day Senators Franks and Walsh were scheduled to rule on the Department of Justice Response to Misconduct in Law Enforcement.

I was front and center at the hearing to hear the official ruling on the legislation.

I sat at the long wooden table, hair pulled back neatly in a bun, pearl earrings, navy blue Hugo Boss suit, over a polished cream silk blouse by Theory with a smart-lapel, and an elegantly draped front.

House Judiciary Committee Chairman Benjamin Franks (R-Va.) and Crime, Terrorism, Homeland Security, and Investigations Subcommittee Chairman Dennis Walsh (R-Wisc.) took the stand to make the final ruling on the Justice Department's response to the House Judiciary Committee regarding misconduct in local Law Enforcement Agencies.

Minutes before Senator Walsh was to make his statement, he received a text: a picture of him kneeling in the restroom at the Green Lantern. He quickly swiped the cell phone closed and inconspicuously scanned the room.

A wrap of the gavel, and Senator Walsh leaned in to his microphone.

"Although they are late to tackling this problem, we are pleased that officials at the Justice Department share the American people's concern about instances of misconduct at the Department of Justice and are taking steps to address this problem.

"The Justice Department's response makes clear that the DOJ's Office of Professional Responsibility failed to fully investigate the officers who murdered and subsequently covered up these acts and as a result, other responsible parties failed to appropriately discipline those involved.

"In the future, Justice Department employees who break the law must be fired. We will not tolerate further episodes of 'police officers gone wild.' In matters of civilian safety, we will take appropriate actions to ensure that all American's civil rights are protected by the officers sworn to do so." Senator Walsh shuffled papers around until he found one specific page.

"We needed to understand what broke down in these investigations and why DOJ employees were not sufficiently held accountable for their actions. The American people deserve answers from their government about this atrocious behavior and demand change to ensure such lapses in judgment don't happen again."

"Mrs. Jackson," Senator Walsh said. "You have been fighting hard to see this bill come into fruition. The End Racial Profiling Act of 2015 (ERPA) was introduced to Congress by the NAACP and failed twice, a failure on the side of law enforcement to provide real protection against abusive policing practices.

"On behalf of the Crime, Terrorism, Homeland Security, and Investigations Subcommittee, I would like to applaud you for your efforts in fighting for its merits and raising its profile; and assure you that from this day moving forward, misconduct in Federal law enforcement agents will not be tolerated." Senator Walsh placed his papers down and turned to face his colleagues.

"And now, I call for the vote to approve the ERPA bill."

As each Senator verbally casted their vote, I stood holding my breath. 156 Yeahs, 0 Nays.

I breathed in a deep, cleansing breath. *The Anti-Racial Profiling Bill Passed.*

I nodded. Unable to speak. Barely able to breathe.

I couldn't believe this moment was real. Tears filled my eyes, everything was blurry, and everyone was a blur. One rap of the gavel, and I was calm, at peace. The crowd behind me cheered.

In the midst of the hugs and handshakes, I snuck out the chamber. I took the back entrance and exited the stairway to the waiting vehicle. I dialed Francisco.

"Hey you?" I whispered.

"Hello, Precious. What's wrong?"

"Nothing. The bill passed."

"You did it!" Francisco said. "I am so proud of you." I smiled.

"I kept my promise to my son." I sighed deeply.

"And now? Are you ready to go off the grid?"

I stood on the steps of the Capitol and looked around. My heart was light.

"I have one stop to make, but after that. Yes. I am ready."

Candace screamed as soon as I walked through the door.

"You did it!" Candace threw her arms around me as I stood resigned. "What? What's wrong? You did it. You got the bill passed."

I sat in between Candace and Geovanne on the couch. I grabbed Candace's hand and squeezed it. I reached over and squeezed Geovanne's hand.

"We did it." Tears streamed down my face. "We did it. You, Candace, and you Vaughn--*Geovanne*. The NAACP, all of those people who protested, and held our government accountable this past year and a half. *We* did it." I opened my clutch and pulled out tissue. I dabbed my face.

"Then why are you acting so . . . sad?" Candace said. "This is what you've been fighting for. This moment." Candace squeezed my hand. "For Jared."

I wiped more tears. "That's just it, Candace. It's over." I blew my nose. "I'm done. I've done what I promised my son I'd do. And now—I just feel, empty I guess. Lost." I dropped my head in my hands and cried.

"When I heard my son say to that cop, *You don't know who you're fucking with*." I smiled. "I heard my dad." I laughed. "He used to say that all the time. He was the rebel rouser. He was so hood." We laughed.

"My mom was the opposite. She was strong, and smart. But her strength, her power was in her silence. My dad told you, my mom showed you." I paused, but the tears kept flowing. I wiped my face and blew my nose.

"Jared is gone. Linda is gone. There's nothing left here for me. And, I know I should be happy, but being in this place just sucks all the air out of my lungs." I shook my head.

"I can't begin to know how you feel Adrian. But I can tell you how I'm feeling. As a black woman in America, raising a black son, I feel like today, there is hope for Trey." Candace's eyes sparkled.

"Today, there is a law that says Trey is a little bit safer." She smiled. I nodded.

"And that's huge for us. I'm not naïve. Those cops are still racist. This country is still racist. But at least now we have a law that says we can do something about it."

Candace shook my shoulder. "You should be celebrating! You should be happy." Candace laughed. "I am so happy that I was a part of this. I know it was small in comparison to all you've done and sacrificed. But, I feel good knowing I've actually been a part of something that will change the course of America as we know it." Candace grabbed both of my hands inside hers. "Thank you, Adrian Jackson, for fighting for my son's life." She hugged me.

"Well!" I said, wiping tears with the back of my hand. "I guess my job here is done." I handed Candace a copy of the day's proceedings. "Here, this is for you. And Trey. Show him what his mom was a part of when he gets older and can understand."

Candace took the paper and started reading it.

"Geovanne?"

"Si, Senhora. I am ready when you are."

I nodded.

15 THE RIMSHOT

It was a beautiful California day. The sun's rays dominated the clear blue sky. A light breeze filled the air, but gave no real relief from the bright white rays of the blazing sun.

The tall woman dressed in a black baseball cap, sweats, and sneakers darted in and out between the headstones with long, purposeful strides. She walked up a paved road that led to a small pond.

Firmly implanted in the embankment was a large green weeping willow tree. She moved up and down the walkway until she reached her destination: a beautiful sand stone colored granite headstone.

She paused, then knelt before the smooth square rock. She placed a copy of the official proceedings on the soft green grass. She leaned in and brushed the dirt off the marker.

"They didn't know who they were fucking with did they Jared?" She knelt for a moment, traced the carved letters of his name, then stood and kissed the top of his headstone, rubbed it, turned and walked away.

A loud crack filled her ears. In that second, the bright blue sky went to black.

Her limp body hit the ground like heavy metal. She lay face-down, sprawled across Jared Jackson's grave with a single bullet to the back of her head. Blood splattered across the print out that lay beneath her shoulder.

Congressional Record:

Containing the Proceedings of the Electoral Commission

Appointed under

The act of congress approved April 16, 2016, entitled "An Act to Eradicate and Regulate the Act of Racial Profiling of Men of Color, and the decisions of questions arising thereon, for the term commencing March 4, A.D. 2016;

Being Part IV, Volume V.

———————

Two Hundreth Congress, Second Session

———————

Washington:
Government printing office.
2016.

ELECTORAL COMMISSION.

———————

PROCEEDINGS OF THE COMMISSION APPOINTED UNDER THE ACT OF CONGRESS APPROVED APRIL 16, 2016, ENTITLED "AN ACT TO ERADICATE AND REGULATE THE ACT OF RACIAL PROFILING OF MEN OF COLOR, AND THE DECISIONS OF QUESTIONS ARISING THEREON, FOR THE TERM COMMENCING MARCH 4, A.D. 2016"

Antoinette

I watched through my scope as the ugly American fell to the ground. My nipples tingled and my face felt flush as the warm blood raced through my veins. All signs of a good kill. I pulled out my phone, zoomed in on the body, snapped the photo, and hit "Send".

I dismantled my high-powered weapon, packed it up, and was in my vehicle in under six minutes. I drove out of the Inglewood Mortuary and Cemetery smiling and humming "I want a rim shot, hey, digi, digi. A rim shot hey, c'mon."

Ten minutes later, I pulled into the Marriott hotel near LAX. My flight was leaving at 6:00 am the next morning. I'd order a nice steak from room service, take a nap, then maybe check out the bar to see if I could find anyone interesting enough to take back to my room.

Inside, my room, I stepped into the shower. I closed my eyes and enjoyed the steam as it filled the small glass area. The hot water ran over my head and down my shoulders. As I reached for the shampoo, the shower door swung open, I was yanked out of the shower by the top of my head.

Disoriented and in pain, I tried to free myself from the hand dragging my wet and naked body out of the bathroom, down the short hallway and into the hotel room.

I twisted and turned, but only succeeded in causing a chunk of my hair to separate from my scalp. I couldn't see my assailant's face and I couldn't get my bearing to position myself to fight.

Francisco

Just as she was about to turn to try and stabilize herself, I slammed her up against the foot of her bed.

"Ow! Foder!" She pulled the heavy wet black hair away from her face and locked eyes with mine. She was startled. Then quickly her face turned cold.

I tied her up, then scrolled through her phone. Once I saw the confirmation I walked over to her.

"Voce esta louco cadela. Eu nao te amo."

"Yes you do! You do love me. You were just distracted."

'E assim, sua solucao e matar todas as mulheres que me distrait?"

Antoinette gave me a smug look and shrugged..

"Well, I hope you're happy now. You have my full attention."

I shook my head, pulled out my .45 revolver, inserted a hollow point bullet in the chamber.

Antoinette's look turned from smug to panic.

"Voce nao faria. You wouldn't," she said in two languages.

I aimed the barrel at Antoinette's head and pulled the trigger. The loud cracking sound of Antoinette's skull splitting only lasted 3 seconds. Her body slumped over to the right. Blood oozed from the gaping hole in her head.

I text'd Geovanne

< It is complete.

I fought back tears as I carried the large body to the man-made lake in Inglewood Mortuary Cemetery, only a few hundred feet away from Jared's plot. My throat burned from constraining the roar I forced myself to swallow. Things weren't supposed to have gone this way. I struggled to figure out how things could have gone so terribly wrong. I just couldn't make sense of it all.

I placed cement cinders inside her warm up jacket and the bottom of her sweat pants, and rolled her heavy body over into the dank, dark green, algae-laced water. It went against every code and protocol I had been taught, this feeling I was experiencing at that moment.

But I felt a deep sense of sadness, guilt and remorse. I had been unable to protect her; and as a result, her lifeless body would be found, unidentifiable--due to the time submerged under water and the damage done to it by the fish, detrital feeders, and physical and chemical micro-organisms that prey on organic matter.

I text'd Francisco.

< It is complete.

Francisco

I read Geovanne's message and placed the phone in my pocket. As the airplane took off, I closed my heavy eyes.

I sat quietly as the Senate Chambers cleared.

I walked down the long corridor and made a right. I turned and pretended to talk on my phone as an administrative assistant walked by. I slipped by the Senator's aid who was flirting with the clerk in the break room.

I pulled out another phone and dialed it as I opened the door. A cell vibrated on the desk in front of me. Senator Franks appeared from a door to the left.

Startled, he stopped in his tracks. "Oh. Can I help you?" He looked around. "Are you lost? These are private chambers." Senator Franks went to reach for the intercom, but I grabbed his hand. "What are you doing? I'm calling security."

The phone vibrated again.

"Pick up the phone," I said.

The Senator looked at the phone. "That's fine. They'll call back." I reached over and picked up the phone and handed to the Senator.

"Answer it."

Senator Franks swiped the burner phone. "Hello?"

I put the other burner phone to my ear. "Look at the picture I sent you."

Senator Franks stared at me, then pulled the phone away from his ear to look at the screen. He pushed the button to open the text.

"Oh!" He dropped the phone. Senator Franks sat there, terrified. "Who are you?"

"I am the person who killed your assassin." I removed my gun from my waist. I sat on the edge of the desk. "I bet you were disappointed to learn Adrian Jackson was still alive, weren't you?"

Senator Franks sat quietly.

"When you learned that Senator Walsh called off the hit, you put one out on your own, and you thought she had successfully accomplished her task." Francisco leaned in the Senator's face.

"She confirmed and sent you a picture of the dead body and everything."

"Was it staged?" he screamed. "It was fake?"

"No. Unfortunately, she killed her target," Francisco said, screwing on a silencer.

The Senator panicked. "Well . . . the bill passed Monday. Did you see that? I voted for it."

"You voted for it because everyone voted for it."

"Yes, but I could have easily voted against it."

"No you couldn't have, otherwise you would have," I said. He crossed his arms over his chest. "So tell me. Why did you want Adrian Jackson dead?"

The Senator sat quietly. I placed the gun between his eyes.

"She was a nuisance--and"

Blip.

Senator Franks' body fell forward on the beautiful mahogany desk. His eyes were open. Blood poured from the hole in the center of his forehead.

I unscrewed the silencer, placed the gun in my waist, and slipped out the same way I'd come in.

"Good evening. The Los Angeles coroner *has* confirmed that the female body retrieved from the man-made lake at the Inglewood Mortuary Cemetery *is* that of social activist Adrian Jackson."

B-roll of a female body being pulled out of the lake.

"Adrian Jackson became very vocal around racial profiling and discriminatory practices by law enforcement agencies after her son, Jared Jackson was murdered and his killer, Peter Carpenter failed to get indicted."

B-roll of Adrian testifying on Capitol Hill.

"Jackson went on a crusade to enact legislation that prohibited racial profiling and prosecuted law enforcement officers who were found guilty of discriminatory acts such as racial profiling and murdering unarmed innocent minorities.

"Some believe Jackson's campaign spurred the killing spree of the sons white police officers who killed unarmed African American and Latino victims, but there was never sufficient evidence to officially tie her to the murders or the serial killer.

"Just as some speculate, because she was killed execution-style, that she was killed in retaliation by the police. Although no evidence officially ties anyone in law enforcement to this murder either.

"Only days after the legislation she fought so hard to get passed was approved, Adrian Jackson paid the ultimate price for leading the charge in making racial profiling a crime in America. The irony, she was visiting the grave of her murdered son.

"A vigil will be held tonight at 7:00 pm, in Leimert Park to honor the life of the slain social activist. But you as you can see," the camera panned across the front of the cemetery, "mourners have already begun to build a shrine at both the East and West gates."

The camera zoomed in on a picture of Adrian and Jared on a poster that read 'Together Again, RIP'

"I'm Ellen Leyva, reporting live, from Inglewood Mortuary Cemetery, Channel 7 Eyewitness news."

16 THE MOMENT FOR WHICH YOU HAVE BEEN CREATED

President Barack Obama stood in the pulpit at West Angeles Church. He scanned the enormous room packed with wall-to-wall people—there had to be well over a thousand people.

The President took a deep breath, and steadied his nerves. On the front row was Reggie and his fiancé, JR and all the people from Running Springs. Behind them were the employees from Dietrich Advertising.

"My brothers and sisters, it pains me as the President of these great United States to stand before you, as my last act as the leader of the most powerful country in the world, to eulogize a woman who should still be with us today."

"Well," a voice from the congregation chimed.

"And, it pains me as an African American man, to stand before you, to put to rest, one of our most fearless civil rights activists to date."

"Amen!" a young man shouted.

"But mostly, it pains me, as a human being, a member of this free society in 2016, to stand before you, to try and sum up the amazing life of one of the world's most staunch advocates for humanity, decency, and human rights."

The church thundered with cheers and clapping.

"I am happy to say that the last piece of legislation I signed as the Commander and Chief was an Executive Order enforcing and expanding federal bans on discriminatory policing and strengthening police accountability mechanisms nationwide."

The church stood for a full two minutes clapping. President Obama nodded. "Yes, it was the Executive Order Adrian fought fearlessly to get signed, and I am so happy it's the last official act that I did as President of the United States."

"And so, as we gather here today, beloved. I encourage you to remember, that Adrian Jackson gave up her life, like so many before her—of course there are the notables, Malcolm X—who I, I have to tell you . . . she reminded me so much of, with her zeal, and her unapologetic love for her people."

The church clapped. The President smiled.

"I remember the first time we met in the White House. I was, kind of nervous." The church laughed. "No seriously. I'd seen her on the talk shows, watched her bring down the most formidable opponents on CNN, Meet the Press, and Fox News." He smiled and nodded his head.

"She was the same height as Michelle, about 5'11"— but . . . for some reason, she seemed . . . taller." The church laughed. "Bigger." He became somber. "I remember saying to myself, I kind of know why these people are afraid of her. She had a presence that just sucked up a room, you know?"

There were nods, and people dabbing their eyes throughout the church.

"But, when she walked in. Instead of walking up to me and just taking my head off . . . she stopped. Dead in her tracks. It was a most peculiar moment.

"She said, 'Oh my, Mr. President, I am so sorry! And turned away. The First Lady, knowing exactly what to do, walked up to her and embraced her. They just stood there . . . as beautiful, fragile, strong, vulnerable, smart and amazing women."

The sanctuary errupted in.applause. President Obama nodded.

"They stood there holding each other up--like African American women do. American women, with a painful history.

"But what I saw in those women, those American women, were

their connection to Africa. Their pride and courage, their love and acceptance, their compassion and humanity. And my heart filled with a love that words cannot begin to express."

The church clapped and clapped and clapped.

"Michelle whispered something in Adrian's ear. I can't confirm it. But I think Michelle must've said something like, *Girl, You better pull yourself together and handle your business!*"

The crowd went wild. The women stood with raised hands,, jumping up and down. The men nodded their heads and laughed.

The President said. "Adrian Jackson presented the most succinct, most concise, and poignant points on why I should enact an executive order that prohibited racial profiling that I'd ever heard.

"She painfully recounted the numerous ways members of Congress, the media, and just plain ol' disrespectful folk disrespected me, the title I carried as Commander and Chief—the office I held. And then she broke it down. Talked about our young men who don't have a chance. Whose lives are in jeopardy, just by walking out the door.

"And it's because of that fight my brothers and sisters, Adrian Jackson lost her life." President Obama shook his head. His eyes filled with tears. The churched clapped. "I am a praying man."

"That's right!" awoman shouted.

"And when I heard of Adrian's . . . murder. I prayed." He paused and thought for a moment. "I didn't quite know what to pray *for*, my heart was heavy, and so I just . . . I prayed and asked God, *Why?*" The church clapped. "Why, didn't you protect her? "She'd lost so much already. Her parents to medical illness, her husband to a war we should have never been fighting."

"Amen!" "Yes Lord!". and other outbursts came from the crowd.

"Her only son. *Lord, Why?*

"And I'll tell you, I'd had this same conversation with several of my aids and closest friends, and they had their opinions. Some said that maybe God was being kind, taking her away from all the evil in this world.

"Others said that she was at peace with the ones she'd lost. And still others said that it was because the world is not ready for truth and real systemic change.

"But when I prayed, God dropped this passage into my spirit. And if you will indulge me for just a few minutes . . ." President Obama smiled. He turned and looked atBishop Blake, "You know, I've always wanted to say that."

The church laughed with the President.

"If you will . . . indulge me for a few minutes, I want to share with you what God dropped in my spirit. And let me say this. Of all the things I've prayed about, none have been answered so clearly, so . . . profoundly as this prayer."

"Preach!" a woman shouted.

"I am humbled and deeply honored, that God would give this answer to me, to share with you today, in honor of our beloved sister Adrian Jackson.

"The passage God dropped in my spirit was '*For Such a Time as This.*' He scanned the congregation. "For Such a Time as This. For all of you avid and astute Bible readers, you know that this passage comes from the book of Esther." Members of the church nodded. "I had to look it up." The church laughed.

"That's alright!" one lady shouted.

"That's alright?" The President chuckled. "Thank you. I did. I looked it up, and it's a story about Esther, a Jew who for one year had been a concubine with 200 other virgins, to be considered as the 2nd wife of the King.

"Esther in all her beauty was the one he chose.

"Now, of course, there's a lot more to this story, but to cut it down, Esther's cousin, Mordecai, told Esther that she needed to talk to the King and tell him not to kill the Jews." Obama looked back at

Bishop Blake who gave him the thumbs up.

"The thing about that is, wives were not allowed to approach the King. Doing so would get you beheaded. But Mordecai, desperate, told her: *Perhaps you have come to this place, to this moment, to these people, to this challenge, for just such a time as this.*"

The camera zoomed in on President Obama. "Perhaps? Perhaps Esther was called, at that place, that moment, to those people, to that challenge, for such at time as that. To save her people from destruction.

"But this is the passage that God dropped in my spirit in answer to my prayer about our beloved Adrian Jackson. And I thought on it long and hard.

"Perhaps Adrian came to this place . . . to this moment . . . to our people . . ." The crowd stood. The cheering was so loud it reverberated throughout the buidling. President Obama nodded and waited patiently for the cheering to subside. He pointed his index finger. "To this challenge, for such a time as this.

"A time when a black man was the President of the United States. The first time in the country's history. A time when, innocent lives of black and brown Americans were being taken, without a second thought, or apology.

"As a matter of fact, they were being gunned down, and their killers were walking free, time after time." The church clapped. "For such a time as this.'" He scanned the crowd. "When her son would be brutally murdered in front of her. For such a time as this, when hundreds of thousands of people would rise up in protest and say, "No More! Black Lives Matter!"

More thunderous applause.

"Adrian would be our Esther. She had some things. She lacked other things. She had beauty. She was well traveled, well educated. She was ambitious and a successful businesswoman. She had a very powerful position. But she didn't have any power over her own life, not after one human being took the life of her son. She went into a tailspin.

"She didn't have any security in the face of those who planned to kill her and her people."

"Think about Esther, think about Adrian . . . and then think about yourself. You have some things. You lack other things. Maybe you have the gift of great intelligence. Maybe you don't have great brains, and are free of the burden of feeling you have to be clever all the time.

"Maybe you have good looks. Maybe you don't have good looks, and are free of the projections and expectations that good looks can bring. Maybe you have had a calm and stable family life, and understand what trust and promise-keeping and security mean.

"Maybe you have known none of these things, and experience hardship and anxiety and fear that may come to be of value to others who sense a little of the panic that both Esther and Adrian must have felt.

"Maybe you have a prominent public role, as an elected official or an executive or some other job that puts you behind a big desk. Or maybe you have the freedom of being out of the limelight, your actions not being perpetually judged and your words not being endlessly evaluated.

"Think about yourself, what you uniquely have and what you uniquely lack. And then think about the context *you* are in. Think about the ways you feel powerless.

"Think about the number of times you have said, "What Los Angeles needs", or "What Ferguson needs", or "What the American church needs", or "What my family needs", or "What the world needs". Think about the number of times you have thought there was nothing or no one that could do anything about it.

"And then feel, hear this exasperating man Mordecai tap on your shoulder, saying, 'Perhaps you have been given these skills and experiences, these privileges and deprivations, so that just at this very moment you could do what no one else could do, you could be what no one else could be.'

"God made Adrian just as she was because he wanted someone just like her. Maybe all this happened and she came to be here for just such a time as this."

"People, we don't know the whys. We don't know *who* will bring us to that place. That time. But like our sister, Adrian, we have to step up to the call."

The church clapped.

"The world doesn't get any better by sitting back and hoping that it will get better. The world changes because *we* make it change."

The church stood up on its feet.

"Adrian made it change! She fought, she pushed, she showed up, time after time! She was the change she wanted see in world."

The sanctuary resounded with thunderous applause.

"And as I close. As I honor the amazing life, the amazing accomplishments of this one woman, I leave you with this: What about you? Perhaps God has put *you* right here, right now, for such a time as this? There is still so much more to do, ladies and gentlemen. One law doesn't solve bigotry, and hate. One law doesn't create respect of human life. There is still much to do. And I dare say, What about you?

"We know without a doubt, this was Adrian's task on earth. We know, that she was brought to us. But our work does not stop because we lay this powerful sister's body to rest, our work is fueled because we lay this powerful human being's body to rest."

The church stood and cheered for two full minutes.

"I'm no preacher." President Obama turned and looked at Bishop Blake. "But I did alright, right Bishop?"

The Bishop laughed and waved his hand.

"I think that was a wave of approval, I don't know." He chuckled. "I'm no preacher," he whispered, paused, and looked out into the crowd.

"But I am a black man, an African American, an American, a

human being. And today, I am so proud to have known such a remarkable woman . . ." President Obama glanced across the church. "Thank you Adrian Jackson, for accepting the call, *for such a time as this.*"

18 OFF THE GRID

Francisco and Geovanne would meet at the Hawthorne airport near Crenshaw Blvd. and the 105 Freeway, and take a small chartered plane back to Brazil. The flight home would be somber.

"You executed perfectly, Senhor Azevedo," Francisco said, looking out his window.

Geovanne sat across from him. He sat quietly.

"Obrigado Senhor. However, we both know I failed this test."

Francisco stared out of the window. The plane tilted forty-five degrees to the right, then straightened up. He thought long and hard about this assignment, and Geovanne's actions throughout. Francisco knew he had failed Geovanne as an instructor.

"Your failure is my failure. By example, I have shown you how to get killed, how to take on an assignment with a person you are physically involved with, how to become emotionally-tied to victims, how to lose sight of the end-game, and, put your direct reports in imminent danger." Francisco looked into Geovanne's eyes.

"Is this why you left the family, sir?"

Francisco nodded.

"You have to have the heart for killing," Francisco replied. "I have the skills, the mind, and the hands, but not the heart. Not anymore."

"And me? What do I have?" Geovanne inquired. "Am I General material?"

Francisco analyzed Geovanne's face for a moment. "Yes, you have exactly what it takes to be an excellent General: courage, patience, strategic thinking, fearlessness, and a good read of people. I will recommend that the Comandante give you the title of General, Geovanne."

The two flew the rest of the flight home in silence.

Geovanne knew he should be elated knowing he would advance to such an honorable rank. But he couldn't shake the sadness that loomed deep inside him.

Francisco watched Geovanne as he struggled with this phase of his life. He knew, first hand, what he was going through.

It was his turning point after Pilar. This would be Geovanne's true test. If he could return to his role, unfazed by this loss, this sense of emptiness, he would be an excellent commander.

If not . . . He knew it was always best to learn these things early in your career. It could cost you your life. Although, if you asked the Comandante, Francisco was confident he would say his decision had certainly cost him his life.

✊ ✊ ✊

Francisco entered his flat. It was a beautiful beach-front apartment located fifteen minutes away from Natal town centre.

Cotovelo was a small and calm beach with clear, calm waters, and a few high end houses. Cotovelo was a beach formed by cliffs and therefore common to find locals there bathing.

While just as luxurious as San Paolo, Natal town was more of an exclusive community, and where Francisco stayed when he did not want much human interaction. Fourteen hundred forty miles south, southwest felt like a completely different continent in terms of pace and density.

Francisco walked straight to his shower. It faced the private beach, and sat up high on a cliff so there was no need for curtains or blinds.

In the morning, the sun illuminated the room. At night, Francisco bathed underneath the lunar light.

Today, the weather was 87 degrees, with the humidity of 67. In this type of tropical weather, he showered 2-3 times a day – which was the reason for such a luxurious design.

He peeled off the black silk short sleeve shirt and grey slacks and kicked off his black loafers. He stepped into his walk-in shower, turned on the two rain showerheads, handheld showerhead, and massage jets that sprayed high velocity streams from all angles. Francisco stood as the water massaged his aching muscles. He closed his eyes and tried to quiet the noise in his head.

Francisco felt the pulsating of the jet streams against his body. They reminded him of the warm wet pulsating feeling he felt being inside of Adrian.

He ran his fingers through his hair. It made him think of Adrian pulling his mane, guiding his tongue in and out of her vagina.

Francisco shook his head. He turned to see a beautiful woman walking up the beach, tall, full-figured—light complexioned. Her hair was short and blonde and curly. Francisco closed his eyes and placed his head up under the water.

His mind kept returning to Adrian. He could see her smile, vividly, and hear her laugh. He could see the brown specks in her vibrantly green eyes, and hear the rhythm of her breathing as she lay next to him sleeping. Despite his best efforts, his mind was hell bent on thinking about this woman.

He felt a gentle kiss in the middle of his back, followed by tender kisses down his spine. Francisco smiled. Arms slid around his waist, pulling him back into full breasts that pressed up against his back.

He grabbed the left hand and kissed her palm. With the right, she grabbed his erect dick and slowly stroked it. He tried to turn and face her, but she moved her hand down to the base of his shaft and held it, preventing him from turning.

Instead, she stroked him. Slow and steady, until he grew rock hard. Then she increased her speed and tightened her grip. She felt his veins expand with each stroke.

He turned to look into her eyes, those sad green eyes. He kissed her round cheeks, sprinkled with cinnamon brown freckles. He traced the long slope of her nose, down to the tip, and covered her mouth with his, feeling the comfort of her tongue luxuriating inside his mouth.

He kissed each breast until her nipples were tender and rigid, and then he took the fullness inside his mouth. He sucked them so perfectly he made her whimper with ecstasy.

Francisco lifted her in the air and slid in between her thighs and inside her wet walls. He could feel her, pumping—back arched, arms around his neck, legs around his waist . . . pumping, longing, yearning, eagerly taking all of him inside her. Sloppily kissing him, pulling his hair, grabbing his shoulders, scratching his back, moaning, screaming, grunting—loving him, wanting him.

Francisco moved to the back of the shower and sat on the shower bench. She bent her legs and pushed up on her knees.

She lowered herself down on his shaft and pumped up and down, over and over; bodies slapping, colliding, melding into one. Pumping with the same rhythm, the same wild and feverish pace, pounding—ass to pelvis, pussy on dick, pumping, grinding, explosive—release!

"Ohhh!" Francisco moaned. The ejaculation of the warm, thick juice made him fall back, almost breathless. He opened his eyes to find her staring into his.

He smiled. She smiled. Her green eyes were light, bright, beaming. His heart raced.

"Ola, meu amor, *Isobela.*" Oh how I've missed you."

She kissed him slowly, tenderly. "Ola, Precioso. Yep, that's about all the Portuguese I know."

They laughed.

"I will teach you." Francisco kissed the tip of her nose. He stared at her for a while. He examined every inch of her face.

"What, you don't like the blonde?"

"I like it just fine," Francisco said, running his fingers through the curls. "It suits you. Do you miss it?"

"My hair?" She smiled. "Nah. I'm actually growing quite fond of the length. I think it's . . . liberating."

"Good. Good." Francisco smiled. "And . . . how does it feel being off the grid?"

Adrian paused, giving the question serious consideration. It gutted her knowing that amazing people died because of her: Linda, Candace. She knew she couldn't be the cause of any more people dying.

Watching her 'funeral' at the airport had her in tears. The amazing tribute--*from the President of the United States!*—and the hundreds of people who attended the service.

She looked at Francisco and her heart couldn't help but smile. He'd done so much just to make this day possible. He'd figured it all out, made it so she had no reason to stay in America.

And she had accomplished what she set out to do: Get legislation passed that made it illegal for a human being—no matter who he was—to target, harass, or kill another human being because of his race. She was free to leave that part of her life behind, and start a totally new adventure.

"It feels absolutely fabulous!"

EPILOGUE

Geovanne text'd Francisco to let him know he'd gotten Adrian off to the airport safely.

Back in California, he had to wrap up a few loose ends before they closed out the case.

Geovanne called Candace, but she didn't answer her phone. He returned to the hotel room to pick her up.

"Candace?" He scanned the room and saw a note written in red lipstick on the mirror.

Gone to Inglewood Cemetery to finish this for Adrian. Be right back.

Before Geovanne made it to his car, Francisco sent him a text:

< Geovanne. Candace was just killed at Jared's tombstone. I'm sorry.

< Antoinette believes she's Adrian. I am tailing her.

< Will identify the initiator and then eliminate her.

< You know what to do.

Francisco had been trailing Antoinette for days. Thiago notified him that after the first contract on Adrian had been fulfilled, another one had been placed soon after; and Antoinette had accepted the assignment.

After Francisco was sure the initiator had received the confirmation email fulfilling the contract, he terminated Antoinette and had Thiago trace the call. It led back to Senator Franks.

Geovanne ensured the Coroner confirmed the body from the cemetery lake. Official records would state that 'Adrian's body' had been badly decomposed by the water, but was confirmed by dental records.

Candace's official death record would indicate that she had been fatally stabbed twenty-seven times, a crime of passion that totally disfigured the victim. Final autopsy report indicated that the Coroner required dental records to confirm victim's identity.

The body was that of an unclaimed Jane Doe of similar height and description Geovanne had obtained from the morgue.

Planted evidence on Tyler Fontaine, II would lead to a murder conviction, leaving Tyler Fontaine, III (Trey) in the custody of his grandmother.

Two weeks after Candace's funeral an officer showed up at Mrs. Williams's home. He delivered an official letter indicating Tyler Fontaine, III as a recipient of the Jared Jackson Memorial Fund.

The letter said that his mother had applied for and was granted a scholarship for Trey in 2015. Those funds would be placed in a trust that would be allocated monthly until the funds were depleted.

"Lord Jesus!" the grandmother cried. She raised her hands up to the sky and praised God. "Trey!" she shouted. "Trey! I told you yo mama was looking out for you, son." Trey walked into the living room, bewildered by the grandmother's statement.

The officer knelt down and motioned for the young man to come over. Trey walked over and stood in front of the officer who gave him a hug. "Congratulations, young man. I know your mother is very proud of you. You must grow up to continue to make her very proud, okay?"

"Yes sir," the young boy replied.

The officer stood and tenderly rubbed the boy's head. He smiled, placed the official 8 point police cap on his head, and turned to walk off.

"Thank you, officer?" the grandmother said. "I'm sorry, I don't recall your name."

"Geovanne."

"God bless you, Officer Geovanne."

He turned to woman and smiled. "You raised an amazing woman."

Mrs. Williams smiled. "Why, thank you. How would you know that?"

The officer looked down at the little boy, "Because she raised such a handsome and smart young man."

The woman smiled at Trey.

www.ingramcontent.com/pod-product-compliance
Lightning Source LLC
Chambersburg PA
CBHW021314250626
47155CB00002B/526